DEVIL
IN OHIO

DEVIL IN OHIO

DARIA POLATIN

SQUARE
FISH

FEIWEL AND FRIENDS
NEW YORK

An imprint of Macmillan Publishing Group, LLC
120 Broadway, New York, NY 10271
fiercereads.com

Square Fish and the Square Fish logo are trademarks of Macmillan and
are used by Feiwel and Friends under license from Macmillan.

Our books may be purchased in bulk for promotional, educational, or business use.
Please contact your local bookseller or the Macmillan Corporate and Premium
Sales Department at (800) 221-7945 ext. 5442 or by email at
MacmillanSpecialMarkets@macmillan.com.

Library of Congress Cataloging-in-Publication Data

Names: Polatin, Daria, author.
Title: Devil in Ohio / Daria Polatin.
Description: First edition. | New York : Feiwel and Friends, 2017 | Summary: Mae moves in
with fifteen-year-old Jules' family and seems to be taking over her life, but Mae's past in a
nearby cult soon threatens them all.
Identifiers: LCCN HYPERLINK "tel:2017007306" 2017007306 (print) | LCCN HYPERLINK
"tel:2017033903" 2017033903 (ebook) | ISBN 9781250113603 (Ebook) |
ISBN 9781250113610 (hardcover)
Subjects: | CYAC: Cults—Fiction. | Family life—Ohio—Fiction. | High schools—Fiction. |
Schools—Fiction. | Child abuse—Fiction. | Kidnapping—Fiction. | Ohio—Fiction.
Classification: LCC PZ7.1.P6428 (ebook) | LCC PZ7.1.P6428 Dev 2017 (print) |
DDC [Fic]—dc23
LC record available at https://lccn.loc.gov/2017007306

ISBN 978-1-250-18077-3 (paperback)   ISBN 978-1-250-11360-3 (ebook)

Originally published in the United States by Feiwel and Friends
First Square Fish edition, 2018
Book designed by Rebecca Syracuse
Square Fish logo designed by Filomena Tuosto

3 5 7 9 10 8 6 4

LEXILE: HL680L

To those who have been hurt, and come
through the other side even stronger.

To my mother and sister, for everything.

AUTHOR'S NOTE

*This book is based on a true story. Not my story, but someone's.
What matters is that most of it actually happened.*

Just be glad it didn't happen to you.

PROLOGUE

AS SHE PEELED THE CATATONIC GIRL'S HOSPITAL GOWN off her back, the nurse's face paled: red lines, brimming with blood, had been carved deep into the teenage girl's porcelain skin. The congealed liquid was starting to tighten, crack. The maroon lines were precise, stick-straight. There was no way the girl could have done this herself.

This had been done *to* her.

The nurse gazed at the nest of lines. The slices formed a five-pointed star. An upside-down one. Around that, a circle was engraved.

Sign of Satan.

Slowly—carefully—the nurse replaced the thin cotton gown. With an unsteady hand she pulled out her cell, stepping backward across the linoleum as if repelled from the girl's damaged body. Cell phones weren't normally permitted for use on the hospital floor, but this seemed like an emergency.

When the person on the other end of the line answered, the nurse whispered fiercely—

"You better come quick."

PART ONE

The world breaks every one
and afterward many are strong at the
broken places.

—Ernest Hemingway, ***A Farewell to Arms***

CHAPTER 1

THE TAN CORNFLAKE LOOKED LIKE A LONELY ISLAND in the translucent sea of 2 percent milk. As I watched it drift across the screen from behind my phone, I wondered why, as soggy as the flakes got, they never seemed to sink.

My phone wasn't great with close-ups, which was why I needed a new, real camera, but I could sharpen the shot in a filter—if I could just get the framing right.

"No phones at the table," my little sister, Danielle, reminded me from over her own bowl of cereal. She was eleven, and a tattletale. She was also right—our mom didn't like us to talk, text, or snap pics at the table, but this shot was lining up so perfectly.

CLICK—

I rebelled against the world in my own small way.

(It's) Still Life was what I was calling the series. It was a collection

I was putting together for my application to a digital photography program at the Art Institute of Chicago next summer. I wanted to magnify the everyday moments we took for granted, examine what we dismissed as mundane.

Dani's eyes narrowed. I didn't want to grant her a win, but it was too early to fight. I slipped my phone back into the pocket of the vintage corduroy pants I'd scored at Goodwill and stared, daring her to tell Mom.

Dani turned back to flipping through her *InStyle* magazine without further confrontation.

"I'll be there as soon as I can. Thanks, Connie."

My mother had a weird look on her face as she ended the call. She was completely inept at hiding her feelings. It was a trait she had unfortunately passed down to me.

Having your face reveal exactly what you're feeling is an extremely unhelpful characteristic, especially as a fifteen-year-old. I had paid dearly for this feature in awkward situations of yesteryear—the time I let my face show that Lucas O'Donnell already having a date to the eighth-grade graduation dance was heartbreaking; or that my neighbor Stacy Pickman *did* look fat in those jeans. But the worst was the time I was standing outside the gym last fall with my best friend, Isaac Kim, when I inadvertently let my jaw drop hearing Larissa Delibero describe the blow job she'd given Eric Mann. In great detail. Larissa caught my stunned look and commented, "Obviously someone's never given a BJ." Her pack of cheerleaders laughed, egging her on. "Might wanna check out some porn before you get a boyfriend. *If* you ever get a boyfriend."

Larissa was correct: I had never given a BJ. Sure, I had kissed a few boys, but I hadn't ventured much beyond that. The thing was, I wasn't even sure I wanted to anytime soon.

"Jules," Isaac had whispered, "you need to get that face under control."

That night I had started practicing *not* showing every ounce of what I was feeling on my face. Each night, I stood in front of the mirror, thinking about happy things, sad things, upsetting things, all the while keeping my face in neutral. Since then I was better at it. Admittedly still not great, but at least not as bad as Mom. Baby steps.

"What's the matter?" my older sister, Helen, asked my mother, entering the kitchen, texting. She was sporting a tweed jacket and skirt, which was a little matchy-matchy for my taste, but it worked perfectly on her. She had inherited my mom's tall, slender frame, so everything looked good on her. She also had Mom's straight auburn hair. I had our family's signature auburn locks too, but unfortunately my hair had a hard time making up its mind if it identified as straight (like Helen's) or curly (like Dani's), so it occupied a frizz-filled middle ground no amount of product seemed to be able to tame.

Not taking her eyes off her phone, Helen plopped her book bag down on the kitchen table, sloshing my cereal so hard that it nearly spilled over onto my sleeve.

"Hey," I protested, but Helen ignored me, laughing at something on her screen. Ignoring me was pretty much Helen's M.O.—at home and at school. She was an effortlessly smart senior, kept a

4.0 while also being captain of the field hockey team, and was queen of her clique. My hours of homework yielded Bs—plusses if I was lucky—and I barely got to play at my volleyball games. And while I wasn't exactly *unpopular*, I wasn't setting any records for social status either. Sure, I had Isaac, who was a great best friend, and a few girls I knew from volleyball. I'd tried to be better friends with other girls in the past, but for some reason it never seemed to work—I always said the wrong thing or didn't say enough. I'd secretly hoped that the jump from middle school to high school would magically catapult me into the next level.

Spoiler alert: it didn't.

Lately I'd been trying to convince myself that the fact that no one paid attention to me was actually a good thing. It meant I could blend in, take my photographs without being noticed, watch the world from the safety of my screen. High school was just something I had to get through. It was okay that I didn't seem to fit in now. I'd do better later, in college—in Life. Then one day I'd be a successful photographer in New York City or San Francisco, and no one would remember that in her high school days, world-famous editorial photojournalist Jules Mathis hadn't exactly fit in.

Or at least that's what I was telling myself.

"Is something going on at work?" Helen reached for the French press of coffee that Mom had brewed for Dad. Drinking coffee was something I'd wanted to try—it seemed grown-up, more sophisticated than drinking soda or juice—but I couldn't get past the smell, which to me was like chocolaty dirt.

"Nothing's wrong," Mom practically sang, forcing a smile.

I took a bite of my soggy cornflakes and glanced at Dani, hoping she'd acknowledge Mom's obvious evasion of the truth, but she was consumed with her glossy magazine. This past summer Dani had lost a bunch of weight and had become obsessed with reading about celebrities.

"What's wrong, honey?"

My dad arrived through the swinging kitchen door and saw Mom's Everything's Fine face.

"Everything's fine, Peter." Mom smiled, not looking him in the eye.

"Liar," he wagered, kissing her on the cheek. Mom didn't respond. She just reached into the cabinet for a box of tea, proving my dad right. My parents were high school sweethearts and knew each other better than they knew themselves. True love? Kind of creepy? I could never decide.

"I have to go in to work early," she explained, plunking a bag of Earl Grey into her travel mug of hot water. "You mind dropping off the girls?"

Mom hadn't bothered to ask Helen to take us, even though Helen and I went to the same school, and Danielle's middle school was right across the street.

"Sure thing," Dad said, reaching for the French press before he realized it was nearly empty. "Where'd all my coffee go?"

DING! Helen's phone sounded—probably her boyfriend, Landon, texting that he was waiting outside to chauffeur her to school.

"Thanks, Daddy!" Helen flashed a grin and zipped out the door with a smug smile, her streak of perfection unbroken.

Mom capped her travel mug and skipped her scrambled eggs

in favor of her work files, stuffing them into her bag. "Pizza okay for dinner?"

"I'll just have salad," Dani said, eyeing a too-thin model in her fashion bible.

"Danielle, you can eat a slice of pizza," my mom encouraged. Mom was a psychiatrist and had covertly coached Dani through the change in physique. My guess was Mom had seen her share of eating disorders at the hospital where she worked.

"Okay," Dani gave in. "With pepperoni."

"No mushrooms," I requested—I just couldn't get over their texture.

"You got it," Mom assured me, hurrying out of the kitchen. "Have a good day, everyone!"

She'd forgotten her travel mug of tea. It was unlike my mom to leave in such a rush. Whatever call she'd gotten from work must have been important.

"Can we run through my sixteen bars for my audition one more time?" Dani asked Dad.

"I don't want you and Jules to be late, sweetheart," he countered.

"Please? You're so good at playing the piaaa-nooo?" she belted. "It'll take two sehhh-connnnds?" Dani could get a homeless guy to give her money if she asked the right way.

"Okie-doke. Just one time through," Dad caved as he followed her out.

I was left alone in the kitchen. This seemed to happen a lot in my family, everything kind of swirling around me. Me ending up alone.

As the upbeat strains of "Defying Gravity" from *Wicked* floated in, I experimented with a few filters on the photo I'd taken of my unsunk cereal before posting it on Instagram. I liked posting images that told stories—a forgotten mitten on a playground, a couple holding hands, a kid staring at the cookie aisle. I loved the way photos let you express something without having to actually say anything.

I captioned the photo #unsinkable, along with #julespix #(its) stilllife #picoftheday, and posted it.

A "like" immediately popped up, causing my stomach to flutter. Someone had noticed me.

I checked to see who had liked the photo.

ig: futurejusticekim

My face fell. It was from Isaac. While I appreciated the "like," somehow it didn't make me feel as special knowing that it came from him. And just like that, I went back to being average again.

CHAPTER 2

THE TEENAGE GIRL'S THIN FRAME LAY ON THE hospital bed, her sleep anything but restful. Her small lungs lifted upward with a short, jagged gasp for air as her sedated body struggled to keep itself oxygenated.

It had been a long night for the girl—ambulance, EMTs, ER doctors. She'd landed in the trauma unit, where the staff worked to stem the bleeding from the wounds on her back. The police had been there too, trying to find out what they could about the incident, but the girl was so depleted she could barely speak, and when the police ran her description through a missing persons database, they came up empty. They hoped that a social worker from Child Protective Services might be able to obtain more information.

And they needed it.

The girl had fiery rope marks on her wrists, ankles, and the back of her neck, telling the tale of forcible restraint. What was even more disturbing, though, were the extensive bruises that covered her body. Purple and blue swirls of blood circled just under her skin's surface like weather patterns of hurt.

The hushed conversation around the hospital had surged during the morning shift change: Who was this strange girl who'd been found by the side of the road with the sign of Satan carved into her back? And more important, what had happened to her?

The girl expelled a labored breath, her rib cage sinking back toward the bed.

"How ya doin', sweetie?"

Connie—a veteran nurse who lived for her patients—shuffled in, tired from being up all night. Although she was supposed to have left the hospital hours ago after her night shift, she had traded shifts with a colleague so that she could stay near the new arrival and make sure she was okay. The girl didn't stir.

Stepping over to the bedside, Connie checked the patient's chart. She adjusted the girl's IV of antibiotics. Although the girl's pitch-black strands of hair were still caked with mud, they managed to keep their raven luster, even under the hospital fluorescents. Her milk-white skin had been wiped clean, although a few specks of dirt still spotted her cheeks.

Connie leaned over, stretching her stout frame across the sleeping girl to get a glimpse at her back. Despite the white bandages that had been placed over the girl's wounds, blood had seeped through the barricades and now painted the thin hospital gown. She'd have to change the dressing after she checked her vitals.

Connie placed a gloved hand on the girl's shoulder. The girl's eyelids flickered, then slowly separated.

"Open for me?" Connie held a thermometer near the girl's mouth to check her temperature. The girl let the nurse get a reading.

"Have to make sure you don't get a fever. Last thing you need is an infection," Connie warned. She checked the thermometer. "A perfect 98.6! Good girl. You hungry, sweetie?"

The girl's thick lashes swept up toward Connie. Weary with sedatives, she shook her heavy head no. She sank her ear back down onto the pillow, her eyes fluttering closed.

Connie decided not to fight it and let the girl drift back to sleep.

"I'm here, Connie!" Dr. Suzanne Mathis raced through the doorway. "Got here as fast as I could," she explained, pulling her white hospital coat around her. "Is this—"

Suzanne's gaze fell on the sleeping girl. As her eyes took in the blood-spotted gown, the waifish body, the bruises, her expression clouded over.

"She's about Julia's age, right?" Connie asked Suzanne.

Suzanne nodded, but her face paled at the thought of her daughter Jules being compared with this injured girl.

"Are her vitals stable?" Suzanne asked, stepping toward the bed.

"They are, but she's been mostly nonresponsive. Poor thing's been through a lot."

Suzanne perused her chart. "Do we know her actual name?"

"Came in with no identification so it's 'Lauren Trauma' till we know more."

"The police couldn't figure out anything more?" It was unusual for someone to arrive with absolutely no identifying factors.

Connie shook her head. "Not yet. This one's a mystery."

"How's her back?" Suzanne asked, noting the blood-speckled bandages.

"It's—" Connie started, but wasn't sure how to finish. "I've never seen anything like it," she concluded.

The girl's chest rose and sank, rose and sank. The two women watched their patient, mesmerized by her mysterious arrival and clearly traumatic past.

"She's like a broken angel," Connie sighed.

Suzanne finally tore away her stare. "I'm going to get some tea. Page me when she wakes up?"

Connie nodded. "Will do."

Suzanne took one more look at the patient's sleeping face. She watched as the girl's eyelids twitched.

What nightmares lay behind those lids?

CHAPTER 3

THE CRISP AUTUMN LEAVES CRUNCHED UNDER MY SECONDHAND oxfords. They were a little more formal than the Converse I'd sported last year, to go with my recently adopted vintage look. The heels made a satisfying click against the pavement.

As I headed down the sidewalk toward school, I braced myself for Monday morning. Everyone would be talking about how much fun they'd had over the weekend—what parties they'd gone to, who got wasted, who hooked up with who. Friday night I'd Netflix-binged on British comedies with Isaac—one of the only things he and I could agree on to watch. He was a big documentary fan, and I'd recently gotten into old movies. There was something about them that I found comforting. I'd also stayed in on Saturday night, theoretically to babysit Dani while my parents had their date night, but really to rewatch *Casablanca*.

"You again." I heard a voice coming from a yellow school bus. Isaac peered down at me through the rectangular slat of an open window.

"Come on, Rapunzel," I returned. Isaac flicked his chin-length black hair out of his eyes. He was in perpetual need of a haircut.

"Ugh, fine, I guess I'll continue to spend nearly every waking moment with you," he conceded, hopping down the steep steps of the vehicle.

"Who else would you hang out with?" I asked, adjusting the straps of the new tan book bag Mom had gotten me at a Labor Day sale last week. I liked its brass buckle and thick stitching, but the faux-leather straps were already starting to fray. No wonder it was on sale.

"Who else would *you* hang out with?" Isaac countered. Fair point.

As Isaac and I turned up the lawn-lined walkway toward the two-story redbrick building, our steps fell in sync. We'd been best friends since third grade, when he moved from Alaska to Ohio to live with his aunt. I never asked too many questions about why, but it seemed like whatever had happened to Isaac earlier in his life had made him the kind of person to make room for himself wherever he went.

"True or false," Isaac started. "In the United States, campaigns that support candidates for public office ought to be financed exclusively by public funds."

"Do we have a quiz?"

"Wrong answer. It's my next topic." Isaac was super into Speech and Debate, and had competed on a team since middle school.

"Do I even need to ask which side you're arguing?" Isaac was always fighting for the underdog. He was a perpetual man of the people.

"Campaigns should be fought fair and square, with the same budgets on both sides. It's not an impartial selection process if one side gets unlimited private funding and the other doesn't. Additionally, it's absurd the amount of money that's spent, period. Why not put that money to better use? Like toward infrastructure, or public resources?"

"Sounds like a good argument," I assured him.

"I'm going up against Victoria Liu, who is vehemently pro-corporate financing. Like, hello, Citizens United is ridiculous," he argued. "But her dad's a big anti-union guy, which around here is obviously blasphemy, but it figures she'd take that position. Blech. And I know she's gonna try to play hardball with me—she's still mad since I whipped her ass at regionals."

"You guys are on the same team. It's only September; you have a whole year to get through with her."

"I still did way better than her," he smirked, not hiding his ambitious nature. "And don't think I'm just being competitive with her because we're both Asian," he added.

I smiled. "I think you'll kill it."

"I know I will," he replied with unironic certainty. "You should join the team, Jules."

"Yeah right, you know how much I love public speaking," I joked.

"You need to bump up your extracurrics."

"I'm still waiting to hear from the *Regal*."

I had finally convinced myself to submit an application to take pictures for our weekly school paper. They already had an excellent photographer on staff, though—a senior named Rachel Robideaux—so it was unlikely they'd need anyone new. But, channeling the boldness of Holly Golightly in *Breakfast at Tiffany's*, I was trying new things.

I did really want to be a photojournalist. But, full disclosure, I might have had a second reason for wanting to join the paper. And that second reason might have been named Sebastian Jones.

Sebastian was also a sophomore now, and had shown up at school last fall. He'd moved here from Philadelphia and immediately made his mark, scoring the highest GPA in our class. He'd written a *Remingham Regal* article on "The Fifteen-Minute Hack to Improve Your GPA," quickly becoming one of their star journalists, and at the end of the school year he'd been named editor in chief—the youngest in the school's history.

We'd ended up as lab partners last year in Earth Science. His friendly demeanor made him really easy to talk to, which somehow calmed my jittery nerves. As we put together our final project, on plate tectonics, Sebastian had confided in me that he planned to restructure the school paper—and bring in some fresh blood. As far as I knew they hadn't offered any positions yet, so I was still holding my breath.

"They'd be idiots not to take you," Isaac assessed. "You're just as good as Rachel Robideaux, if not better."

"You might be just a *little* biased," I smiled. Secretly, I loved that Isaac's faith in me was as strong as his faith in himself.

"Oh!" Isaac erupted. "This weekend there's a screening of a documentary on America's surveillance state. We're going."

"Only if you do a David Lean double feature at the Independent with me. *Lawrence of Arabia* and *Doctor Zhivago* in seventy millimeter."

"Are they in black and white?" Isaac whined.

"You liked the Hitchcock films," I countered.

"Because those were creepy."

"These are classics. And in color."

"Fine, as long as you buy me popcorn *and* a drink," he negotiated. "Deal?"

But I had stopped listening. Across the swarms of students I had caught a glimpse of something—okay, someone. Sebastian was standing on the side entrance ramp, scrolling through his phone. The newspaper office was near the side doors, and although there was usually a contingency of Goth kids perched on the railing smoking, the ramp was also frequented by a *Regal* staffer or two. I'd seen Sebastian a few times since school had started, and we'd caught up about our summers—he'd been away at a journalism camp like an exciting person while I lifeguarded at the local pool like a boring person. But seeing him in person still made my breath catch in my chest.

"Earth to the Friend Formerly Known As Best." Isaac called back my attention.

I willfully tore my thoughts away from Sebastian. "What? Yeah, I'll get the tickets," I said, trying to cover the fact that I'd spaced.

Isaac folded his arms. He could tell I hadn't been listening, and not listening was a federal offense in his book.

"Where is he?" Isaac searched the crowd.

"Who?" I tried to play it off, but I knew who he was talking about and he knew that I knew.

"It's written all over your face," he retorted.

Damn. "Whatever. He doesn't even like me."

"You two just need to bang and get it over with," Isaac teased.

"Yeah, I'll get right on that. As soon as I can string together a sentence in front of him."

The truth was, Isaac and me discussing banging was as arbitrary as us talking about sailing yachts, living in the landlocked middle of Ohio. Neither of us had any real experience. I'd only been to first base a few times, and Isaac was practically asexual. He never talked about liking girls—or boys, for that matter. Sometimes I wondered if Isaac might come out as bi or gay, but he never brought it up, so neither did I.

"Hey, what should we do for the Social Studies presentation?" Isaac mused, changing the subject as we headed up the stairs toward the front entrance. He took the steps two at a time.

"Isaac, it's not until November," I reasoned.

"I know," he defended. "I was thinking: The Power of the Proletariat in Cold War USSR. Fun, right?"

I cast one last glance at Sebastian. The morning light glinted off his black-rimmed glasses as he cracked a smile at something on his phone.

"Sure," I replied as we stepped through the front doors of the school. "But then you have to promise to watch North by Northwest with me."

"Again?" he sighed.

CHAPTER 4

DR. MATHIS: Testing, testing. Is this recording? I pressed the red dot. . . . Okay, looks like it's working.

[Creaking of bedsprings.]

DR. MATHIS: Oh, you don't have to get up, you can stay where you are. You had a long night.

[Shuffling of some papers.]

DR. MATHIS: So, I am Dr. Suzanne Mathis, attending psychiatrist at Remingham Regional Hospital, and I'm here to assess how you are doing. I am here with patient—

[No answer.]

DR. MATHIS: Would you mind telling me who you are? We don't have any identification on file for you yet.

[No answer.]

DR. MATHIS: Your name? Or do you have some kind of ID that the staff might have overlooked?

[Leaning close] Please note that the patient has shaken her head, indicating that she has no ID.

That's okay. Why don't you have some water?

[After a short silence, a cup clinks.]

DR. MATHIS: I know you've been through something unspeakable. Something you never want to face again, let alone talk about. But I want you to know that I'm here to help you. That is my entire job. To help you work through what happened.

They're calling you "Lauren Trauma." That's your code name in your file. We use it for your own protection, so that only people we give it to can find you. But can I tell you a secret? The ones who we never find out their real name—they're forgotten, they're the ones left behind. And we're not going to let that happen to you.

[A tired, raspy teenage girl's voice finally speaks.]

MAE: Mae. My name.

DR. MATHIS: Thank you for telling me, Mae. That's a beautiful name. Do you spell it with a Y?

MAE: E.

DR. MATHIS: Wonderful. And your last name?

[No answer.]

DR. MATHIS: Okay. We'll stick with Mae for now.

So Mae, tell me what you remember from last night. Besides the doctors and tests and all that. Tell me about what happened before you got here.

MAE: I—don't remember anything.

DR. MATHIS: Nothing at all?

MAE: I remember—the truck driver. He found me. There were bright lights, and then he called the ambulance, I think.

DR. MATHIS: Thank you, that's what I have here as well. He called the ambulance at 12:52 a.m. It is pretty incredible that he

24

saw you. Police said you were lying nearly fifteen feet from the side of the highway. How did you land so far from the road?

MAE: I don't know.

DR. MATHIS: Did you jump out of a moving vehicle? Or head into the woods from the road? Or did you maybe come from inside the woods?

MAE: I was in a car. Van. A white one.

DR. MATHIS: Okay, so you were riding in a van. In the passenger seat?

MAE: In the back. I was thrown from there.

DR. MATHIS: You were thrown from a moving vehicle?

MAE: Yes.

DR. MATHIS: By thrown, do you mean that the van hit a bump or something, or it got a flat tire?

MAE: No, by a person.

DR. MATHIS: You were thrown by a person out of the back of a van.

MAE: Maybe that's why I rolled so far.

[Quiet. Some scribbling.]

MAE: It was two people.

DR. MATHIS: Two people threw you?

MAE: And someone else was driving.

DR. MATHIS: Do you know who threw you?

Do you remember who was driving the van? Or what he—or she—looked like?

MAE: I don't remember. I'm very tired—

DR. MATHIS: Of course you are. Just a little bit longer. Do you remember anything about them? Any of the people involved? Were they tall, short, thin, heavy?

MAE: They were wearing black.

DR. MATHIS: Black sweaters? Jackets? Pants?

MAE: Long black coats.

DR. MATHIS: And what about their faces? Could you see what any of them looked like? Do you remember what color anyone's hair was? Or—

MAE: They were wearing hoods.

DR. MATHIS: Hoods?

MAE: Black hoods.

[Pause.]

DR. MATHIS: Mae, where are you from?

MAE: From?

DR. MATHIS: Are you from Ohio? [Leaning in] Note that the patient has nodded affirmative. Where in Ohio are you from? Somewhere nearby?

[Quiet. A sip of water is gulped.]

DR. MATHIS: Mae, I'm going to help you. I'm going to help you stay safe, and help keep you away from whoever did this to you. It won't be easy, but we're going to have to trust each other. Can you do that? Can you trust me?

MAE: [Pause.] Okay.

DR. MATHIS: Good, thank you. I'll trust you too. Okay, this next part might be difficult, but we're going to get through it. Together. Mae, who did this to you? The carving on your back. Who cut you? Was it someone you knew?

[Leaning close] Please note that the patient is nodding her head yes. Can you tell me who it was? The more I know, the more I can help you. Was it someone from your family?

You're nodding yes.

MAE: Mmm-hmm.

DR. MATHIS: Was it your—father?

[No answer.]

DR. MATHIS: Mae, most abuse happens from within the family. It's nothing to be ashamed of, because none of it is your fault. Do you understand that? None of it is your fault.

Was it your dad, or an uncle?

MAE: Yes.

DR. MATHIS: Which one was it?

[After a long pause.]

MAE: Both.

[Quiet.]

MAE: I need to rest now—

DR. MATHIS: Are you sure you don't want to tell me—

MAE: I'm so tired.

DR. MATHIS: [Leaning into the microphone] Note that the patient has closed her eyes and is no longer responsive.

CHAPTER 5

CLICK.

A crumpled chip bag lay on the puke-colored linoleum a few lockers over from mine. Its silver interior sparkled under the hallway fluorescents. Inspecting the frames I'd snapped, I sharpened the image and bumped up the green highlights, then posted the picture to Instagram, captioning it #trashcan't.

The pic would be a good addition to my portfolio. The summer program application wasn't due until January, but I wanted to get a head start and send my submission in early. The idea of focusing on photography for a whole month sounded like heaven.

At first, Mom had been worried about the idea of me spending four weeks in a big city, but since she went to a yearly convention in Chicago in December for work, I'd convinced her to take me with her. That way I could show her how well I could manage. Then she'd have to let me go.

My stomach groaned, reminding me that I had turned my nose up at the mystery meat on offer at lunch and was starving, so I made my way down the hallway to the cafeteria. When I reached the vending machines, the choices stared back at me, daring me to make a selection. Sometimes, when I got too hungry, deciding what to eat felt like brain surgery.

"Go with the granola bar," I heard from behind me.

I turned to see Sebastian adjusting his glasses. Feeling a blush blooming across my cheeks, I quickly swiveled my attention back to the prepackaged foods.

"But the peanut butter–filled pretzels are hard to beat," I replied, hoping I didn't sound as nervous as I felt. I punched in D6 and a snack plunked to the bottom of the machine. Before I realized what was happening, Sebastian knelt down and retrieved the plastic pack.

"*Gracias,*" I managed.

"*De nada,*" he returned, handing the bag of pretzels to me. I'd forgotten how easy it was to talk to him.

I ripped open the packet and held it out to him. He reached in and popped a protein-filled pretzel into his mouth. I took one too.

"Oh wow," he said through crunches. "Good call, Mathis." The side of his mouth rose into a half smile. I could feel myself staring at his lips, making me feel kind of giddy and queasy, like I'd eaten too much candy.

Pull yourself together, Jules. He is only a human.

Sebastian reached into the pocket of his jeans and deposited a few quarters into the machine. "How's your day going?"

"Despite forgetting the capital of Serbia in Social Studies, not too bad," I answered.

"Belgrade," he said without pause as he punched in his snack selection.

"Ding ding ding."

A bag of peanut butter pretzels dropped. His choice was obviously a sign that he was in love with me and we were meant to be.

"I know what you're thinking," he said.

Oh no. Was it that obvious that I liked him? Had he caught me staring this morning?

"The *Regal*," he said, tearing open his bag of carbs.

Right. The paper. Duh.

"So," Sebastian started, "we're not going to bring on a new staff photographer."

My stomach sank. This was very not-good news.

"Rachel's got it under control, and she's a senior, so I want to give her, well, seniority," he explained.

I felt the strap of my book bag slipping down my decades-old shirtsleeve, which I'd rummaged from my grandma Lydia's old clothes in the attic.

"She's a talented photographer," I said, willing myself not to show my disappointment on my face.

"However, I'm starting a new section on the back page of the paper, and to go with it, there's a new position I'm creating," Sebastian revealed. "A portrait-a-week, *Humans of New York*–style column. Intimate, no-frills portraits of people around school, with short interviews accompanying. A little get-to-know-you type thing, with interesting facts about the subject."

That sounded like a supercool idea, but I didn't know what to say. My brain was sprinting to figure out where he was going with this.

"That sounds awesome," I encouraged. "We see people around school every day, and we know who people are on a superficial level, but not what's underneath. Why they are the way they are. Sorry, I'm rambling," I apologized.

"Exactly! It's about connecting with people you don't know."

"'People You Don't Know.' That's what you should call it," I spitballed.

Sebastian cocked his head, his shaggy brown hair falling across his forehead. "I like the way you think, Mathis."

"I like the way *you* think," I returned. Oh God, I was so bad at this.

Luckily he didn't seem to notice. "So the column might be something you're up for? You'd take the photos and also do the interviews."

I froze, willing myself to come up with a response. Sebastian continued, "You have such a great eye, Jules. Your images really tell a story." He was looking right at me, his warm brown eyes staring into mine. "You'd be a perfect fit."

"I'm in," I blurted, trying to sound more confident than I felt.

"Excellent! Why don't you come in after school tomorrow and interview with the rest of the team."

"I'm there." I beamed. Then corrected, "I mean, I'll be there. Tomorrow. Not, like, now. You know what I mean." *Stop. Babbling.*

"Can't wait." Sebastian popped a pretzel and headed down the hall.

Neutral face. Neutral face. Neutral face.

CHAPTER 6

"YOU HAVE NO RIGHT TO DO THIS!" the tall man shouted.

"Sir—" Dr. Mathis cautioned the imposing man in a tone one usually used on cornered animals about to attack. "Please don't raise your voice at me."

She was standing across from the man in the hospital lobby, the sliding doors shut against the crisp fall wind. There were a few waiting patients trying not to stare at the escalating dispute.

"Now listen, lady—" he snarled.

"*Doctor*," Suzanne corrected, quickly deciding not to share the rest of her name with the man. He was wearing a long brown work coat, and a low-pulled cowboy hat covered most of his face. He had a menace to him that made you not want to ask what he did for a living.

"I don't give a rat's ass who you are," he challenged, pacing closer to her. "I know she's here. You have no right to deny me."

His proximity forced Suzanne to take a step backward. She cast a quick glance at the few people watching. The receptionist behind the desk looked on, concerned.

Suzanne squared her shoulders and forced herself to face the man.

"We're only allowed to release the patient's information to listed next of kin. It's hospital policy," she said, trying to appeal to the man's rational side, in case he had one.

He didn't.

"Screw your policy!" he spat out, making little effort to control his fury. And although crimson from sun damage, his face grew even redder. "I'm takin' her out of this place!"

"I'm afraid that's not possible." Suzanne stood a little straighter as he towered over her.

He leaned closer, his beady eyes only inches from Suzanne's face. "Are ya? Afraid?"

Suzanne took a deep breath. She wasn't going to take the bait.

"While I would like for you to have your needs met," Suzanne said slowly, steadily, "we are not legally allowed to release her to you."

"I've had enough of your lies. Lemme talk to someone who can actually do something," he demanded, taking one last step toward Suzanne. Her back was now up against the reception center wall, making it impossible to move any farther away from him. The man had her trapped. She cast a glance toward the receptionist, who picked up her phone.

"Code purple," the woman whispered into the receiver.

The man's eyes remained focused on Suzanne, who stared back, boldly meeting his gaze. "She's not medically cleared for discharge."

With that, the man whipped his fist into the air, incredibly close to Suzanne's face. He held it there.

The room tensed.

There was a long moment where neither Suzanne nor the man moved an inch.

Then he spread his hand open slowly, softly stroking Suzanne's cheek.

Suzanne flinched but kept still as she could as the man's rough hand moved across her face. She could barely breathe.

"You're just a scared little lamb, aren't you," he taunted.

"Dr. Mathis!" A security guard hurried into the lobby. His entrance caused the tall man to step back from Suzanne, breaking the spell that had fallen over the room.

"Sorry, I was helping Mrs. Engle out to her nephew's car," the hefty security guard explained. "What's going on here?"

"It's okay, Jerry," Suzanne said, pulling her white lab coat around her waist, regaining her composure.

"We have some trouble?" Jerry asked the man.

"Nah, we're just gettin' to know each other," the man said with a wry smile.

Jerry wasn't as tall as the cowboy hat–wearing man, but he did have a handgun tucked snugly into his belt.

"Why don't we step outside, sir." Jerry was clearly not just asking.

Two cops suddenly appeared. "This the code purple?" one of them asked, reaching for his gun.

The tall visitor raised his hands in compliance. "Calm your horses, I'm leavin'," he growled. He stepped toward the lobby doors, then turned back and flashed his dark eyes at Suzanne.

"I'll be back for the girl. You can't keep her forever."

CHAPTER 7

JUST WHEN I THOUGHT I'D GOTTEN A LEG up in the being-noticed department—Sebastian had thought of me to write and photograph the new column!—I was immediately forgotten again.

Mom hadn't arrived to pick me up at school, and because of volleyball practice I'd already missed the late bus. I'd texted and even called her, but she didn't answer, which was weird, 'cause she always answered, even if it was a *busy right now call you back* text.

I'd texted Dad too, but I knew that was useless. He was terrible with all things phone-related, and I was sure he was working anyway.

I had been forced to get a ride home with Stacy Pickman, who lived next door and was on the volleyball team with me, and her complaining had been nonstop. Ever since my face had revealed that I thought her jeans were too tight a few years ago, she tried to ignore me in school, but the truth was Stacy had even fewer friends than I did—meaning zero—so she couldn't be too choosy. And she'd never turn down the opportunity to have a captive audience to complain to.

She complained about how spotty the Wi-Fi was in the cafeteria, how gym class should be shorter, and how upset she was that the weather had already turned cold. It seemed pointless to me to complain about things you couldn't do anything about, but for Stacy no topic was off-limits. To drown it all out, I'd taken to counting churches as we passed them. Twenty-four.

When we finally got home, I nearly fell out of the car in my desperate attempt to escape. "Bye, Stace!" I called, slamming the door to her parents' old Ford sedan. I knew she hated being called that, but I couldn't resist. She had just been complaining about trees. Trees.

I headed down the stone walkway toward our house. It looked pretty much like the other houses on our block—two-story family homes in unassuming colors. American flags waving on the porch. Typical suburbia. Behind the row of residences were some woods. We'd played there when we were little, but I never saw any neighborhood kids back there anymore.

I was surprised to see Mom's car parked in front of the garage.

If she was home already, why hadn't she answered my text? Or returned my phone call? Maybe her phone had run out of battery. But she always carried a backup battery, in case there was an emergency.

When I reached the front door, I noticed it was slightly ajar.

This was some *Rear Window*–level creepiness.

"Mom?" I called, pushing the door open and stepping into the vestibule. "Are you home?"

My voice echoed off the wooden staircase. I stepped into the living room. Empty.

My mind was starting to race. Was she still at work? But then why was her car here?

"Jules!" My mom swooped through the swinging kitchen door into the living room, startling me. She wore her Worried face. Uh-oh.

"I'm so glad you're home!" she blurted, her words coming out faster than usual.

"You left the door open." I slung my book bag onto the couch. "And why didn't you answer my text?"

"What text?" she asked, moving over to a vase and nervously picking out the dead flowers.

"I sent you a text that I needed a ride. Stacy had to drive me," I explained, with emphasis on the Stacy. Mom wasn't crazy about her either, and thought her parents ought to do a better job at regulating her expectations of the world.

"I'm sorry, honey. Work was . . ." She trailed off.

She seemed like she had a lot on her plate, so I dropped it. "Don't worry about it," I said, reaching for the TV remote. "Is Dani home?"

"She just got back from her audition and fro-yo with Taryn. Apparently it went well!" she replied, intercepting my reach. "Helen won't be back until later."

I stared at the remote in her hand. "Can I not watch TV right now?"

She took a deep breath. "I want to talk to you about something."

Mom's "talks" were never good. They were always about things that were uncomfortable: there was the time we had a "talk" about my grandma dying; the time Mom and Dad told me they were converting our playroom into an office for Dad; and worst of all, the S-E-X talk, which was a festival of awkwardness. My mom's tactic for dealing with awkward situations was to move through them as agonizingly slowly as possible. With that particular talk she had expounded on the details of various forms of contraceptives and every single sexually transmitted disease known to mankind, all of which made me not want to think about sex for a very long time. Or maybe just become a nun.

But this was something different. Mom seemed distracted. Almost skittish. Something was definitely not right.

"Are you okay?"

"Of course!" she said brightly, clearly lying.

"Did I do something wrong?" I asked, scrolling through possibilities for her peculiar behavior.

"Not at all," she answered quickly. "You're—*I love you.*"

While appreciated, my mother's sudden profession of love was disconcerting.

"Mom, seriously, what's up? You're freaking me out."

Mom smoothed down her already straight hair. "Why don't you come into the kitchen?" She then called upstairs, "Danielle, could you come down, please?"

Mom moved over to the swinging door and held it open for me. Wanting to get to the bottom of the weirdness as quickly as possible, I stepped through.

The kitchen was eerily quiet, like one of those soundproof rooms where the padded walls absorb any noise. It felt airless.

Sitting at our kitchen table was a teenage girl.

She looked about my age, and had shiny black hair, which hung long and wet down her back. Her thin shoulders slumped forward, which gave the impression that she was trying to protect herself. From what, I didn't know. She was wearing a too-large pink sweatshirt adorned with a cat painted in glitter. It looked like it had been sitting crumpled up somewhere. The large top made her seem even thinner than she already was, the shirt cuffs sagging around her delicate wrists. Her pants were those blue scrubs that people at my mom's hospital wore. It looked like she'd been outfitted by the hospital's lost and found.

"Have a seat," my mother requested.

I sat down across the table from the girl. Her face was pale and looked almost ghostlike under the lamp that hung over the kitchen table. Her enormous eyes were bright green, and focused on the plate in front of her—a peanut butter and jelly sandwich Mom had probably made for her. The food lay untouched.

Although she looked like she hadn't slept in months, and she didn't seem to be wearing any makeup, this girl was really beautiful. Like model pretty. I felt a wave of jealousy and quickly tried to shove it down. I didn't even know this girl; there was no reason for me to make snap judgments about her. But who was she and why was she sitting in our kitchen?

Mom read my mind.

"Jules," she started, perching herself on a chair. "This is Mae. Mae, this is Jules—my middle child."

I resented being called the "middle child," but for whatever reason Mom wasn't acting like herself, so I didn't say anything about it.

"Hey." I half waved to the girl, who didn't look up.

"Hello," she mumbled back, pulling the cuffs of her sweatshirt over her wrists.

Sitting across from this Mae girl felt . . . strange. She had a strong pull, like there was something kind of magnetic about her.

I didn't know why this girl was at our house, but she was obviously uncomfortable, so I did my best to bridge the silence.

"Cool top," I offered as an ironic icebreaker.

Mae looked down at the glittery feline on her sweatshirt. She then swept her large green eyes up to face me, and stared.

My breath caught in my throat. I didn't know what to say. Something about the way she looked at me made me feel exposed, like she could see inside my brain.

"I—I was kidding," I stammered, looking away. Creepy stare: check. No sense of humor: check.

"Mom, they're posting casting tomorrow online. I'm so nervous!" Danielle had arrived. She saw Mae.

"Hi!" She grinned.

"Danielle, this is Mae. Mae, this is my youngest daughter, Danielle."

Mae barely nodded. "Nice to meet you," she said, so softly we all had to lean closer to hear. Danielle grabbed a bag of dehydrated peas from the cabinet and joined us at the table.

"You can call me Dani," my sister offered, holding out the bag of snacks to Mae. Mae looked at the packaged food with curiosity but declined.

Mom looked at me, urging me with her eyes to continue interacting with Mae, like somehow I should be the one to hold down this awkward conversation. I wasn't sure what else to say to her.

"Danielle auditioned for her school musical today," I said, deflecting the herculean task of talking to this quiet stranger to my chatty sister, who was an Oscar-winning movie at talking to people, while I was a student film.

"I'm up for one of the leads," Danielle piped in, taking my bait. "It's *Wicked*."

Mae looked at Dani, her face contorting into confusion.

"That's the name of the musical," my sister clarified. "It's really good. It's based on a book, which is based on *The Wizard of Oz*, and it was on Broadway."

These all seemed like foreign words to Mae, but that didn't stop Dani.

"I'm up for the role of Elphaba, one of the two main parts. I really really really want to get it but if I don't I know I'll at least get a supporting role."

I was sure Dani would get a good part—she was admittedly a great singer, and had taken dance lessons since she could walk.

"You sing?" came a feeble voice from across the table. We all looked at Mae. "I used to sing," she continued.

"At school?" Danielle asked.

Mae shook her head no.

"Church?" I guessed. Dani, Helen, and I had all sung in our church choir when we were kids.

Mae considered. "Sort of."

"That's wonderful, Mae," my mom interrupted before Mae could say any more. "Thank you for sharing that with us.

"So, girls," she continued, folding her hands on the tabletop. "Mae came in to my work."

I tried to hide the surprise on my face. It was strange for my mom to bring a patient home. Mom barely even talked about work at home, let alone brought an actual patient to the dinner table. Her profession required strict confidentiality, and she took that very seriously.

I looked at Mae's fair skin and seen-everything eyes. Other than being on the thin side, she looked fine.

Mae turned her attention toward the sandwich and poked it with her bony finger. Underneath her baggy sleeve I caught a glimpse of purple marks on her wrist. How did she get those? Was that why she was in the hospital? Had she tried to kill herself?

Maybe she wasn't so fine after all.

I suddenly felt guilty for being so judgy about her before. Who knows what this girl had been through. She was Mom's patient, so obviously something wasn't right. I should try to be nicer to her.

Before I could say anything, Mom cleared her throat, then looked at Danielle and me.

"Mae is going to stay with us for a few days."

Danielle and I stared at our mother, bewildered. Talking about her work at home was one thing, but bringing a patient home to *stay* with us?

"Why?" I said before I could stop myself.

Mom scolded my rudeness with her eyes. Then she explained calmly, "It's not an option for Mae to return to her home, so she's going to stay with us until another suitable option opens up."

I couldn't believe what I was hearing. A psychiatric patient was going to be staying with us? This was completely bizarre.

"It'll just be for a few days," Mom said, looking down at a place mat. She swept up some crumbs, then paced over to the sink to rinse them off her hands.

"So, we have a houseguest!" Mom concluded, upbeat, turning off the water.

I glanced at Mae, who almost smiled, the edges of her naturally red lips turning nearly imperceptibly upward.

This whole situation didn't seem to faze Danielle.

"Cool, wanna stay in my room?" Dani proposed. "I'll sleep on the trundle."

Mom wiped her hands on a dish towel. "Actually, I thought Jules could stay with you, Dani. Then Mae can have her own room," she explained. "And some privacy."

It was strange enough that an unknown person was going to be living with us, but I had to give up my room? What bothered me wasn't so much the fact that I was being displaced, but that Mom had made the decision without consulting me. She always liked to talk things through. Why would she just announce this without discussing it as a family first?

Mom could see that my face had clouded.

"It's only for a few days, Jules," she said. "You don't mind, right?"

It sounded more like a strong suggestion than a question.

I considered. So what if I slept in my sister's room for a night or two. If it was just until Mae found somewhere to go, it wasn't a big deal. And maybe then Mom would get me the new camera I desperately needed.

"Sure, I'll stay with Danielle," I conceded, glancing at Mae.

"Want to listen to my *Wicked* audition?" Danielle chirped to Mae. "I recorded it on my phone!"

Before our new houseguest could answer, I spotted something on Mae's shoulder.

"What is that?" I pointed.

A deep red blotch had appeared through the pink cat sweatshirt, the stain creeping up her back over the top of her shoulder.

"Is that blood?" Danielle gasped. She hated the sight of blood and swore it made her dizzy. I dreaded what was going to happen when she started getting her period.

Mom hurried over with a dish towel and placed it over the blooming bloodstain. Mae must have felt something, but she didn't move.

I stared as Mae closed her eyes, going almost motionless in response to the pain. I'd never seen a reaction like that. When someone was hurt they usually cried, but Mae just—stilled.

Why was this girl bleeding from her back? Had she been beaten? Abused?

"Jules, would you find some clothes for Mae to borrow?" Mom requested. "And please change the sheets on your bed."

"Sure," I answered, standing. I couldn't stop looking at Mae, wondering where she had come from, what had happened to her. I tried to read her face, but as opposed to my mother's, Mae's facade was placid, blank. From looking at it, no one would guess she was currently bleeding through her sweatshirt.

"Let's change your bandages," Mom said tenderly to Mae.

Mae didn't respond. She just sat there, unmoving.

I felt bad for her. She was obviously injured, but there was also the possibility that she had done something to cause the injury, which scared me.

The whole thing was confusing. Who was this strange girl who had come into our home?

CHAPTER 8

MAE DIDN'T JOIN US FOR DINNER.

She said she was too tired, so Mom let her rest. Dad was working late, and Helen was at Landon's. Dani was worrying nonstop about whether she'd get the lead in the musical.

I stared at the tomato sauce–covered triangle on my plate: there were mushrooms on my pizza. Yes, I knew it shouldn't be the biggest deal in the world. Starving children in Africa and all. But it bothered me. My mom had completely forgotten about me—again.

Dani didn't mind—she was chowing down, discussing why she deserved to get the part and *not* Taryn, even though Taryn was her best friend.

"She doesn't know how to hit the high notes right. You go like this," my little sister explained to my mom, knowing that I couldn't care less. She contorted her mouth into an extra-wide almost-smile.

"And then flatten your tongue, -ike -is," she added, her tongue apparently flattened. "That's how my notes sooooooooar," she sang.

I shot her a look: *Really?* She smiled back at me with faux innocence, then dug into a bite particularly ripe with fungus. I grimaced.

"What?" she asked. "Jules, are you insulting my food choices?" she baited me, eyeing Mom.

"No," I returned. "I just don't like mushrooms, which no one seems to remember."

Mom, who had been staring blankly at the tablecloth and hadn't eaten a bite, finally looked at me. I glanced down at my slice.

"Oh, I'm sorry, honey," she remembered. "I forgot to order some plain."

"Whatever, I can pick them off," I compromised, not wanting to get into an argument about it.

Mom's gaze moved toward the leaves of arugula on her plate, but she didn't eat. Why was she so out of it?

"Mom," I started, picking up the crust end of my pizza slice. "After dinner I want to show you the website for an exhibit we can see in Chicago."

Mom turned her threadbare attention toward me.

"For our trip," I explained. "These photographers re-created iconic images from classic Hollywood films with African American models. It looks super cool." Photographers Omar Victor Diop and Antoine Tempé had a stunning collection of photos I really wanted to see in person and not just on my laptop screen.

Mom pushed a smile onto her cheeks. "Sure, honey," she said, and finally speared a cherry tomato.

I was really looking forward to this trip to Chicago. Yes, for the pure excitement factor of traveling to a new place and checking out as many museums and galleries as I could possibly squeeze in, but also to spend time with Mom. She and I never hung out one-on-one anymore. I knew I was a teenager and shouldn't have cared about hanging out with my mother, but it had been a long time since we had, and I was hit with a wave of nostalgia, that in a few years I'd be out of the house—and hopefully out of the state—and hanging out with my mom would be a thing of the past.

"You want me to make you some pasta?" my mom offered.

"No thanks." Mom sometimes got distracted like this for short periods of time when she was ultrafocused on something, so I didn't want to cause any more trouble for her.

I diligently took a bite of my pizza crust, the puffy dough warmly comforting. Glancing over at my mom, I saw the cherry tomato still lingered on her fork. Something was definitely wrong.

"Mom, what's the deal with Mae?" I asked. Maybe if she told me more about what was going on it would snap her out of it.

"While I would like to tell you more, Mae needs some privacy right now, honey" was all she'd answer.

Whatever. I had my interview at the *Regal* to think about. I couldn't be concerned over what was worrying my mother. I had to nail this interview tomorrow with Sebastian. That way not only would I have a recurring reason to hang out with Sebastian, I could also get Isaac off my back with this whole extracurricular thing.

After dinner I camped out in the living room to get my homework done. Mae was in my room, and I wasn't quite ready to brave

Danielle's neon-pink ecosphere of musical theater posters and pre-teen video chats.

Even though she was just resting upstairs, Mae's presence somehow made our house feel off.

BLIP, BLIP.

It was Isaac, video messaging me. I clicked yes to the call on my laptop, happy to see his face pop onto my screen.

"*Señorita*," he greeted me.

"*Señor.*"

"Wanna see me do my debate speech?"

"Wanna see me hang up?"

"Fine, your loss. And hopefully Victoria Liu's," he added in an evil-geniusy way.

"You guys are on the same team—you have to stop hoping she loses."

"Do I?" he asked, only half kidding.

"Whatever," I grumbled, scrolling through my Instagram.

"What crawled up your butt?"

"Ew. Nothing." I lowered my voice. "It's just been a weird night."

Isaac leaned toward the camera. "Regular I'm-a-teenager-and-life-is-weird weird, or a different kind of weird?"

"Different kind of weird."

"How so?"

I modulated to a whisper. "Okay, when I got home today—"

Before I could tell Isaac about the arrival of Mysterious Mae, I heard Dad walking in the front door.

"Hi, Dad!" I called to him, which also signaled to Isaac that I no longer had privacy.

"Hey, Jule-Jule," my father hollered back, entering the living room and loosening his tie. I could tell he was tired.

"Hi, Dad," Isaac sang from my computer.

Dad leaned down to see Isaac on my screen. "What's happening, Isaac?"

"Besides a debate with my nemesis Victoria Liu, who I will wipe the floor with, and trying to find an extracurricular to put on your daughter's academic résumé, not much."

The corners of Dad's eyes crinkled into a smile. "Well, keep up the good work."

"Peter!" we all heard my mother's strained voice call from the kitchen.

Mom burst into the living room, then composed herself.

"Before you go upstairs, can we talk for a minute?" she asked my father. She glanced at me. Then added to my dad, "In the kitchen?"

"Sure," he replied as he headed over and gave her a kiss on the lips.

"Cold glass?" she offered for the beer she would probably pour for him. He followed her into the kitchen.

"Yes, please," he replied.

The door swung closed behind them.

"Since when do your parents have secret meetings?" Isaac investigated.

"I'll call you back," I answered, quickly shutting my laptop before he could ask any more questions.

I tiptoed over to the kitchen to eavesdrop, careful not to touch the swinging door.

Through the door I heard muffled conversation. Mom was speaking way too calmly. It was the voice she used when she wanted us to go along with whatever new therapy study she was testing out on us. I heard snippets:

"Last night . . . work . . . news . . ."

Suddenly I heard a glass break.

Dad's frosted beer glass, I presumed. I wondered which of my parents had dropped it. I then heard clamoring and the sound of broken shards being swept. Over the shuffling and scraping, my dad's voice was beginning to rise. My parents barely ever argued. Was Dad actually getting mad at Mom? Was it about Mae?

The swinging door suddenly shuddered, thudding against my knee. Someone must have passed close to it on the other side.

I quickly moved away from the door. I'd ask Dad about it tomorrow, and hopefully he'd tell me more than Mom had. It wouldn't help my case if I were caught eavesdropping. My detective skills were obviously lacking. I'd have to brush up and rewatch *The Maltese Falcon.*

I grabbed my laptop and crept upstairs.

Sharing a room with Danielle wasn't ideal. She was really messy and she went to sleep much earlier than me. And she was known to snore. Like a chain saw, shaking-the-walls snore. The good news? She was also the deepest sleeper ever. One time on a family trip to Florida she'd slept through a fire alarm at our motel.

Thankfully, she'd taken the trundle and left me the regular bed. After I'd finished my homework, gone through what I was going to say in my interview one more time, and brushed my teeth, I was about to climb in. Then I realized I'd left my headphones in my room. If there was any hope of me getting sleep I'd need noise-canceling sound protection.

I shuffled out of Dani's room and crossed the hall. The door to my room was cracked, a shaft of light slicing the carpet. Mae must still be up.

I knocked lightly on the door.

No answer.

Should I knock again? Maybe she had fallen asleep with the light on. I didn't want to disturb her, but I really needed those headphones if I was going to survive a night in Dani's room.

I gently peeked my head into my room.

Mae was awake, and standing in front of my full-length mirror. She was wearing my old robe, a baby blue terry-cloth one, which I never wore anymore and shared with friends if they needed it on a sleepover. (Not that I had a lot of sleepovers. Or friends. Okay, Isaac wore it once when his aunt went out of town.)

Mae was squinting at her reflection, as if trying to recognize herself. It was like she didn't know who she—

EHHHNNNT—

—creaked the door. Mae whipped around, her bright eyes wide.

I could feel the blush rushing to my cheeks. My mom had brought home this girl with cuts on her back to protect her, and here I was spying. *Classy, Jules.*

"Sorry," I apologized. "Didn't mean to scare you."

She looked down toward the off-white carpet, pulling the bath-robe tight around her shoulders. "It's okay," she replied quietly.

Awkward. Silence.

Which was understandable, her being a complete stranger sleeping in my bedroom. But one of us would have to speak first.

Okay, I could do this.

"Find everything you need?" I asked. "There are extra towels in the bathroom."

She nodded. "Thank you."

"Sure." Quiet descended again.

"I just came to get some headphones." I motioned to a pair of wireless aqua-blue ones on my desk.

"Of course," she said, taking a small step backward as if giving me space, even though we were all the way across the room from each other.

I gently padded over to retrieve the headphones. It was strange to feel so uncomfortable in my own bedroom.

Mae looked at the headphones.

"Dani snores," I explained.

"They're pretty," she mused, as if she'd never seen a pair like them.

"Thanks." I had pined over and gotten them for Christmas, which meant I could listen to my music as loud as I wanted without either of my sisters complaining.

"Feel free to borrow them when I'm at school tomorrow, if you want to listen to music or something."

Mae gave a mild shrug in what I assumed was a thank-you.

I looked at my desk, which I'd left messier than I'd have liked. "Sorry, I should have straightened things up."

"You didn't know I would be here," Mae stated, her tone matter-of-fact.

I looked over at her. She was staring at me, like she was studying me. It gave me a creepy feeling all over.

More dead silence filled the space, creating a weird, quiet standoff.

"I'm sorry to intrude," she continued. "On you and your family."

"Oh, it's fine." I didn't love her staying here, but I didn't want her to feel bad about it. It didn't seem like any of it was her fault.

Mae looked around my room slowly, inspecting everything with laser focus.

"Seems like you have a nice life," she concluded.

A chill swept over my body, giving me goose bumps under my flannel pajamas. I guess I did have a nice life, but having someone point it out like that, with curiosity—jealousy, almost—made me feel uneasy. I wanted to get out of there, but this also seemed like my chance to find out what was really going on.

Be bold, Jules.

"I guess it is," I returned, trying to sound casual. "So, where are you from?"

Mae turned away from me and sat down on the bed, as if the question itself had made her tired. Maybe I'd overstepped.

"You don't have to tell me if you don't want to—"

"Tisdale," she answered, burrowing her toes into the carpet.

"Cool," I said, not knowing anything about the town. "Is it far?"

She took a deep breath and sighed, like she was resentful that I had asked her the question. "About an hour away, I think."

Now I felt weird about prying.

"I've lived in Remingham my whole life," I shared nervously.

"My parents are from here. Well, my dad is. My mom moved here in high school. My grandparents are here too—on my dad's side; we do holidays with them. My mom's side isn't around anymore. Her mom passed away a few years ago, and her dad—I think he died a long time ago. She never talks about him." I tapped a headphone with my index finger self-consciously.

Mae didn't respond. Her back was toward me. Under the collar of the blue robe I could see part of a white bandage. I wondered if she'd have to sleep on her stomach to avoid pressing on whatever was on her back.

"Are you okay?" I asked, my focus still on the bandage.

The wind rattled against the windowpanes.

Mae looked down at her unpainted toenails. Then she turned and stared me dead in the eye.

"I will be."

I didn't know what to say to that. After a few moments of silence, I excused myself and said good night.

There was something off about Mae. Not like I thought she was a vampire or a werewolf or anything. She just seemed out of place in the regular world. I didn't know what to make of her.

As I passed my parents' bedroom en route to bed, I could hear faint arguing coming from behind their door. My parents never fought, which only added to the strangeness of the whole situation. Was Dad mad at Mom? Was there something about Mae that Mom had shared with him and not us? What was wrong with Mae?

Back in Danielle's room, I stepped around her sleeping on the trundle and climbed into bed. I crawled under the pink covers and pulled up a Billie Holiday playlist I often listened to while I worked. I liked listening to classic jazz—it calmed me down when I was feeling anxious, which was more often than I liked to admit.

I put my headphones on and pulled up a search window on my phone. I quickly realized that I didn't know Mae's last name. I did some sleuthing on social media, but no one came up that looked remotely like her.

Then I typed in "Tisdale, Ohio." Maybe where she was from would tell me more about her.

Tisdale popped up on my search. I scanned through a few entries about the town. There wasn't much info: farming town . . . founded in eighteen-something . . .

Then I clicked on the last link. My screen loaded an image:

An upside-down five-pointed star, surrounded by a circle.

The symbol looked familiar, but before I could think of what it meant—

CRASH!

CHAPTER 9

IT WAS A BRANCH. A HEAVY ONE.

It had fallen from the oak tree in our front yard last night. The wind was blowing so hard it knocked the dead bow into the bay window of our living room, shattering the glass. Dani slept through the ordeal (surprise, surprise), and Mom went to comfort Mae. I helped Dad sweep up the glass and tape a tarp over the window. Neither of us spoke much. I could tell he was preoccupied with whatever was going on between him and my mother, and it was the middle of the night, so it didn't seem like the right time to ask any questions.

By the time I got back to bed I was too tired to investigate any further. I needed to get some sleep before my meeting tomorrow.

But I tossed and turned all night. I kept sinking in and out of a nightmare where I was standing in our garage and it was pitch-black. I tried to feel around for a way out, but the walls were too smooth and felt like they just kept going around in a big circle.

Needless to say, the next morning I was exhausted. Trudging into the kitchen, I could barely keep my eyes open. Mom had prepared breakfast, leaving pancakes on the counter.

I decided what I needed was caffeine. Today was the day I would start drinking coffee.

I went over to the French press and poured myself a cup. It smelled smoky and acidic and totally gross, but I didn't care. I had my interview later today and I had to stay awake.

"Since when do you drink coffee?" Helen entered in a gray blazer over a navy wrap dress.

"I need it. I have an interview today."

"It's strong," Helen warned, without asking what my interview was for.

"I know," I shot back, although I had no idea if strong meant caffeine level or flavor or both. I poured what was left of the coffee into a huge mug so that there was none left for her.

Helen glanced at the empty French press. "I'll have Landon stop and get me some," she shrugged. "What happened to the window in the living room?"

If Helen didn't know about the branch, she probably didn't know about Mae yet. I'd heard her come home pretty late last night. Maybe Mom hadn't had time to talk to her. Although you'd think Mom would've at least texted a heads-up. *Hey, there's a strange girl with a bleeding back sleeping in our house.* Was there an emoji for that?

"A branch," I informed her flatly. "Do you even know what's going on?"

Before Helen could answer, Mae entered the kitchen.

I startled. Mae was wearing my clothes.

Mom had asked me to loan her some, which I had, but it was still weird to see the full effect. Mae had on a pair of my dark jeans and a black boatneck sweater Mom had bought me in eighth grade. I'd thought it would make me look sophisticated, but when I wore it, it always felt bulky and never sat quite right on my shoulders. On Mae it fell off her left shoulder, effortlessly high-lighting her elegant collarbone. Over the top edge I could see a white bandage.

Mae must have caught me staring, because she quickly adjusted the sweater to cover her shoulders.

I glanced down at my coffee and forced myself to take a sip.

"Hello, I'm Helen. Are you a friend of Jules's?"

Mae looked at me. *Was* she a friend of mine?

How was I supposed to answer that? I mean, we didn't even know each other yet.

Luckily, Mom interrupted the awkward moment before either of us had to respond. Mom was dressed for the day in taupe slacks and a blue blouse.

"Oh good, you met Mae," Mom said to Helen. "Mae will be stay-ing with us for a few days."

Mae was leaning her hip against the counter, as if she needed it for support. Looking at her long torso, I wondered if she had bled on my bed.

"Great boatneck," Helen complimented. Mae ran her fingers over the bottom of her side-braid, which hung down to her elbow. Even though she had dark circles under her eyes and no makeup on, she still looked gorgeous.

"Oh, thanks," Mae returned quietly. "Jules lent it to me."

"It looks better on you than her."

"Thanks a lot," I shot at Helen, even though I knew she was right.

"Where'd the coffee go?" Dad asked, entering and seeing the empty container. He looked more tired than usual.

"Jules took it all. Bye!" Helen grabbed a protein bar and waltzed out.

Dad turned to me. "If you're going to drink my coffee, Jules, at least make some more." There was a hint of annoyance in his voice.

"I wasn't sure how to," I defended myself.

"It's all right," he said, softening. Dad could never stay mad at us for very long. "I'll show you how sometime."

"You look nice," Mom complimented him, running her hand down his arm. "Is this the new suit we got?"

"Um-hmm." Dad nodded, more tight-lipped toward her than I'd ever seen him.

Mom reached for her travel mug, then realized, "Your meeting! I forgot that was today."

Dad didn't reply, but it was evident that he was a little hurt she'd forgotten.

"The regional manager is going to love you," Mom said as she prepared her Earl Grey. "I'm sure they're going to give you the promotion." From what I gathered, Dad was going up for the position to oversee a merger at the bank he worked at.

"Let's hope so," Dad replied warily as he spooned fresh coffee grounds into the press.

"Peter," Mom started, "I know you have a big day, but would you mind dropping the girls off at school again? Mae and I have to take care of some paperwork at the courthouse."

"Sure," Dad agreed, rolling up the bag of coffee. "Mae, are you hungry?"

He might have been irritated, but my father was a midwesterner through and through—constitutionally incapable of being anything less than polite to a visitor.

"No," Mae answered quietly. "Thank you."

"Mae and I are going to get breakfast at the diner," Mom explained as she capped her to-go tea.

I knew the diner she meant. Mom used to take me there for lunch whenever I'd visit her at work. I loved the periwinkle vinyl seats, the shiny tabletops. But what I loved most about going was that when I was there, I had my mom all to myself. There never seemed to be time for just us anymore.

There did, however, seem to be time for Mae.

I looked at the strange girl in our house. Overnight, she had managed to cause a rift between my parents, my mother was now taking her out to breakfast, and she was wearing my clothes.

But what really bothered me was that I had no idea who this girl was.

CHAPTER 10

"THIS WILL DEFINITELY LEAVE A SCAR," CONNIE CONCLUDED, staring at the girl's back. "But looks like the lacerations are healing well," she added in an effort to find a silver lining. "And your vitals are looking good."

"That's great!" Suzanne exclaimed. Connie looked up at her, hovering over the examining table looking on. Mae was sitting on the edge of it, gown open in the back so Connie could clean the wounds. Mae didn't say anything, just stared at a tree branch out the window of the Medical Floor room, a floor up from the trauma unit she'd been in previously.

"Now this is gonna sting a little." Connie dipped a cotton ball into some disinfectant, then admitted, "Okay, maybe more than a little."

Mae wrapped her fingers around the sides of the mattress, steeling herself.

Connie pressed the cotton to Mae's cuts, cleaning the wounds quickly and efficiently. Mae didn't move a muscle.

"So," Connie started as she wiped down the blood-caked wounds. "They found you a place in foster care real quick, didn't they. I've never seen Child Protective Services work that fast! Have you, Dr. Mathis?"

Connie glanced at Suzanne, who forced herself to answer.

"Mae didn't stay in foster care. She stayed with me."

The nurse stared at Suzanne, her cotton ball now frozen in mid-air.

"I'm a registered foster care provider," Suzanne informed. "Peter and I did it before we had the girls. We got the judge to approve it this morning."

"But you took her home last night." Connie resumed cleaning the wound, trying to keep her voice down in front of Mae, even though it was useless because Mae could obviously hear this entire conversation.

Suzanne folded her arms across her white lab coat. "So I was supposed to leave her here with that man coming around—"

"What man?" Mae whipped her attention toward Suzanne, who realized she'd put her foot in her mouth. "Did someone come for me?"

Connie applied sanitizer to her hands, suddenly becoming very busy cleaning up the supplies.

"Yes," Suzanne explained slowly. "A man tried to check you out of the hospital. Yesterday afternoon."

"Well, I'm just about finished here," Connie concluded, forcing an upbeat tone. "Lots of patients left to see. Call me if you need anything!" She fled the room.

An uneasy silence settled in.

Suzanne stepped over and perched on the edge of the bed next to Mae, whose palms still gripped the mattress. They sat there for a few moments in silence. Finally, Mae spoke, her voice low.

"What did he look like? The man?"

Suzanne dug her hands deep into her coat pockets. "He was tall," she started. "He had gray hair, and his skin was very tan. Kind of reddish."

"Did he have a hat?" Mae didn't remove her gaze from the floor.

Suzanne nodded. "Yes. A cowboy hat."

Mae started to shake, wrapping her arms around each other as if she were trying to make herself smaller.

"Is that one of the men who hurt you?" Suzanne ventured.

Slowly, Mae nodded yes.

Suzanne absorbed this. Then she asked, "Is he your father?" She tried to sound calm, but her escalating pitch betrayed her dismay.

Mae continued to shake in silence.

"It's okay, Mae," Suzanne soothed. "I'm going to protect you."

At this, Mae looked at Suzanne, her eyes pleading.

Suzanne forced herself to hold the girl's gaze. "You won't have to go back home to him, I promise," she said firmly.

Mae released her arms, her shaking starting to subside. She took a deep breath, then tilted her head to the side, resting it on Suzanne's shoulder.

Suzanne was surprised by the contact and remained very still.

Mae's thin shoulders slowly rose and fell unevenly as she breathed. Suzanne waited out the quiet, giving Mae time to process.

After a while, Mae spoke again. Her voice wavered—

"He isn't my father."

Mae lifted her head from Suzanne's arm and faced the far wall, her body becoming very still.

"He's the sheriff."

CHAPTER 11

AT LUNCH ISAAC AND I SAT IN A corner of the cafeteria and picked at stale ham sandwiches, while Isaac complained about Victoria Liu's tendency to end sentences with a question mark.

As Isaac cited numerous examples of Victoria's grating vocal pattern, I experimented with filters on a photo of a limp fry drowning in industrial-grade ketchup. I thought I'd save it to post at the end of the week and call it #frydie.

"It's just, like, legitimately annoying? To talk like that? All the time?" Isaac mimicked the upward inflections of his self-proclaimed nemesis.

I nodded as he continued, but inside my head I was giving myself a pep talk about my meeting with Sebastian and the *Regal* staff.

"Are you even listening to me?" Isaac asked.

He knew that I wasn't, so I didn't pretend. "I'm just nervous about my interview."

I tugged at the collar of my wool dress, feeling warm in the crowded cafeteria. "And I didn't sleep."

Isaac rolled his eyes. "Great, so you're going to be grumpy all day."

Which reminded me—I hadn't had a chance to look up that upside-down star symbol from the Tisdale link! I tapped around on my phone to find it. I'd seen the sign in TV and movies and thought it had to do with something bad, but I wasn't sure exactly what.

Scrolling down, I read a few descriptions. The sign was a pentagram.

My eyes fell on:

"An upside-down pentagram was used in Renaissance-era occultism. It continues to be associated with the devil, and is often considered the sign of Satan."

What.

The.

Eff.

Pentagram? Did this girl worship the devil? Or had she lived with people who did? Most of the people I knew were Christian and went to church. Different kinds, yes, but none of them were the devil kind.

"If you're not going to eat those nuggets, I'm getting in there," Isaac claimed, pointing to my plate.

I quickly clicked off my screen.

"Go for it," I said, covering my alarm at what I'd just read. I couldn't deal with this right now—I had to focus.

I stared at my tray. I wasn't really hungry. I was, however, dead tired. I reached for the cup of coffee I'd bought at the café next to the cafeteria. It tasted like charred water.

"We have to discuss our Social Studies project," Isaac pressed, pulling out a notebook. "I started working up thesis ideas."

I couldn't remember the last time I had been this tired. I had to keep myself alert so I could impress Sebastian and his staff after school.

"Seriously, Jules. What is going on with you?" Isaac queried. "And since when do you drink coffee? Late night with your boyfriend?"

"He's not my boyfriend."

"Whatever. He will be, and then you'll forget about me and I'll be all alone," Isaac accused me, only half joking.

"Okay, yeah, that's exactly what's gonna happen," I replied, not having the energy to argue.

Isaac eyed me. "I am going to forgive you because clearly something is going on. And I know it's not your time of the month, so don't even pretend to use that excuse."

"That's creepy," I said, but it was sort of sweet that Isaac knew me so well. I pushed my nuggets over to him as a silent apology. He ate one, accepting my truce. I slurped down a long sip of coffee, wincing at the taste.

"Now, are you going to tell me what's really happening with you or what?"

I hesitated. Should I tell Isaac about Mae? I never kept secrets from him. I even told him when I'd gotten an ear infection in seventh grade and had such a bad reaction to penicillin that my whole body broke out in red spots. But I didn't feel like talking about Mae right now. I'd already been up all night because of her. I didn't need her interfering with my life any further.

"I'm just nervous about my interview at the paper," I finally replied.

For the first time ever, I had lied to my best friend.

CHAPTER 12

THE *REMINGHAM REGAL* OFFICE WAS BUZZING WITH ACTIVITY. There were students typing rapidly on laptops, a guy in the corner at a large monitor editing a clip of some football footage. There was a standing chalkboard with story ideas, and a second one that two freshmen were wiping down.

My heart rate picked up with anticipation. Or maybe it was just jitters from all the caffeine I'd consumed. Likely both.

"Jules!"

Sebastian stood up from a desk, finishing up reading something on his tablet. He turned to one of the editors. "Looks great, Greta. Let's proof it and get it in for the print edition."

He grinned at me. "Come sit!" he said, indicating the communal worktable in the center of the room. I slung my bag onto a chair and sat down.

"Naomi, Zeke, join us," Sebastian called.

Dressed in all black, Naomi was a tall, slim senior. She paced over to the table, followed by Zeke, a lanky junior in a backward paperboy hat and plaid flannel.

"Naomi is our social media editor and Zeke, our chief content editor."

"Hey." Naomi extended her elegant hand. I shook it. Her fingers were thin and strong. "You're Helen's little sister," she asked-slash-stated.

I nodded, then waved hello to Zeke.

"I think we met," he remembered. "My mom works with your dad at the bank. We were both at that Christmas party last year? The one with the all-you-can-eat shrimp?"

"Oh yeah," I replied, even though I had exactly zero memory of meeting him.

"So," Sebastian started. "Wanted to share an idea for a new section Jules and I came up with."

Naomi gave a measured smile. Then she and Zeke listened intently to Sebastian, as he talked about what would hopefully be my column. I realized my face must be in Overly Excited mode— I was so close to this all coming together and getting my own column. I made a concerted effort to relax my cheeks. *Keep it together, Jules.*

"The column will include a portrait and short interview each week with a different student," Sebastian explained. "We'll feature it on the back page of the print edition."

"What's it called?" Naomi wondered, her hands now folded delicately on the table. Sebastian looked to me.

"Oh, um—" *Deep breaths, Jules!* "I thought we could call it 'People You Don't Know.'"

The upperclassmen took a beat to absorb this. I was sweating. From the wool dress, from the coffee, from the nerves—but mostly from the fact that I was *thiiiis* close to having my own column *and* working with Sebastian—if I didn't blow it.

Finally, Naomi spoke. "I like it."

"It's excellent," Zeke agreed.

I inhaled relief.

"So Jules, tell us a little about your vision for the project," Sebastian said.

Thankfully, I had spent all of Geometry preparing my thoughts on the column. Yes, I would have to get Isaac to give me his notes on the Pythagorean theorem, but at least I was prepared.

"Well, I've always thought of portrait photography as, you know, capturing the spirit of a person," I started. "Exposing the inner world of the subj—"

"There you are!"

I heard a familiar voice, but the sound was so out of place I couldn't believe I was actually hearing it. I turned to see . . .

My mother standing in the doorway, smiling. What in the world was Mom doing at school? It must be some kind of emergency.

"Hi, Jules!" she beamed. If something was wrong, why was she acting so upbeat?

This was so weird.

"How'd you find me?" I managed to say. Mom had been so busy this morning worrying about Mae that I hadn't told her about the meeting.

"I saw Isaac," she explained. "He said you were doing an interview for the school paper. Very exciting!" she chirped to the roomful of students, who were now all staring at an unwanted parent. My parent. Extremely unwanted at the moment.

"What are you doing here?" I hissed.

"Well," Mom started, "I thought you could show Mae around." She stepped aside, revealing none other than our new houseguest, standing innocently beneath the doorframe.

Mae was at *my* school. Interrupting the most exciting moment of my scholastic career—and possibly personal life.

I tried to silently communicate to my mother that I was in the middle of something very important, but she didn't seem to get my telepathic message.

"I enrolled Mae to start here tomorrow," Mom explained. "She's going to be in your class!"

Wait. What? Mom had said Mae was just staying with us for a few days. Why was she now going to my school? And what about that sign of Satan symbol that her town, Tisdale, was associated with? Did Mom know about that?

My leg started shaking under the table. I had to focus on the matter at hand: salvaging this interview. I needed to get my mom and Mae out of there as fast as possible.

"Mom, we're in the middle of an interview," I explained, trying to hide my mounting anxiety from Sebastian and the editors.

Mom didn't take the hint. "Wonderful, that'll be exciting for Mae to see! I'm going to run some errands. I'll pick you girls up in an hour. Have fun!" Mom added as she strode out of the room.

This was not happening.

Mae stood awkwardly in the doorway, unsure what to do. Everyone was watching. Was I supposed to invite her in? I wasn't exactly feeling charitable at the moment.

After an awkward lull, a warm tenor voice piped up. "Feel like sitting in?" Sebastian kindly offered to Mae.

Mae turned to me, as if for approval.

I definitely wanted to say no. But what else could I do? Tell her to go stand in the hallway? It wasn't really her fault that she was here, after all. It was my mom's.

I forced my face to reflect pleasantness. "Sure," I offered with effortful positivity. Seeing that the situation was somewhat resolved, the rest of the room turned back to their screens.

Mae glided over to the table and took a seat. Naomi, Zeke, and even Sebastian stared at the beautiful girl who had somehow inserted herself into our world.

"I'm Mae," she told them quietly. "But I guess you already know that," she added with the hint of a smile.

Sebastian, Zeke, and Naomi laughed.

"Super nice to meet you," Zeke returned, a little too eagerly if you ask me.

"So, back to the 'People You Don't Know' column!" That came out louder than I had intended, but I was trying to draw the attention back to the matter at hand. Me.

I jumped to the important part of my pitch: "I thought what I'd do was take in-context portraits of the subjects, so the image they present is related to who they are. But it doesn't have to be obvious. Like a basketball player doesn't need to be on the basketball court. Maybe I take his picture in the library because he's a history buff but never told anyone that."

"Great idea," Sebastian encouraged me.

"Then for the interviews, I'd ask a set of five questions that maybe you wouldn't have thought to ask each subject."

"Interesting." Naomi nodded. "Tell us more about that."

The meeting now back on track, we continued to discuss the details of the column, how and when it would run in the paper. Naomi said she wanted to brainstorm a social media aspect to it, like maybe for one week the questions to the subject could be crowd-sourced, which I thought was super smart.

"If we're all on board, let's get started!" Sebastian concluded. "Come up with some sample questions and send them my way. Since it's our first edition of the column, we'll give ourselves a few weeks to get things sorted. We distro on Mondays, so you'll e-mail final files to Brianna the night before," he said, gesturing to a girl with cat's-eye glasses a few desks away.

"Works for me!" I agreed.

Despite the interruption, I'd pulled it off. I'd be working at the paper on an awesome project. Not to mention, with Sebastian.

"And," he added, "looks like we already have our first subject!"

"What do you mean?" I asked. How could that have been decided? We hadn't even discussed it yet.

I slowly turned and followed Sebastian's gaze. He was staring at Mae.

CHAPTER 13

OUT ON THE FRONT STEPS OF THE SCHOOL, MAE AND I were awkwardly waiting for my mom to pick us up. But of course she was late. She was probably trying to force me and Mae to bond. *Paper-thin tactic, Mom.*

Mae was leaning against the brick by the double doors, as if trying to camouflage herself with the wall. Meanwhile, the caffeine I'd drunk at lunch still hadn't worn off, so I was pacing up and down the stairs like a psycho, trying to burn off the energy. I almost wanted to run across the street to the field and do drills with the boys' soccer team.

I snuck a glance at Mae. She'd tried to refuse when Sebastian suggested she be the first subject of "People You Don't Know," but Sebastian insisted, and he had a unique combination of confidence and optimism that made people go along with him.

Mae hadn't said a word since we left the *Regal* office.

I'm sure it was my mom's brilliant idea to enroll her at the school and stick her on me. Whenever Mom had a task that was uncomfortable she always left me, the easygoing middle child, to do it, probably because I was too quiet to complain.

And yet I couldn't wrap my brain around the fact that Mae was going to be in classes with me. I really didn't know what her situation was, but what if it actually had something to do with devil-worshipping? I wasn't far enough up the social food chain to survive something like that. Especially not at our suburban, churchgoing school. Around here it was better to be a criminal than someone who didn't go to church—Satanic worship had social extinction written all over it.

"You did a good job."

From the bottom of the stairs I looked up to see Mae, who had moved to the top of the staircase, now towering above me. She was twisting her braid through her fingers.

"In your interview," she finished.

I was surprised she'd been paying attention. She had spent the whole meeting staring intently at a container of pencils on the table.

"Thanks. I was pretty nervous," I admitted, kicking the bottom step with the sole of my oxford.

"Didn't seem like it," she said, a matter-of-fact compliment. "Have you been taking photographs for a long time?"

"My dad gave me his old camera when I was seven, so I guess since then."

"That's nice of him," she replied. I looked at her. Something about the way she said it sounded kind of judgmental, almost. I guess I hadn't thought about it like that—I was so used to my parents giving me things, mostly at birthdays or holidays, providing for me, that it never felt that special. But I guess she was right. It was nice of my dad. Not all parents give their kids cameras when they're seven.

"If you want, I can show you my feed," I offered.

"For cattle?" she asked, confused.

Um, no, not for cattle, I replied in my head.

"On Instagram," I clarified. "Just pictures from my phone, but I post them."

Mae looked like she didn't quite understand the words I was saying.

"Are you on it?" I asked. "Instagram?"

She shook her head no, looking perplexed by the whole conversation. How could she not know about Instagram?

"Do you have a phone?" I ventured to ask.

"No," she answered. "I wasn't allowed."

I didn't understand. "Were you not allowed any phone, or just one with internet? Like, you have a phone for emergency calls, right?"

Mae shook her head no.

"Why?" I had to get to the bottom of the strangeness.

Mae thought about it for a moment, how to explain it. "People in my town didn't really like it."

"Like what?"

"Technology," she stated, as if not liking technology was an option in our wired world.

I took a few steps up the stairs. "Were you Amish or something?"

"No," she answered. "We just had—our own way of doing things. People said we didn't need it."

"If you didn't have phones and stuff, how did people keep in touch?"

Mae twisted the soles of her purple Mary Janes on the cement. I realized they were new. Where had she gotten new shoes? Had my mom bought them for her?

"People mostly congregated at the church. Or the schoolhouse," Mae muttered.

Schoolhouse? What was this, *Little House on the Prairie*?

"What kind of church?" I wondered, fishing for info. "Episcopal?"

"Not exactly," Mae replied. "We kind of—did our own thing."

"How so?"

She didn't answer.

I joined Mae at the top of the stairs. Now that we were standing on the same level, she still stood a little taller than me. Although she was pretty quiet and mild-mannered so far, standing right next to her I got a weird sense that she was much stronger than she appeared to be.

"Was the town kind of old-fashioned or something?"

"Yeah, I guess."

I pushed on, wondering if the confidence of the meeting going well—plus all the coffee—was making me bolder.

"Why?" I pressed.

She thought about it for a while, then eventually figured, "They've done things a certain way for a long time, so they just kept doing them."

"Like what kind of things?"

Before I could get more answers, I recognized a voice—

"I thought you were gonna text me!" I turned to see Isaac bounding out from the building. "How'd the interview go?"

I forced a smile. "Good!" Although just barely.

"Did your mom find you? She was looking for you with—" As he approached, he noted Mae. "Her," he declared. He regarded Mae for a moment, then introduced himself. "I'm Isaac."

Mae seemed to clam up, and offered an anemic nod hello.

"This is Mae," I told Isaac. I didn't know what else to say.

"O-kay . . ." He eyed me. He knew I wasn't telling him the whole story, and he didn't like being out of the loop.

I had to tell him something. "She's—staying with us for a few days," I explained. I wanted to say more but didn't want to be rude in front of Mae.

This was not enough information for Isaac. "Well then," he said with a flip of his hair. "You taking the late bus?"

"My mom's picking us up."

"Cool." He turned and practically ran down the steps, clearly annoyed.

"I'll call you later!" I yelled after him. "Promise!"

He didn't answer. I felt like crap. I could tell Isaac was not happy with me. He was my best friend, and here I was making him feel excluded because of Mae. I knew he'd get over it, but this girl had been in my life one day and was already ruining things. The rational part of me knew that it wasn't her fault.

But then again, it kinda was.

CHAPTER 14

REMINGHAM REGIONAL HOSPITAL, TRAUMA UNIT

CONFIDENTIAL CASE FILE

DATE: September 12, 2004

PATIENT NAME: Joseph Trauma

AGE: 10

CASE SYNOPSIS:

SYMPTOMS: Extensive slashes covering the child's back. Five-pointed star-shaped laceration in the center of the back, with a circle encompassing the star, which points downward. Multiple layers of scar tissue beneath the wounds, evidence of repeated abuse.

TREATMENT: Patient refused ingesting liquids, solids, or medication, received emergency treatment for pain management and antibiotics intravenously. Skin graft surgery scheduled for dermal recuperation.

RESULT: Presurgery, patient's parents attempted to remove child from care. Child Protective Services intervened and matter was set for judgment by the court. However, child disappeared from the hospital premises and after police investigation, family could not be located.

REMINGHAM REGIONAL HOSPITAL, TRAUMA UNIT

CONFIDENTIAL CASE FILE

DATE: April 30, 2009
PATIENT NAME: Henrietta Trauma
AGE: 12

CASE SYNOPSIS:

SYMPTOMS: Patient arrived highly disturbed, had multiple lacerations on her back and bleeding from restraints on hands and feet. Patient was treated for extensive physical and

emotional trauma, including possible sexual assault. Patient
displayed evidence of multiple personality disorder.

TREATMENT: Psychiatric treatment, pain management
medication, antipsychotic medication.

RESULT: After wound care was addressed, the patient was
released to guardianship of her uncle on contingency of
continued psychiatric care. Before discharge was complete,
patient took her own life.

Suzanne stared down at the files. While she had never learned
the patients' real names, she vividly remembered the two cases
from years ago. Both children had suffered extensive abuse.

She sifted through the folders and, although she couldn't
find a birthplace for the girl, discovered where the boy was from:
Tisdale. And he had a pentagram carved onto his back, just like
Mae.

Tisdale must be the same town where Mae was from.

KNOCK, KNOCK.

Suzanne snapped the case files shut and looked up. Joanne
Montecito, the hospital administrator, stood in the doorway.
Suzanne surreptitiously hid the files under some papers on her
desk.

"May I see you in my office, Dr. Mathis?" Joanne requested.

Suzanne plastered a smile on for her boss, knowing she didn't
really have a choice. "Sure."

"Unacceptable," concluded Joanne as she sat across from Suzanne, now in the administrator's sea-green office. That, combined with the fluorescents, cast a gloomy light over the small room.

"Dr. Mathis, that kind of thing just isn't done. Do you know what kind of hot water you could get us into?"

"It wasn't safe here," Suzanne countered, folding her arms across her chest.

"Safe?" Joanne scoffed. "See how safe it is when the hospital board finds out that one of our employees took home a patient! You know they already have it out for Psych. Do you have any idea what kind of budget cuts I'm dealing with? I'm trying to keep them from cutting whole departments."

"I know you are, and I'm sorry about that," Suzanne empathized to calm her. "However, I am a registered foster care provider. And I got the judge's approval on the case."

"But you took her home before you got the approval!"

Suzanne avoided eye contact at the truth of Joanne's accusation.

"And approval or no," Joanne continued, "you were the patient's attending psychiatrist."

"I transferred her treatment to Dr. Brenner," Suzanne countered.

"Without checking with me first!"

Suzanne nodded. "I—apologize for that. It was a heat-of-the-moment assessment. That man came in, and he was very threatening. I had to make a judgment call."

"I really don't approve." Joanne pulled at the bottom edge of her fuchsia suit jacket. "And," the administrator continued. "And," she said again for emphasis, "you engaged with a visitor in an inappropriate manner."

"Inappropriate? What was I supposed to do, discharge her to him? He was clearly threatening me and Mae."

"Obviously no, you were not supposed to let him near *the patient*, but you should have let security deal with it."

"I would have if Jerry was in the building," Suzanne defended, her voice rising.

"No need to lose our tempers," Joanne cautioned. "We have to follow protocol around here."

"I was following protocol." Suzanne leaned forward. "Do you know that more than one person cut her? On her back?" she pressed.

Joanne didn't make eye contact.

"The girl was abused. Severely. It's not safe for her to return home."

"No one's arguing with that," Joanne agreed. "We just—have to take certain precautions."

"Precautions like not sending Mae to a group home where she'd be thrown in with a dozen other girls. Precautions like giving this child a chance to heal. Precautions like keeping her safe from a violent man."

Suzanne took a breath to pacify herself.

Joanne placed her palms on the desk. "Look, all of us are trying to look out for the patient's best interest, and every other patient we have at this hospital. I understand your concern about the girl," she went on. "But you are treading on dangerous territory here. The Board of Psychiatry is going to need an explanation," she warned.

Suzanne stood, taking a hard candy from a glass dish on the desk. "I know what I'm doing."

She popped the candy into her mouth and headed for the door.

"You can't save everyone, Suzanne," Joanne called after her. But Suzanne had already gone.

CHAPTER 15

THAT NIGHT I TRIED TO ASK MY MOM about Mae going to my school, but she said she had too much on her plate at the moment to talk. She was poring over work files at the kitchen table, completely absorbed.

I video chatted Isaac. He was still annoyed at me, but I redeemed myself for my earlier offense of not telling him about Mae by listening to his entire speech in support of repealing Citizens United for debate, and promising to watch a doc on Cold War USSR for our Social Studies presentation.

Then I told him everything I did know about Mae, which wasn't much. He was intrigued that she was from a town that had satanic associations.

"I know you don't like to talk to strangers, but you need to get some info out of that girl," he pressed. "Give her the third degree."

I supposed he was right. "It's still annoying that she's staying in my room."

"Well, you said she'd probably be gone by the end of the week," he said.

She wasn't. Mom had told us Mae was only going to be staying for a few days, but it was now Friday and she was showing no signs of leaving.

Around the house, I mostly kept to myself. The news that Mae was possibly from a satanic cult had freaked me out. I wanted to ask Mae more about what she had hinted at, but every time we were near each other some kind of outside force seemed to interrupt before she would say anything about it.

Helen and Dani were in their own worlds—Dani had gotten the lead role in *Wicked*, and Helen was in full-on field hockey season. Dad was distracted with whatever was going on at his work. No one in my family seemed that bothered by it. Mae was just a girl who our family was helping out for a few days.

So far I'd avoided the whole issue of the profile I was supposed to do on Mae for "People You Don't Know." Sebastian had given us a few weeks to get the first column done. I kept telling myself I'd ask about taking her picture tomorrow, then putting it off. I'd also been trying to come up with the five questions for my column, but Sebastian wasn't happy with any of them yet. "Right track, but let's get more specific," he kept saying.

Meanwhile, Mae trailed me around school like a shadow. I was hoping that over the last few days something more about her home life would have slipped out, but Mae was always silent, too busy watching us.

People were starting to wonder, though. I was actually grateful for my low social profile. I didn't know what to do when people's attention was on me, and this kind of attention wasn't the kind I wanted anyway. But a few people in my classes still asked me how I knew Mae and why she was following me around. I'd said she was distantly related to my mom's family and she was staying with us for a few days. I knew that wouldn't satisfy the students of our gossip-starved school for very long. Word spread quickly around a place not known for any huge events outside of football games and who was dating who, so I knew something this big would catch like wildfire if anything about where Mae was from did come out.

Since it was Friday, I was hoping that if I laid low for the rest of the day, the big football game this weekend against our school's rival would distract people, and maybe she would be gone by Monday and I wouldn't have to deal with answering any questions.

But then Language Arts happened.

Ms. Ramsey was rambling on about *Pride and Prejudice*, and something about reputation and the social constructs in rural nineteenth-century England.

"Okay, guys. So let's do a little survey!" The twentysomething teacher took a sip from her third Diet Coke can of the period.

"Raise your hand if social constructs have affected your life."

A few people raised their hands tentatively.

The teacher stepped through the desk aisles in her furry snow boots. A little overzealous with the wardrobe, I thought, given that it was still only September.

"Come on, guys—social constructs. They're a big deal, am I right? Who's dealt with 'em?" Eventually everyone had raised an arm into the air.

"Exactly!" she gleamed.

Ms. Ramsey then looked at Mae, who was sitting in the far back corner of the room.

"So Mae: How have social constructs affected your life?"

Mae's face went blank. She hadn't been singled out in a class yet. Most of the teachers seemed to be giving her time to adjust before calling on her. But my guess was that Ms. Ramsey was just as curious about Mae as the rest of us and was using the question to get to know more about the strange, striking girl.

"Have expectations of others in a social setting had an impact on you?" Ms. Ramsey rephrased.

Mae was looking down at her fingers, which were running through the bottom of her hair. She usually kept it tied back in a braid, but today she'd left it down.

Finally, Mae answered in a low voice. "Yes," she admitted.

Ms. Ramsey perched on the edge of her desk, causing her short skirt to ride up her tights. "How have you experienced those effects? Could you give us an example?"

All eyes were on Mae. She was wearing a purple knit sweater of mine. I didn't wear it much anymore because it had started to feel snug around my stomach and chest, but it fit Mae perfectly. She'd pulled the sleeves down over her palms.

"I—grew up in a very small town," she started. "People talked about what you did."

Ms. Ramsey waited for Mae to go on. So did the rest of the class.

"That's very common in small towns," Ms. Ramsey encouraged her, trying to guide the conversation forward. "So tell us more about that. Did you feel pressure to think or act a certain way because of the socially agreed-upon expectations?"

Mae considered this for a moment, then continued, "Well, you had to act in a way that they liked if you didn't want them to get—upset."

My pulse quickened. I was terrified of what else Mae was going to say, and how that would make me look by association. Was she going to tell them that she was from a town associated with a cult? Would people think that I might somehow be involved?

Ms. Ramsey inquired, trying to sound casual, "And where is it that you grew up?"

Mae took a deep breath.

"Tisdale," she stated.

A snicker came from across the room.

"Tisdale?" Jason Kessler had a smirk on his face. He was wearing his personal daily uniform of workout clothing. "That's where the devil worshippers live."

People turned to him. "My dad's a lawyer," Jason proudly explained to the class, who were listening attentively. "He had this case where a guy who owned a store sued these farmers for not delivering what he'd paid for. The farmers were from Tisdale. When my dad questioned the farmers they blamed the wheat not growing on their sacrifice not being accepted or something totally insane like that. They, like, worship the devil."

Giggles burst out from various parts of the room, but it seemed more like nervous laughter.

"Okay, Jason, that's enough." Ms. Ramsey brought the conversation back toward the issue at hand. She cleansed her palate with more soda.

"So Mae, do you find that some of those same social constructs are universal?"

Mae thought about it for a moment, then turned to me.

"Yes. Jules has been explaining them to me."

The whole class stared at me. It was true, I had been trying to explain things to Mae. The internet. Social media. Packaged foods. I wanted attention at school, but not the attention of being associated with Weird New Girl. I seriously wished I were invisible.

"So is it true?" Jason piped back up. "Are you guys devil worshippers?"

"Jason, enough," Ms. Ramsey interjected, but I could tell she wanted to know just as badly as everyone else.

"What, I'm just asking a question," Jason faux-scoffed. "Aren't we supposed to be developing inquiring minds?" he challenged her.

Ms. Ramsey looked to Mae, uneasy. She wasn't sure what to do here.

Mae went ahead and answered the question, clearly hoping that would stop her having to give any more answers.

"People—believe what they want," she stated simply.

"Do you believe in Satan? Do you worship the devil?" Jason pushed.

Mae was sitting very still. The room was pin-drop quiet, which never happened. Even Ms. Ramsey was watching Mae, transfixed. Finally, Mae replied—

"No, I don't believe," she said definitively. Then she added forcefully to Jason, "I never did."

Mae's face tilted down toward her desk, and in a kind of chant she whispered—

"They can't make me they can't make me they can't make me they can't make me . . ."

I shrank in my chair. No one knew what to say, even Ms. Ramsey.

Mercifully, the bell rang. A relieved din rose as everyone left class, happy to get as far away from Mae as possible.

I moved through the lunch line, accepting a too-thin turkey burger and opting for a lettuce bun. But I couldn't resist the French fries—sometimes you needed comfort food, and this was definitely one of those times. Over at the condiment table I loaded up a few white paper containers of ketchup. I knew it was filled with chemicals and kind of gross, but for some reason I loved the sugary red sauce.

Mae trailed behind me. I hadn't been sure how to talk to her before, but after what had happened in class, I *really* didn't know what to say to her. Mae tried to get closer to me, probably because I was the only person she knew, but I kept as much distance between us as I could. However every time I turned around she was there—closer—like a creepy game of Red Light, Green Light.

As I stepped away from the condiments, I noted there was a seat left at the volleyball girls' table, but a right side hitter strode over and took the seat. Damn.

I considered crashing Isaac's debate practice in the auditorium, but I didn't feel like being around conflict. I turned back to see Mae moving through the lunch line, watching me. She quickly averted her gaze, pretending she hadn't been staring, and paid the lunch lady with money my mom had given her.

I surveyed the room, trying to decide where to sit. There weren't many other options. I thought about going outside, but it was raining. Would it be better to sit alone, or should I just give in and sit with Mae? After all, people already associated me with her—

"AHHHHHHHHHHHHH!!!"

I spun around. Jason Kessler was staggering through the cafeteria, his mesh shirt oozing red liquid from his chest.

"She tried to kill me! Devil Girl tried to kill me!"

He was pointing at Mae, who stood frozen, holding her lunch tray. Jason clutched his neck with his red-stained hands.

"I'm gonna dieeeeeeee," he howled as he sank to the ground. Chairs scraped as people craned their necks to get a better view. "I'm dyinnnnnnggg!!"

The whole cafeteria stared at Mae. Her face was pale. Had she really tried to hurt him?

Suddenly, Jason popped up from the floor and addressed the gawking crowd.

"Thank you, thank you," he said, bowing, the red ketchup he had smeared over himself dripping to the floor.

Realizing what Jason had done, the room started laughing. A gigantic, goofy grin spread across Jason's face.

A hair-netted cafeteria worker came over and started mopping up the carnage.

Mae's cheeks had quickly gone from white to nearly as red as the tomato paste that now stained Jason's shirt. People were laughing and pointing at Mae. She tugged at the back of her sweater. Under the bottom edge I caught a glimpse of a white bandage. I think my mom had helped her change it last night, because they spent a long time in my room together with the door closed.

Mae glanced up and locked eyes on me, begging me to do something.

I felt awful. I had no idea what to do. Was there anything I could do to help this situation? And did I actually *want* to do anything?

"You little *shit!*" a bossy voice boomed across the cafeteria.

Larissa Delibero, sophomore cheerleader and apparent expert blow-job giver, marched over to Jason. I'd heard she and Jason had dated briefly over the summer but broke up right before school started under circumstances that were unknown to me. I guessed it had not ended well.

Larissa shoved Jason in the arm and yelled, "You're such a dick!"

Jason wouldn't stop snickering as Larissa pushed him away from the limelight. He returned to a grouping of his friends as the whole room now watched Larissa and Mae.

Mae stood there like a statue. She had been outed by Jason and was now about to be humiliated by Larissa. I was standing a few feet away. I thought about helping her, but my legs felt frozen. Even though I'd watched countless classic films about others taking valiant actions to save people, nothing prepares you for what to actually say or do when those situations happen in real life.

Larissa folded her arms over her tight cheerleading top and

inspected Mae. Mae's jaw was clenched, like she was trying to hold back tears.

Everyone in the cafeteria stared. Larissa was one of the most popular girls in school. She had the power to grant this newcomer instant acceptance, or banish her to untouchable status for the rest of her high school days.

Finally, Larissa spoke.

"Your hair is shiny," she evaluated Mae. "What do you do to it?"

"Oh," Mae said, surprised. "I put oil on it."

"Oil?" Larissa's face scrunched, grossed out.

Mae naively nodded yes to the oil, the weight of the social ramifications of this transaction unbeknownst to her. Larissa looked back at her group of friends at the table, who wrinkled their noses in solidarity with their leader.

"Like, *oil*?" Jessie Herrera, a bubbly, curly-haired acolyte of Larissa's piped up. The table full of cheerleaders looked on, awaiting the verdict that Larissa would pass down on this new girl.

"Castor oil," Mae added, almost as a question.

Larissa's well-plucked brow furrowed.

I had pretty much stopped breathing. Not that I was a fan of Mae, but Larissa could be pretty cruel, and if things went down badly, the rest of the school would follow suit. The social wrath would certainly rain down onto me as well.

There was a long silence.

"Ohmygod, you have to tell me where to get that!" Larissa finally concluded. "I *neeeed* my hair to be that shiny."

A chorus of "totallys" and "me toos" rang out from the cheerleader table.

The room seemed to collectively exhale. Larissa had deemed Mae cool enough to talk to and had actually given her a compliment.

"Sit with us," Larissa insisted, linking her arm in Mae's. I saw a nearly imperceptible flinch as Larissa's hand passed close to Mae's secretly bandaged back.

Mae wasn't sure what to do. She looked at me.

"I was going to sit with Jules," Mae said.

Which was a lie. Mae knew I hadn't been planning to sit with her. But she was giving me the benefit of sharing her moment in the spotlight with Larissa. Her niceness made me feel even worse that I hadn't done anything to help her.

Larissa turned to me, perplexed. I'm sure she didn't remember that she had reverse slut-shamed me, or that we had algebra together last year.

"I'm Jules," I said, and added, "Mathis," for clarity.

Larissa looked me up and down. She pointed at the blue-and-white-striped sweater dress I'd found in the attic. Another one from the Grandma Lydia Attic Collection.

"Where'd you get that?"

"It's vintage," I managed to sputter.

For one heart-stopping moment, Larissa deliberated. Then—

"Cool," she said appraisingly, and waved me over to join them too.

Mae and I went to sit with Larissa and her cheerleader friends.

"Sit here," offered Christine Symkowitz, a tall, athletic blonde who I'd had science class with for two years but had never said a word to me before. They scooted around to make room for us at the table. Girls who had never even acknowledged my existence were now making a place for me.

Larissa dove in, sitting down next to Mae. "Okay, you have to tell us. You grew up in a cult, right? How bizarre was that!"

And somehow, just like that, Mae was cool.

And, by association, so was I.

PART TWO

And so it is, that both the Devil and the angelic Spirit
present us with objects of desire
to awaken our power of choice.

—Rumi, "By the Sound of Their Voice"

CHAPTER 16

"*THAAAAAN, PAHT* THE *LINAHHHR* RIGHT ON THE *ADGE* of your *lahd—*"

"Why is she talking like that?" marveled Mae at the overdyed blonde on my phone screen giving a tutorial on how to apply liquid eyeliner.

"I have no idea," I returned, adjusting my seating on the bed. I'd forgotten how soft the mattress was, since I'd been staying in Dani's room the last few weeks while Mae stayed in my-slash-her bedroom. I didn't mind it that much—Dani pretty much lived in her own world, and I'd started spending more time with Mae. Mom had said finding Mae a new foster home was taking longer than expected, so I'd decided to make the best of the situation. Besides, Mae and I were hanging out more at school, since we were in all the same classes, and it was actually kind of fun to have her around at home. Mae had included me in her newfound popularity from moment one, which was very cool of her—especially since I hadn't been particularly nice to her when she first arrived. Also, I was used to being on my own around the house, but ever since Mae had defended my outfit to Helen before school one morning, I liked having her as an ally at home. And although I had Isaac, it was nice to have a girl friend.

We watched the screen skeptically as the talking head ran through tips on applying the goopy dark liquid. I had never been good at applying makeup, but it was a task that I had forced myself to get better at, resigned that it was something I would probably be doing for the rest of my life. I usually didn't wear much—just enough so that my eyes "popped," as Isaac said, and so that I didn't look like an insomniac zombie all the time.

More important, I'd never been invited to hang out with upper-classmen, so this seemed like the perfect occasion to up my grooming game.

Larissa Delibero had invited us to a party at senior Chelsea Whiff's house this Saturday night. Well, she invited Mae, and me by association. Over the last couple of weeks, Mae and I had been hanging out with Larissa and her #squad, which despite my initial skepticism of their cool-girl aloofness had been a lot of fun. At Larissa's insistence, we all went to the store together to buy makeup. I hadn't realized makeup buying was a group activity—it was usually something I did on my own, as an afterthought when I was at the drugstore—but I admit that it was actually helpful to have friends there to remind you that no matter how on-trend it is, blue mascara or pink eye shadow are terrible ideas. Larissa swore by liquid eyeliner, so I bought some, even though I'd never used it before. Mae had asked me how to apply it, but I had no idea, so we turned to YouTube.

"Should we try?" Mae ventured, heading toward the bathroom.

I followed. I wasn't usually one for taking adventurous actions—especially when the consequences could go terribly wrong. Looking at this dangerously thick inky liquid, I had a sudden image of me smudging it and it running down my face and not being able to go to the party 'cause I looked like a disgraced pop star.

But Mae seemed excited about it, so I thought why not give it a try. Brave New Jules.

In the bathroom, Mae clicked the video to start again. Before she came to our house she'd had no experience with the internet, but I'd shown her how to use it and she was a quick study.

Mae tried to emulate the girl, steadying her hand to apply.

"It's cold!" Mae said as she touched the applicator wand to her lid. I laughed. She had a black dot on her eyelid.

"Can you fix it?" she asked.

I was nervous about messing it up more, but knew I couldn't leave her looking like a warped Snapchat filter.

I sorted through my small, stain-caked makeup bag, plucking out a regular eye pencil.

"Let's do this. I think black will be good," I figured, holding it up to Mae's face. "And you can smudge it a little and do a smoky eye."

"So it looks like there's smoke on my eye?"

"It's supposed to be sexy." I shrugged.

Mae's eyes widened for a millisecond but then recovered. She was definitely touchy about anything related to sex. From the little I had learned about her old life, it seemed like the world she'd grown up in was pretty strict, even prudish.

"Close your eyes?"

I looked at her flawless skin. In the few weeks she had been here I had not seen her get one pimple. I didn't get them often, but still, we were human teenagers. And her cheeks had a natural pinkness to them. She really didn't need makeup at all.

Gently placing one hand on the edge of her lid, I steadied the palm of my pencil hand. Her skin was soft. I placed the pencil tip on the corner of her lid and ran it across her eyelash line with more confidence than I'd had doing most things in my life. It came out straight.

I then focused on the other eye and did the same. Success.

"Now we smudge."

I ran my ring finger along her eyelid, making small circles. I added some shadow too and evened it all out. When I was done, I admired my work. Mae looked beautiful—grown-up and sexy, but not like she was trying too hard.

Mae stared at her reflection, unsure.

"You didn't wear a lot of makeup growing up," I guessed. She shook her head no.

"Me neither. My parents didn't let me wear it until I was twelve. Mom didn't want us to have a distorted sense of self, or 'overglorify outward beauty.'"

"Dani wears makeup, though." I was surprised that Mae had noticed that, but she was pretty observant. She had noticed that I ate untoasted bread at breakfast sometimes, and that my dad always liked to sit on the left side of the table, so she had started taking the seat next to him.

"Yeah, she won't be twelve till next month," I answered, "but she convinced my mom to let her when she lost all her baby fat so she could make a grand entrance when she started school this year."

It occurred to me that I never even thought of asking my mom to let me wear makeup before I was twelve. I never considered questioning rules. I always just went along with everything to maintain the status quo.

"I guess it never seemed like an option to not follow the rules," I admitted to Mae.

"Me too," Mae confessed. "But then I couldn't do it anymore."

She thought about it, running her finger along the smooth edge of the sink surface.

"How do you mean?" I asked gently.

"I used to follow a lot of rules. And then it became—too much . . ." Mae trailed off and stared at the sink, picking at a dried piece of toothpaste. She would zone out like that sometimes, and it would take a little prodding to get her back into the conversation.

"What do you mean it was too much, Mae?"

She snapped out of her zoning and turned to me. "Sometimes things are meant to break you. And they do. But," she added fiercely, "you can use it. To make yourself stronger."

A quiet descended while her words settled.

"Ooh, let me try!" Dani interrupted, busting into the bathroom. Dani was wearing a pink velour jumpsuit, which she was sporting nearly every day now—her official rehearsal gear, which I think she must have seen some pop star wear.

"We're getting ready," I told my sister. Translation: Get out.

"I just need my elastics. Chill." She reached for the cabinet and pulled out a wad of neon rings.

"Is that Helen's perfume?" she sniffed. "I'm telling!"

"She gave it to me," I said defensively. Which she had. Or more she had put it into a bag Mom was bringing to Goodwill and I had slipped it out.

"Your eyes look cool," Dani complimented Mae.

"Thanks, Amelia." Mae smiled, then realized she had called my sister the wrong name.

"I'm sorry—Danielle." A shadow fell across Mae's face.

"No biggie," Dani returned, tying her curls up in a pony.

"Who's Amelia?" I asked. It didn't sound anything like "Danielle," so seemed like a weird name to confuse with it.

Mae picked up a brush and ran it through her raven locks. "Just someone I used to know," she answered quietly.

"*A-meeee-liaaaa*," Dani sang, to the tune of *West Side Story*'s "Maria."

"Get out," I ordered, having had enough of my annoying little sister.

Dani rolled her eyes, grabbing my lip gloss on her way out. "Thanks okay byeeeeee!"

"Hey!" I called after, which I knew was useless. I could hear her snickering down the hall.

After putting on our makeup we got dressed in our joint room, Mae changing in the closet. When we were all ready we inspected ourselves in the full-length mirror.

Mae pulled at the sleeves of the maroon knit sweater dress I had lent her over her palms. The dress looked good with her pale skin and dark hair. I was sporting a new/old navy button-down sailor dress I'd discovered in the back of my closet. I vaguely remembered Helen giving it to me as a hand-me-down a few years ago. It was a little tight but I wore it anyway. I adjusted my white-piped dress hem. It was short enough to look cute but long enough to not feel slutty—the holy grail middle ground of an outfit.

Our heads were side by side in the mirror, Mae's a little higher than mine. I was impressed with our going-out A-game. *Good job, us*, I thought.

Then Mae glanced at my neckline.

"That's so beautiful."

I reached for the pendant on my necklace. The gold half heart was warm between my fingers.

"Thanks; my mom gave it to me for my thirteenth birthday. She has the other half. I know it's cheesy, but I still like it."

Mae stared at it, the heart glinting in the light. I remembered Mae had mentioned that she wasn't allowed to wear jewelry.

"Here, try it on."

I stretched my arms behind my neck, unhooked the clasp, and held it out to her.

Mae stared at me. "Really?"

"Yeah," I assured her. Careful not to touch her shoulders or back, I reached the necklace around her. She held her dark hair up as I fastened it around her pale neck.

Mae admired the pendant now hanging on her chest, beaming like she had just been crowned homecoming queen.

She looked at me through the mirror.

"Thank you, Jules."

I smiled back. "No problem."

Mae's eyes didn't move from mine. "You're such a good friend."

CHAPTER 17

COUNTRY MUSIC WAFTED FROM A JUKEBOX IN THE corner of the bar. The smell of long nights and spilled beer filled the air. Neon signs and whiskey placards were the only decorations on the wood-paneled walls, save for a lone deer head.

Suzanne pulled her thin overcoat a little tighter around her body, scanning the small crowd of dedicated patrons. Her eyes followed the lineup of drinkers at the bar until she saw:

Detective Nelson.

His rumpled gray suit had been a feature he hadn't changed in all the years she'd known him, and he wore it no matter what the season. She'd met him after Helen was born, when she first started working at the hospital, where he was assigned to cover cases. Now in his fifties, his hair had grown gray, and there was less of it.

She made her way across the sticky floor and slid onto the bar seat next to him. He turned and faced her, then back to his beer.

"You didn't return my calls," Suzanne stated, by way of explaining her presence.

Nelson shook his head at Suzanne's tenacity. "You don't ever quit, do you." He waved to the bartender. "Bill, this woman needs a drink, if not two."

Suzanne ordered a glass of wine, which set the bartender off to find a wineglass—and a bottle, for that matter.

Suzanne picked at a cardboard coaster. It wasn't exactly bad what she was doing, coming here. However, she knew that Peter probably wouldn't approve of her tracking down a detective at a dive bar on a Saturday night to talk to him about a patient.

"Cheers," Detective Nelson said, holding up his drink as the bartender set a glass of red wine down in front of Suzanne.

Suzanne clinked his glass with hers and sipped her wine to calm her nerves. The wine tasted extra acidic. She guessed the beverage was not served here often.

Nelson took a long pull of his pint, then his watery blue eyes looked up at Suzanne.

"What brings you to this fine establishment, Dr. Mathis?"

Suzanne launched in. "I want to talk about the girl at the hospital. The one with the carving in her back."

Nelson nodded knowingly, as if he was afraid that's what she was there about.

"There was another boy. He came in years ago, when I first started at the hospital. He had the same carving. He was from Tisdale—just like Mae."

Suzanne waited for the impact of that to settle in. Nelson sipped the amber liquid, not betraying his thoughts.

Suzanne took a deep breath, pressed on. "The town—I think it's a cult. And they're committing violent crimes against minors."

ZZZZTTT, buzzed Suzanne's cell on the peeling lacquered surface of the bar. Suzanne instinctively pressed the button to silence the ring, then looked at the display.

PETER.

Suzanne wasn't sure why he was calling, probably just to check in, but she didn't want to answer the call right now. She needed to focus on getting Detective Nelson to look into Tisdale.

"I need your help finding out more about—"

"I can stop you right there," Nelson interrupted. "That town is not in my jurisdiction, so I don't have access to information."

"But we have to find out what's going on there. Mae has been abused; other children have clearly been abused as well. Who knows how many more children are going through the same thing?"

Nelson turned his beer glass clockwise a couple of times in his thick fingers. "Dr. Mathis, I investigated this town years ago when that boy came in."

Suzanne's surprise showed on her face.

"These people are nutjobs. They think they're direct descendants of the devil," he cautioned. "You don't want to have anything to do with them. They like to keep to themselves, so help them keep it that way."

"But my patient—" Suzanne countered.

"People've escaped out of there before, but they never end up testifying. They're too scared to say anything. The town's got some kind of, I don't know, hold over them, I guess. Mind control."

"Mind control . . ."

"They mess with their heads, and then the victims just go right on back 'cause they don't know anything else. Then, lo and behold, no one hears from them again."

"Classic cult mental programming," Suzanne assessed, taking a big sip of her wine and grimacing from the taste.

The country song on the jukebox ended, and a more upbeat one started.

"Someone has to do something about it," Suzanne determined. "We can't just let people get away with this abuse."

"I've seen a few people go down that road. People have tried bringing charges against them in the past. But what ends up happening—is no good." Nelson shook his head. "End up getting themselves into trouble."

"What kind of trouble?"

"You don't want to know."

Suzanne doubled down. She had to get him to help her. She leaned forward on her barstool, brought her voice low. "What if we could find him?"

"Who?"

"The boy who had the pentagram carved into his back. The one who came into the hospital years ago. He probably still has the scar—that's evidence. And we have Mae. We could convince them to testify. What could be a stronger case than those scars!"

"Dr. Mathis—"

"If you can't help me look into the town, then at least help me look into his case. Find out his real name for me."

Detective Nelson didn't answer.

"Please," she went on. "You want to help people, right? That's why we do what we do."

Nelson heaved a sigh, then looked at Suzanne. "Dr. Mathis, you have a family to take care of. Keep your eyes on that."

He reached for his beer, ending the conversation.

ZZZZTTT, buzzed Suzanne's phone again. Peter. Suzanne stared at her phone screen as his name flashed.

"I think you'd better answer that," Detective Nelson advised.

Suzanne didn't. The phone kept ringing, until it eventually went to voice mail. Suzanne sat there, not leaving.

"They never did get your father, did they?"

Suzanne's face blanched.

"After he came to find you?" he continued.

Suzanne drained the rest of her glass. "No," she managed, finally finding her voice.

Then she stood up, put some money on the counter for the bartender, and walked out.

CHAPTER 18

GROSS WAS ALL I COULD THINK AS I took a tiny sip of beer from a red plastic cup. But besides vodka and a questionably colored punch, it was the best option at the party. Plus Sebastian had poured them for Mae and me when we arrived, so it seemed like the obligatory thing to do to take them. It had been a nice surprise to see him. I wasn't sure if he was coming and had been too nervous to ask him when I'd seen him in the *Regal* office the day before.

Mae and I were now standing on the crowded back porch of Chelsea Whiff's house. Chelsea was a senior who I had never spoken to, but she was super popular—the house was packed. Word was her parents were in Mexico building houses with their church group. Since it was all the popular kids, I would have expected to see Helen there, but I'd heard her tell my mom that Landon was taking her out for their four-year anniversary dinner. Mr. and Mrs. Perfect.

I was glad Mom hadn't questioned it too much when we'd asked to go out tonight. She seemed a little out of it and simply nodded when I told her we were meeting up with Isaac to go to a movie and that his aunt was driving. She probably wouldn't have minded us going to a party, but I didn't want to get into questions about it since I was sure there was going to be alcohol there.

I hadn't mentioned the party to Isaac. I'd meant to, but kept forgetting—maybe even a little on purpose. Isaac didn't like these kinds of parties, and part of me thought he'd be judgmental about me going. Larissa had picked us up in her dad's Chevy SUV. Although most of us had our learner's permits, that meant we couldn't drive after midnight without supervision. But Larissa's dad apparently didn't care, and let her use the car anyway.

I looked over at Mae, who was standing next to me on the porch, so close I could feel her body heat. Her beer was still full.

"Tastes like pee," I joked.

Mae laughed out loud.

"Not that I've ever drunk pee," I clarified. "Like what pee smells like."

"My brother drank pee once."

"Nasty. Why?"

"He was stuck in the woods all night and ran out of water. He got thirsty and said it was the only option."

I remembered she'd mentioned she had a few brothers. "Your older brother?" I asked.

She nodded.

"What is his name?"

Mae's mood darkened. "Haskell," she answered reluctantly. Then she got quiet, retreating into her own world.

"Mae!"

From the other side of the porch, Larissa made her way over to me and Mae. She was sporting short overalls with only a bra underneath, which was yellow. I wondered how she wasn't freezing.

"Ohmygod, Travis is here and we already talked for, like, an hour. I need to make out with him," Larissa declared, taking a large gulp of her drink. Travis was a star basketball player who all the cheerleaders swooned over. He was tall and African American and model-handsome.

Larissa turned her glassy eyes toward me. "Cute dress, Jules!" she admired, slapping her hand on my shoulder. "You're like a sailor. Love it."

"Thanks," I smiled. "I like your bra."

Jules! What a weird thing to say. I was so excited to get a compliment from Larissa I'd just blurted it out. Shit.

"Um, thank you for noticing," she slurred, then thankfully moved on. "Guys: let's go inside. It's way better in there." She then whispered so loud that it wasn't actually a whisper, "Travis is inside!"

Larissa grabbed my hand and led us through the thick crowd into the house. I followed her lead willingly—Sebastian was inside too, and I hadn't really gotten to talk to him before.

Mae trailed us as we passed through the kitchen, weaving among a sea of sway-standing drunk kids. A skeleton-thin girl in our grade—Sophie, I think her name was—waved at Mae, who waved back. I didn't know they knew each other, but was glad that Mae was making friends.

"Hey, lard-ass!" Larissa had spotted Jason. He was taking a Jell-O shot with a pretty, doe-eyed freshman by the Sub-Zero fridge. Sure enough, he was wearing a mesh tank top and basketball shorts. The freshman was squeezing Jason's bicep.

"Don't even bother," Larissa drawled to the girl. "He has a tiny dick!"

Jason flipped Larissa the finger as nearby partygoers snickered. We continued into the living room. I surveyed the mostly upperclassmen crowd. Everyone looked more grown-up than me. Or at least what I thought I looked like. I'd hoped my makeup and Larissa-approved outfit aged me up a little so I didn't look so fifteen.

Isaac and I had never been invited to parties. Not the cool ones, at least. We'd made fun of how superficial they probably were, but now that I was here and having fun in the electric buzz of the crowd, I really liked it. I felt energized by being part of a group.

"Jules!" I heard a familiar voice call. It was Sebastian, standing with Zeke. He waved us over.

Sebastian was wearing his contacts instead of glasses and had a T-shirt with a picture of James Dean on it.

"*Rebel Without a Cause*," I noted as we approached.

"Big fan," he returned.

"It's a great one. Although *East of Eden* is my favorite."

"Me too!" Sebastian grinned. I couldn't help smiling back.

"You ladies look stunning," Zeke piped in. He was wearing that backward paperboy hat again, which I wanted to reach for and turn right-side around, or just take the damn thing off.

"That's a nice necklace," Sebastian said admiringly to Mae.

"Thanks," she returned. "It's Jules's." I took it as a compliment that Sebastian liked my jewelry, even though Mae was wearing it.

"You guys enjoying your weekend?" Zeke small-talked.

"We went to a field hockey game last night," Mae offered. Dad had dragged us to one of Helen's games.

"My sister's," I explained to Sebastian.

I realized I was smiling way more than the situation called for. *Keep it cool, Jules.*

"What about you, Sebastian? What have you been up to this weekend?" I asked with effortful casualness.

"Good weekend so far—went running with my dad, edited a few articles, caught up with a friend from Philly. How's it going with 'People You Don't Know'? When can I see the portraits?" he wondered, ticking his eyes to Mae.

"We haven't done them yet," I admitted. I'd intended to take Mae's picture, I just kept putting it off.

"Oh," he said, surprised.

"I'll take them soon," I assured him.

Mae glanced at Sebastian, then looked away. It seemed like she didn't want to take them just as much as I didn't.

"Jason is dead to me!" Larissa declared, arriving and disrupting our social square. "He totally came up behind me and tried to pour a vodka shot into my mouth."

"*Another* vodka shot," clarified Jessie Herrera, arriving in

Larissa's wake. Jessie was wearing her signature halter top, which conveniently showed off her rather large boobs.

"I don't even think he was aiming for your mouth," added Christine Symkowitz, applying lip gloss, which she was addicted to.

"Whatever, he got vodka all over me." Larissa extended her chest toward us as evidence.

"Want me to beat him up?" Zeke offered, clearly joking. I didn't think he could beat up a paper bag. He was no match for gym-rat Jason.

"Yeah, punch him in the face and I'll Snapchat his big black eye," Larissa aimed at Zeke, her words running together.

Larissa surveyed the room. "This party is so over. We should blow this joint."

"You already have," joked Christine, at which Jessie snickered. Larissa let it fly and waved them off.

"I have an idea! Why don't we do a photo shoot?" Sebastian pitched.

My stomach did a flip turn. "Tonight?" I balked.

"What photo shoot?" Jessie asked. "Someone should take my picture, I look super cute tonight."

Christine rolled her eyes. "You already posted eight selfies."

"Of Mae—for the *Regal*," Sebastian explained. "Jules is writing an article about her."

"Yasssss!" Larissa exclaimed. "You look sooooo pretty, Mae. Your hair is, like, extra shiny. Why isn't mine that shiny?" she mused. "I tried that castor oil and everything."

"I don't think that's a great idea." I glanced at Mae, trying to figure out what she thought about it. I didn't want to put her on the spot.

I also didn't want *be* on the spot. The idea of people watching me take pictures made me nervous. Photography was a private thing for me.

"Do you have your camera?" Sebastian wondered.

"I've been using my phone," I explained. "My old Nikon broke, and I'm holding out for the Canon 5D Mark III for Christmas."

Sebastian seemed disappointed, so I tried to counter. "Plus I usually don't usually take my camera to house parties."

"Let's do it," Mae jumped in. I turned to her, surprised. Mae didn't seem to like attention on her, but maybe the two sips of beer she'd drunk had given her some liquid courage.

"Awesome!" Sebastian beamed.

"Travis and some people are going to the cemetery," Jessie informed us. "Apparently the town's digging up tombstones to move them and someone said you can see the coffins."

"Ew," Larissa exclaimed. "Wait, Travis is going?"

Jessie nodded.

"The cemetery would be a cool setting for a photo shoot," Sebastian mused.

"We're going," Larissa pronounced.

She grabbed Mae's hand and led her toward the door, followed by Jessie and Christine. Mae glanced back at me. We both shrugged. Guess we were going to take her portrait at the cemetery, then.

"Shall we?" Sebastian said, offering his arm.

I looked down at it—even though the last thing I wanted to do was go to a graveyard and take Mae's photo right now, I couldn't turn down hanging out with Sebastian.

I linked my arm in his.

"Don't mind if I do," I returned, as if I was Scarlett O'Hara in

Gone with the Wind and he was the dashing Rhett Butler. I knew my face was betraying how happy I was as we walked out of the party arm in arm, but I didn't care.

We piled into Larissa's SUV and headed for the cemetery. Sebastian took the keys from Larissa, insisting he would drive. He was completely sober. Drinking gave him a headache, he'd explained, so he didn't do it much.

Mae and I were squished into the way-back, which was fine because Larissa was talking so loud now she was practically shouting. Jessie and Christine were next to her to absorb the fallout. I reminded myself never to drink vodka shots, or any kind of shots for that matter.

I glanced down at Mae's left palm, which was resting on her bony knee. She had a small, scarred dot in the middle of her hand. I noticed she had one on the other palm as well.

"What happened to your hand?" I asked quietly.

Mae quickly pulled her sleeves down over her palms.

"I fell," she answered simply, then turned away from me and looked out the window.

On both hands? It was weird to have a scar in the exact same spot on both palms. But she clearly didn't want to talk about it, so I didn't push it.

When we arrived at the cemetery, we filed out of the vehicle. Travis was already there, surrounded by his group of jock friends.

Larissa headed over to him and began shamelessly flirting. The boys had a bottle of tequila. I saw Jessie take a big swig, then pass it to Christine.

"Lighting looks good over there, Jules." Sebastian pointed out a large mausoleum, where the full moon reflected off the limestone.

He started to follow me and Mae over. I realized him looking over my shoulder would definitely make me jumpy and I would never get the shot.

"I got it," I assured him. "We'll catch back up with you in a few."

Mae and I continued across the damp grass to the mausoleum. As we wove our way up a small incline through the gravestones, I avoided looking at the engravings. It always creeped me out that the names of people were displayed feet above where their dead bodies lay decomposing.

I wondered if Mae had lost anyone close to her.

"Do you do this often?" Mae asked as we arrived at the stone structure.

"Do photo shoots and hang out in cemeteries? Never. And I don't really even go to parties," I admitted.

A peal of laughter drifted over from where the group was down the hill. I glanced over my shoulder and saw Larissa sitting on a headstone, her legs wrapped around Travis.

"It's fun, though," Mae said. "I like being with people."

"Me too," I agreed. "Fun being part of a group."

"A *good* group," she clarified. "It's really different than how I grew up, but I like it here."

"You are super brave—being adventurous and trying new things." It was a compliment to Mae, but also something I had been thinking lately about myself—challenging myself to be more confident and open at school, with all the new attention.

"Yeah, exactly." Mae nodded, taking that in. "I'm being super brave."

We had arrived at the mausoleum, and Mae smiled at me.

It seemed to go on forever.

Moving on, I pulled out my phone and inspected the best angle for lighting. This was the first column, so I wanted to get the picture right. I suddenly became mad at myself for waiting so long to take Mae's portrait. Night wasn't the easiest time to photograph, especially on a camera phone. If you used the flash it got all washed out, so I wanted to try to get enough light without it. Luckily the moon was full.

"Why don't you stand here," I suggested, gesturing to where the moonlight was brightest.

Mae stepped over to the spot, then looked at me without smiling. She seemed like a person in one of those old-timey portraits where they all looked like someone had just died.

I had to get her to loosen up.

"Why don't you try—shaking out your hair."

"My hair?"

"Yeah, just shake your head a little."

She did, awkwardly.

"And your arms," I added. "Just swing them around a little bit, try to loosen up your body." It was a technique I'd seen a photographer use on a model on some cheesy reality show, but it worked.

Now both a little more relaxed, I got ready to shoot. Looking at my screen, Mae's face nearly glowed in the moonlight.

"Tilt your chin down?"

She did. I snapped a shot and looked at down at it. Without even trying, Mae looked modelesque—like a filter had removed any imperfections from her face, even though I hadn't used one.

I continued snapping photos as we tried a few different poses. "Put your hand on your hip? Yeah, that's great. Now lean back a little?"

Mae shifted back toward the stone but immediately recoiled. I'd forgotten about the injury on her back. It had been a few weeks, so I thought it was healing, but maybe her scars still hurt.

"I'm sorry," I apologized quickly.

"It's okay," she assured me, brushing it off with a sharp breath. She then turned her body sideways in another pose. She smiled for the camera.

"You're a natural," I complimented her.

I snapped a few more pictures.

"You looked happy," Mae said.

"What do you mean?"

"When he was talking to you. Sebastian."

I stopped, checking the last few shots on my phone. I hoped Mae hadn't noticed my crush on Sebastian, but no luck, since her mind seemed to soak up every detail available.

"He looked happy too," Mae added. "Talking to you."

"He did?" I asked too quickly.

Mae nodded. "You like him," she said.

Was she teasing me? Or just asking? I couldn't quite tell.

"I—whatever. I mean, he's nice," I backpedaled. I don't know why, but I was embarrassed admitting my crush to her. Why was I turning this into a big deal? It wasn't a crime to like someone.

I changed the subject. "The moonlight highlights your cheek-bones."

Mae looked up at the moon for a long moment. She didn't answer. She grew quiet, solemn, staring at the moon.

"Let's just do a few more and we'll be done," I told her.

She turned back to me and I clicked a few more shots. She looked practically perfect in every frame; I knew we'd have plenty to choose from. I clicked back to the camera.

Suddenly, through my screen, Mae's head whipped around.

"What was that?" She was now staring at the edge of the woods, looking like a deer that had picked up the scent of a predator.

I looked over at the placid trees. "I didn't hear anything."

Mae continued to stare past the row of gravestones to the trees.

"Maybe it was the wind," I guessed, trying to brush off her concern.

Mae turned back to me. I could tell she didn't think it was the wind. "Sorry, I get nervous around the full moon," she explained.

"Why, are you a werewolf or something?" I joked.

"No," she answered without irony. "Full moons were kind of a big deal where I came from."

"How so?"

"They just . . . It's special. Like a holiday."

"That's cool," I said. I lifted my phone and took a few more pictures. Through my viewer, I saw her turn her attention back toward the moon, as if she were magnetized by it. Her pale skin glowed.

I clicked a few shots, wanting to capture the bright glow on her cheeks.

Then, through my screen, I saw Mae's lips start moving. I couldn't tell what she was saying.

"*I reign over thee, sayeth the Lord of the Earth—*" she mumbled.

I lowered my phone and watched as she continued, a little louder.

"*—In the power exalted above and below, in whose hands the sun is a glittering sword and the moon a through-thrusting fire—*"

She seemed like she was kind of in a trance, reciting this—poem or something, staring at the moon.

"Mae?" I ventured.

But she made no indication she had even heard me.

"*—Who measureth your garments in the midst of my vestures, and trusseth you up as the palms of my hand and brighten your vestment with Infernal light,*" her voice continued, getting louder and louder.

What the hell was she talking about?

Then she started shaking. I stepped toward her, not sure what to do. Her whole body was convulsing, as if she was having a seizure or something. Panic ran through my body. I didn't want anything bad happening to her, especially on my watch.

"Mae!" I called to her, trying to get her to snap out of it. Her arms were flailing so hard now I couldn't reach her even if I tried. Her voice rose.

"*Can the wings of the wings hear your voices of wonder?*"

Holy crap, this was weird. What in the world was she talking about?

"Help!" I yelled over to the group. Some drunken heads turned from their revelry. Sebastian sprinted toward us.

"—Whom I have prepared as cups for a wedding or as flowers regaling the chambers of lust!"

Mae was shaking uncontrollably now. Her body seemed to lose its ability to stay vertical. She was leaning against the mausoleum stone, slumping down it. I wondered if that hurt her back.

"Stronger are your feet than the barren stone. Mightier are your voices than the manifold winds!" She was almost yelling now.

"Epilepsy?" Sebastian asked, arriving on the scene. The others had followed him over.

"I don't know," I said, panicked. "She just started shaking."

"For you are become as a building such as is not, save in the mind of the All-Powerful manifestation of Satan!"

Jessie reached for her phone to take a video, but Larissa's arm stopped her—maybe Larissa actually cared about Mae.

Sebastian reached for her upper body to lift her off the ground.

"Sounds like Enochian Keys," Zeke offered. "Want me to grab her legs?"

"Let's just get her upright," Sebastian suggested as the two boys reached between Mae's flailing arms.

"Keys are like Bible verses, right?" Sebastian asked.

"More like incantations, I think," Zeke said as they leaned Mae up against the mausoleum.

I had no idea what Enochian Keys were, but I did know they were creepy as shit.

Sebastian knelt down next to Mae. Her eyes were still fixated on the moon.

"Arise! Sayeth the First! Move therefore unto his servants! Show yourselves in power—"

"Mae," Sebastian said gently.

He reached toward her and wrapped his arms around her thin body, scooping her into his arms. "Everything is all right," he said calmly to her. "Everything is going to be all right."

Mae finally tore her eyes from the moon and brought her gaze to the boy who was enveloping her.

"You're okay," he assured her. And somehow, at least for the moment, she believed him. Her shaking body grew still.

Mae stared up at Sebastian, lying limp in his arms. While I'd had my *Gone with the Wind* moment with him earlier, I couldn't deny that Mae's dark features and damsel-in-distress position made her look exactly like Scarlett O'Hara, staring up at her Rhett.

CHAPTER 19

SUZANNE DIDN'T BOTHER LEAVING A MESSAGE. This was the third time she'd called Detective Nelson, and it was the third time it had gone to voice mail.

Pocketing her phone, she climbed out of her car, grabbing her mug of morning tea. She entered the hospital building and strode down the hall of the trauma wing, glancing at a clock. She had an all-department meeting in a half hour and wanted to do some more research before it started, so she quickened her pace.

A first-year psychiatry resident averted his eyes as Suzanne passed. He'd probably heard about Suzanne taking Mae home. Suzanne knew the whole department was talking about it, but she kept her head held high.

"Morning, James," she offered casually as she passed.

Rounding the corner, she turned into her office. She nearly dropped her beverage as she entered the doorway.

There was a man sitting at her desk: the sheriff from the cult.

He was wearing the same long brown coat, and he held his cowboy hat in his hand. His heavy boots were hoisted onto Suzanne's desk. A piece of caked mud had fallen next to Suzanne's keyboard. His mere presence was invasive.

"How did you get in here?"

"Came in the back with a delivery. Friend o' mine supplies the milk around here."

Suzanne took a deep breath and arranged her face. "What do you want?" she demanded.

The man's dark eyes stared at Suzanne.

"Same as you," he returned. "What's best for the girl." He swung his feet down from the desk, wiping the piece of mud from the faux-wood surface onto the industrial carpet.

"What girl," Suzanne challenged him. She was a bad liar and knew it, but she wasn't supposed to give away information about Mae, even though she knew that was exactly who he was talking about.

"Mae Louise Dodd," he said. "Sixteen. Born on January the sixth. Black hair, green eyes, little brown birthmark on her left cheek. Scratch or two on her back."

Suzanne still didn't take the bait. She didn't say anything.

"Her parents," he continued. "They're mighty worried about her."

"So am I," Suzanne returned, still standing. She didn't want to let her guard down by sitting.

"That why she's not in the hospital anymore?" he pressed.

Suzanne couldn't risk her face giving anything away, so she covered it with movement, taking a sip of her tea.

"Where'd she go? 'Cause I know she ain't here."

Suzanne stood her ground, unwilling to confirm or deny anything. She had no idea how he'd found out Mae had left, but was determined not to give him any more information.

"I am not authorized to release information about a patient's whereabouts."

The man ran his hand through his salt-and-pepper hair. "Her family's worried. Whole town is. All we want is to have our girl home."

"After what you did to her?" Suzanne blurted before thinking better of it.

"Families have their own—ways of doing things," he explained. "Outsiders don't always understand."

"I understand abuse," she told him plainly. "That girl belongs as far away from you people as humanly possible."

"Where she belongs is with her family. Her community."

"A community that carved a pentagram onto her back?" Suzanne's anger was rising. "A community that left her on the side of the road to die?"

The man didn't reply. He stood up.

"I'll start checking the foster homes. We'll find her eventually." His tall frame towered over Suzanne. "Don't say I didn't ask nicely," he warned as he tipped his hat and exited the office.

CHAPTER 20

SLAP!

High five from Noah in my math class. We'd never spoken more than a few words to each other ("What did you get for the area of the quadrilateral?"), but apparently he'd read my "People You Don't Know" column, which everyone in school was talking about.

I'd gotten compliments about it all day, which made me understand the phrase *walking on air*. People I didn't even know knew me were telling me how much they liked my interview and how cool the photo was. Score one for Jules. Finally.

And all because of Mae.

I'd ended up using a photo where her face was entirely lit by moonlight, her green eyes shining bright. She looked intriguing, like she was giving you who she was by staring directly at the camera, but something about the way she was looking told you that there was still something hidden—that she'd never fully let you know everything about her.

The photo and article had run in print and were all over social media. I'd gotten tons of "likes" for them—even from Rachel Robideaux, which made me feel amazing.

As Mae and I walked down the row of lockers, everyone was watching us. Except now instead of being leery of the Creepy New Kid and Quiet Awkward Girl, they looked at us like celebrities. My picture had made that happen.

"I'm glad you're here," a nervous freshman mumbled to Mae. "You're really inspiring," she managed to get out before hurrying off down the corridor.

In the column Mae had—without giving away any gruesome details—talked about having felt lonely in her old life, and how she was learning to be brave and adventurous. It was basically what we'd discussed in the cemetery together.

Mae smiled at the compliment, hooking her thumbs under the purple straps of the new Jansport my mom had bought her.

Mom had been pretty cool about us getting home late on Saturday. It had been after midnight when we came in, and she'd been up in her room. She found us in the kitchen making popcorn, so we just pretended we'd gotten home before my twelve o'clock curfew and she went with it. Neither Mae nor I brought up the chanting seizure thing—to my mom or each other.

"Ugh. Ms. Ramsey's interpretation of Austen is exhausting, don't you think?" Isaac asked, catching up to us.

"I don't think she appreciated your theory that Elizabeth

Bennett should move away and start her life over somewhere else," I agreed.

"Yeah, like, I get the societal constraints of the time, I just think people need to do something to change things. Amiright, Mae?"

Mae mustered a smile. She didn't really get Isaac's rants, but she was polite about them.

Isaac had been annoyed when he found out that Mae and I had gone to the party without him. "Would you have even wanted to go?" I'd asked him. "No, but that's not the point." His argument was that I should have told him about it, and he was right. I ceded the point, which he seemed satisfied with, so we dropped it.

"You guys wanna go get froyo?" he asked, pushing a strand of hair out of his face.

"We're actually going to stop by the *Regal*," I told him.

He nodded. "A-plus on the article, Jules. I'm glad you're putting yourself out there. Now the world can see how talented you are. Or at least the school can."

"Thanks, Isaac." I smiled back as we reached the stairwell. Even with all the attention from other people at school, it still was nice to have Isaac's approval. He was my oldest friend, after all.

"Bye, females," Isaac said, waving as he headed off.

As Mae and I descended to the first floor, Jessie and Christine met us at the bottom of the stairs. We stood in the stairwell.

"Loved the article," Jessie complimented me.

Christine reapplied her gloss. "And you looked gorge in that picture, Mae."

Mae smiled. "It was all Jules. She's awesome."

I was sure my face was beaming. I appreciated that Mae had shared her newfound celebrity with me, and was giving me credit.

"You should take pictures for *Teen Vogue*," Jessie decided regarding my career.

"Um, don't make me cry, my mascara's gonna run," I ventured as a joke, which I was relieved to find they laughed at.

Other students stepped around us as we talked, not wanting to disturb our group. Usually I was the one who moved out of the way for people, and I had to admit, it was pretty fun to get a taste of being popular.

"Hang out this weekend?" Christine asked. "Jessie wants to buy a new vibrator."

Jessie thumped Christine in the arm. "Do not."

Christine didn't flinch; her arms were pretty buff. "Whatever, you can just borrow Larissa's again," she grinned.

Jessie fake-gagged. "Ew, that is so gross."

I tried not to squirm at the vibrator conversation. I obviously knew about them, but had never actually seen one in person. Or used one. I knew what they did—theoretically, at least—but the ease with which these girls discussed something that seemed like it was private was making me blush. And Mae probably had zero idea what they were talking about.

"Jessie doesn't need a new one," Mae piped up. "She already has two."

They all burst out laughing. I was surprised Mae had made that joke. She barely knew what the internet was; I didn't think she'd know about vibrators.

Feeling my cheeks flush, plus the nagging fact that we were blocking the flow of traffic on the stairs, made me turn to Mae.

"We should get to the *Regal* soon," I reminded her.

"See you guys later!" Mae called as we went our separate ways from Jessie and Christine. "They're nice," she continued as we made our way to the *Regal* office.

"There they are!" Sebastian welcomed us as we walked in. "Come 'ere," he said.

Before I knew what was happening, he pulled me into a hug.

I felt my face against his flannel shirt, warmed by his body heat. I caught a faint whiff of his smell. Cologne? Pheromones? Whatever it was, it was amazing.

I wanted to stay there forever.

His arms softened, so I quickly released mine as well. Sebastian then turned to Mae. He didn't hug her, but put a gentle hand on her arm.

"Thank you for your honesty," he said to her. "How are you feeling?"

Mae brushed off the incident at the mausoleum like it had never happened. "Oh, I'm fine," she answered quickly. "Low blood sugar," she said to excuse what had occurred.

I stared at her. That was the exact excuse I'd used that morning when I forgot my book bag in the house as we were leaving for school. She sure did pick things up quickly.

Or was she copying me?

"I'm just glad you're okay," Sebastian returned. Mae smiled at him. Was she blushing?

"Really nice work," Naomi complimented us as she strode over.

She wore a chambray zip-up jumpsuit I would have babysat Danielle a month for.

"Thank you so much, Naomi, I appreciate it," I returned. Maybe a little over the top, but it didn't seem like compliments from Naomi were easy to come by.

"Who's next?" Naomi probed.

I turned to Sebastian, who was still looking at Mae.

"What's my next assignment, boss?" I asked, trying to get his attention back to me.

After a moment, he turned. "Up to you, Mathis! You're a pro now. Anyone you thought about doing a profile on next?"

Buoyed by the attention for the article, I had drafted a list of potential new people to interview in Geometry.

"I was thinking Thalia Biggs would be interesting. She's the youngest captain the women's basketball team's ever had and spends her summers volunteering building schools in different countries—last year she was in Belize. And," I added, "it would be cool to get an action shot portrait."

Thalia was in my gym class, and I'd always been impressed by her athletic prowess. Plus she was a super go-getter, so selfishly I wanted to know more about her.

"I like that," Naomi said, nodding, then headed back to oversee a GIF that Greta was creating to hype up the paper on social media.

"Excellent idea!" Sebastian approved. "Let's get a list of questions going. And now that you're an official member of the hallowed *Remingham Regal* staff, you have your very own cubby!"

"Cubby?"

"I know, what is this, second grade? It's more of an in-box, really. Couple welcome papers in there." He motioned over to a stack of shelves. "Names are on the bottom."

I walked over and found my name printed on a sticky label. I knew it wasn't a big deal to have a cubby, but it felt cool to have a place made for me.

Like I belonged somewhere.

One of the papers in the box was for a staff-wide movie night next Wednesday. *All the President's Men*—a great movie about reporters during Watergate.

"Movie night sounds awesome," I said, turning back to Sebastian.

I froze. He was standing close to Mae. They were talking quietly together, and she was giggling at whatever he'd just said.

I made my way back over and held up the movie night flyer. "This looks super cool."

They turned to me. I suddenly felt like I was interrupting something.

Trying to fill the empty space, I hurried on. "We totally have to screen *It Happened One Night*. Everyone thinks of *Citizen Kane* when it comes to classic journalism films, but this is way better. Although *All the President's Men* is definitely a good choice," I rambled, my brain desperately trying to convince me I was being paranoid that something was going on between them.

"Cool," Sebastian said finally. "Haven't seen it."

The three of us stood there awkwardly, waiting for someone to speak.

"We should get going," I said to Mae. "Mom's picking us up soon."

The truth was, I didn't really care if I made Mom wait for us a few minutes. But I certainly didn't like seeing Mae and Sebastian talking to each other, so close they were practically touching.

"Of course," Mae returned, sounding slightly disappointed as I basically pulled her out the door.

From behind me I heard Mae say, "Let me know if you ever need any help."

"Will do!" Sebastian called. "Bye, guys!"

I turned and looked over my shoulder. Was I imagining it, or when I glanced back was Sebastian blushing?

CHAPTER 21

SITTING ON A BEANBAG CHAIR IN DANI'S ROOM later that night, I plowed through my homework. Thankfully Dani was out. I couldn't shake what had happened earlier with Sebastian. Was Mae flirting with him? Was he flirting with her? Or was I just being a crazy person and imagining things, like the psychologically fragile heroine in *The Haunting*?

I had been avoiding Mae since school, burying myself with work. I had zipped through the first act of *A Doll's House* (drama!), finished my Spanish vocab review (¡La Playa!), and did my best at solving a geometry set (B-plus at best). I had e-mailed Thalia Biggs to see if she'd be interested in me doing a profile on her for "People You Don't Know" (she said yes), and I'd messaged Isaac to see how his debate had gone (well, despite gloating from Victoria Liu).

I had one more action item I could do. I drafted a list of potential questions for Thalia to send to Sebastian. I was going to send it tomorrow, but in light of his interaction with Mae this afternoon, I thought I should make a move and e-mail him tonight.

Looking down, I read over my e-mail one more time, made sure it was perfect, then hit send.

Almost immediately, *BLING!* A new message popped into my in-box. It was Sebastian, saying he'd get back to me with notes on the questions ASAP. "Have a good night," he'd added. "And congrats again on the column, Jules. Killer work." Smiley face.

While I wasn't a huge fan of emojis, I appreciated the gesture. And boys didn't usually send emojis to girls unless they liked them, right? Did Sebastian like me, or was he just being friendly? And why would Mae make anything different? Mae was new at school—she was trying to make friends. And Sebastian was ridiculously friendly—he was merely being nice to the new girl. After all, he had been new to town last year, so he could relate.

A wave of shame crashed over me. Clearly, I had been completely exaggerating, majorly overreacting to what had gone on. They had just been two people talking to each other. Plus, Mae knew I liked Sebastian, and she wouldn't do that to me. I was being ridiculous. I had been totally imagining things between him and Mae.

I had to make it up to her, maybe even apologize for being a little cold to her after school, which now felt super immature.

I pushed myself up from the crunchy beanbag chair and paced down the hall to Mae's room. I knocked on the door, but, too anxious to wait for an answer, I opened it.

"Hey, Mae, I'm sorry I—"

And then I saw it.

Mae was standing in front of the full-length mirror holding a towel over the front of her body. But her back was uncovered, her bandages removed to reveal:

A pentagram carved into her back.

My stomach churned as I took in the sight of the upside-down star that had been etched into her pale skin in red scar lines. It was grotesque, like an image from a horror movie. And it was here in my house, in my room, on my friend.

The sign of Satan.

I felt sick.

Mae turned to me, almost daring me to say something. I knew my face must be in Majorly Freaked Out mode. I tried to contort it into something less reactive.

Before I had the chance to say anything, Mae drew the towel around herself and covered her back. Her hair was dripping wet from the shower, the droplets morphing into dark dots on the carpet.

"I . . ." I started, but I didn't know how to complete the sentence. What did you say to a girl with a satanic carving on her back? I'd known something had happened to her—I had seen the bandages—but nothing had prepared me for this.

Mae walked over and slumped down on the bed.

Pull it together, Jules, I demanded of myself. I had to step up here, be a good person. Be a good friend.

I walked over to the bed and sank down next to her. We sat for a few moments in silence.

"That must have hurt an insane amount," I offered, figuring I should just say something honest.

Pulling at the carpet fibers with her toes, Mae nodded. "I almost passed out when they did it."

I didn't ask who "they" were.

"I would've." I shuddered. I could barely even imagine some-one making a cut on my back, let alone carving a gigantic star and circle. "You're doing great with everything, Mae," I compli-mented her. "Especially after all you've gone through."

Mae almost smiled. "Thank you, Jules," she said quietly. I could tell she meant it. I was glad to be able to be supportive to her. She'd given me a lot—a popularity boost at school, a friend at home—I was glad to do something in return.

But there was something still nagging at me that I couldn't wrap my brain around.

"Why did they do it?"

Mae heaved a sigh. I knew it must be difficult to talk about, but I wanted to understand it. To understand her.

"For trying to escape. I tried to leave," she explained.

"Leave home?"

"Leave town, leave the community."

I was trying to put the pieces together. "So you tried to escape the town, and you got caught, and they punished you for it."

Mae nodded.

"Did they bring you to jail or something?"

"No. Church."

My face scrunched. "They punished you in *church*?"

Church was supposed to be a safe place. I mean, I knew there was confession, and some people inflicted pain as a kind of atone-ment in the old days, but I'd never heard of a modern church inflicting pain on their own congregation.

"That's where they do pretty much anything that involves the community," Mae went on. "Where they decide everything, have ceremonies, confessions. Everything is public."

"Why?"

"They say it's to keep it in front of the eyes of the Lord."

"In front of God?"

Mae bit her lip. "Yes, but they believe in a different kind of God."

She let that sit for a moment. I felt my cheeks get hot.

"The devil," I said. That word hung in the air like an ax.

I pushed onward. "So other people watched this happen to you?"

"They make everyone watch."

As I tried to imagine this scenario, I felt nauseous. "Why?" I had to know.

"It's a warning. So other people don't try to leave. It's supposed to teach everyone a lesson. Even the children," she added.

"Kids watched this happen?"

Mae nodded. "I wasn't the only one. They've done it before . . ."

My brain was melting trying to make sense of the fact that human beings would do this to other human beings, in front of a group of human beings. It seemed like something from the Middle Ages, when they still burned people at the stake.

"Why do they mark you?"

"It's a warning. That I'll always be theirs." Mae's head sank. "I'll never be free from them."

I swallowed. I didn't doubt she was telling the truth, but it all seemed too awful to believe.

"Is that what you think?" I asked, my voice trying to contain my unease. "That you'll never be free from them?"

Mae lifted her head, catching her own gaze in the mirror.

"No," she seemed to firm her resolve right there in the moment. "I'm going to prove them wrong."

We sat silently.

"I'm sorry I was weird to you after school," I admitted. "I had it in my head that you and Sebastian were—" I felt stupid even saying it out loud. "Never mind," I went on. "It was dumb."

Mae turned to me, met my hazel eyes with her green ones.

"You're a good friend, Jules," she said, which made me feel extra horrible about thinking she was flirting with Sebastian.

"Thanks," I returned, relieved that we had moved on from the awkwardness.

Then, she put her palm on my hand and held it. Her skin was cold, like a porcelain doll.

"I've—never really had a friend," she revealed.

I felt my chest get warm. It made me feel good to be someone's first real friend. It made me feel—

Special.

Isaac had been my first best friend, but I'd never had a best girl friend, even though I'd always wanted one. But I didn't share that. I pushed past the sappy moment and joked, "Should we prick our fingers and smush our blood together?"

Mae looked at me, confused.

"It was a joke. It's a thing people do to prove their friendship or something. I saw it in a movie once."

"I know what a blood pact is," Mae returned, letting go of my hand as she stood up. "Good night, Jules," she concluded, turning off one of the bedside table lamps and climbing into bed, still wrapped in the towel. I guessed that was my cue to leave.

"Good night," I returned, standing.

CHAPTER 22

BEEP. THE MICROWAVE DINGED AS SUZANNE PULLED THE door open, then poured the hot water into her mug, refreshing her tea.

She was on a quick break between patients and had just talked to a man who was convinced that Tupac was still alive and only he could stop the murder. Suzanne had tried to reason—after she Googled who Tupac was—that it was highly unlikely that the man could have prevented the rapper's death.

Recapping her mug, Suzanne spotted Connie, sitting at a computer terminal in the nurses' station.

"Siamese?" Suzanne ventured as she approached, regarding Connie's crisp new scrub top adorned with cats.

Connie glanced at a cartoon feline playing with a ball of yarn on her shoulder and grinned.

"Aren't they cute? I ordered it online," Connie shared. "Got two of them—that way I can alternate."

"You're always so prepared, Connie." Suzanne glanced up at the wall clock. The long hand was just past the six.

"Lunch looked good downstairs. Can't wait to try that chocolate cake for dessert. I think it had raspberries in it," Suzanne subtly tempted.

Connie looked up at the clock. "Would you look at that? Lunchtime already. Time flies, doesn't it," she chuckled to herself.

She heaved herself off the creaky swivel chair, which was in dire need of being replaced.

"Time to get myself some lunch. Annnnd maybe a little piece of that cake. I did work a double yesterday," she mused, excusing the treat.

Connie paced off. As soon as she was around a corner, Suzanne surveyed the station area. There were a few other nurses at computer terminals, but they all seemed consumed with files or gossip.

Suzanne sank down onto the chair, sitting carefully so as not to make it creak. She reached for the ancient mouse and searched the screen. After clicking a few folders, she finally found what she was looking for.

"Bingo," Suzanne smiled.

She sent the file to print.

CHAPTER 23

"WHAT'S UP?" HELEN PRESSED MY MOTHER.

We were sitting across from her at the kitchen table, where Mom had gathered me, Helen, and Dani. I glanced at the stove clock to check the time. It was the movie night for the *Regal* staff, and Dad was giving me and Mae a ride to Sebastian's house to watch it with the rest of the crew. Sebastian had invited Mae because he'd asked her to help out on some projects—with all the new actions he was taking this year, the paper was short-staffed.

"Well," my mom started, speaking slowly and deliberately. Warning bells immediately went off in my head. Anytime she used that voice it triggered Danger: Mom Talk.

"I wanted to check in with you girls and see how you were doing."

"I'm awesome!" Dani returned without missing a beat. "Rehearsals are going amazing. I'm really finding the role."

"That's wonderful," Mom affirmed. "But I was thinking more about our—home life."

"You wanted to see how we're feeling about Mae?" Helen guessed, always the perfect student.

"Exactly, Helen. I know that Mae has been staying with us a little longer than expected. We're still looking into foster care for her, but haven't found the right home. I think she's doing well here. And since she's been making so much progress—integrating with you girls, making friends at school—I wanted to see if you'd be okay with her staying a little while longer."

This seemed like a logical thing to ask, but I was curious why it meant so much to Mom—I know she liked helping people and all because of her job, but I wondered if there was something more specific, something that I didn't know about.

"It probably won't be that much longer," Mom went on. "We just need to make sure she finds a place that's comfortable for her. Helen, any thoughts?"

"It's fine with me," Helen said, shrugging. If it didn't have to do with her or Landon or her friends, Helen couldn't really care less.

"Dani, what are your feelings about it?" Mom probed.

"I'm okay with it," Dani agreed, oblivious to most things around the house. "But how 'bout Jules stays in Helen's room now?"

"No way!" Helen shot back.

"Gee, thanks, Helen," I cracked.

"I have a lot going on, Jules," Helen insisted, like I had no idea what it was like to be an Important Person.

"Girls," Mom interrupted. "I think the sleeping situation should remain as is for now, and we can discuss it further later."

She then turned to me. "Jules? Are you okay with Mae staying a little longer?"

I wasn't sure what to say. I liked having Mae around, but I admit I was disturbed by seeing that satanic scar on her back. And the freak-out in the cemetery had been pretty scary. And the chanting at school . . . Maybe I should say something about it to Mom.

The kitchen door swung open.

"Jules, your dad's here to take us to Sebastian's—"

I swiveled to see Mae standing in the doorway. She looked so innocent, her face glowing with excitement.

"Oh, sorry," she excused herself, seeing me in a Serious Conversation with my mom and sisters. "I didn't mean to interrupt."

"We were just finishing up!" Mom smiled. "Jules, you okay with—what we discussed?" Mom asked vaguely as to not make Mae feel bad that we'd just been talking about her.

All eyes were on me—including Mae's.

"Of course," I smiled. "All good."

———

Sebastian greeted us with a warm grin at his front door. His T-shirt read THE FUTURE IS FEMALE. If I could have married him right there I would have.

"Come in!" he waved.

His house was cozy and full of books. It looked like the kind of place where he and his parents played Scrabble while talking about art. Sign me up.

"Oh, how cute!" Mae exclaimed, petting a small fluffy dog that had made its way over to her.

"She's a Havanese." Sebastian beamed. "Rescue. Athena."

"Hi, Athena," Mae cooed.

In the den a bunch of *Regal* staffers were packed in, sitting on couches or the floor, eating popcorn and drinking bottled ginger beer.

"My mother loves it," Sebastian explained. "'Looks like a beer but tastes much better,' she says."

"I don't like the taste of beer either," I said.

He cracked the tops off two bottles and handed them to me and Mae. I liked the sweet bubbles and sharp kick of the ginger. Way better than beer.

As Sebastian readied the TV for *All the President's Men*, Mae and I looked for seats. She squeezed into a spot on the floor next to Zeke and a freshman girl.

I felt my phone buzz in my pocket.

where are you?

It was a text from Isaac. Crap, I forgot we were supposed to work on our Social Studies presentation tonight, and canceling had slipped my mind.

been waiting at library for half hour

I texted back—

regal thing
so sorry forgot 2 tell u

I waited for the reply bubble to pop up, but it didn't. I wished he weren't so sensitive, even though he was in the right.

my bad

—I added. Still nothing.

"Jules, sit here." I turned to see Sebastian patting the seat of the big leather armchair that remained empty, presumably for him.

"Where are you going to sit?" I wondered, turning my phone to silent and slipping it into the pocket of my chocolate brown cords.

He looked around the room. "Mae, is there room next to you?"

Mae glanced to her sides—there wasn't really.

"We can both fit," I offered to Sebastian, squishing over to one side of the cushy chair.

"Sure," he said, sinking down next to me.

Um, watching an old movie sitting next to Sebastian had just become my new definition of heaven.

"Great job on Thalia, by the way," he complimented my last "People You Don't Know" column. "Should we do Michael Wells next? He's such an amazing pianist." He clicked the Blu-ray remote play button.

"Awesome idea," I whispered as the opening sounds of the film filled the room. I could feel my right side up against his warm body.

As the film started, I glanced down to the floor and saw that Mae was looking at me. I'm sure my face was beaming.

She smiled at me, then turned back to the film.

My life could not be going any better.

CHAPTER 24

DR. MATHIS: Is this—? Okay, looks like it's working. All right! So, I am here with— Do you want to say your name?

MAE: Mae. Dodd.

DR. MATHIS: Thank you, Mae. So, I know you've been talking to Dr. Brenner at the hospital now. How is it going with your sessions?

MAE: It's fine.

DR. MATHIS: Do you feel like they're helping you?

MAE: Um, I guess. He asks me how I feel a lot.

DR. MATHIS: About?

MAE: Like day to day, how things are going. And about—what happened to me.

DR. MATHIS: Would you be open to talking about what happened to you with me?

MAE: [Pause.] Okay.

DR. MATHIS: Thank you. Mae, why do you think they did this to you? What happened to your back?

[Mae takes a deep breath.]

MAE: They didn't want me to go away.

DR. MATHIS: So they did this to you because they didn't want you to leave, but then they subsequently left you by the side of the road. Why did they leave you there if they didn't want you to go away?

MAE: I had tried to run away. Before. And they found me. That's why they—did what they did to me. So that I would be reminded of them. And feel like I had to return.

DR. MATHIS: They branded you.

MAE: Yeah, like we do to the cows. We mark them. They think if they mark you, you will go back. Everyone else has.

DR. MATHIS: Everyone?

MAE: The other people they did this to.

DR. MATHIS: Can you tell me about these other instances? The other people?

MAE: I'm not supposed to, but . . . there was a girl once. I don't remember much about it; I was really little. And then I heard about a boy, a while ago.

DR. MATHIS: What was his name?

MAE: Victor.

DR. MATHIS: Victor!

MAE: Yes. They . . . punished him after he ran away. And then he did it again, but they found him. Brought him back to town.

DR. MATHIS: Does he still live in Tisdale?

MAE: Yes. He delivers milk.

DR. MATHIS: And he told you about this? What happened to him?

MAE: No, he never talks about it. My brother told me.

DR. MATHIS: Older brother? Younger?

MAE: Older. I have a younger brother too, and a sister. *Had* a sister . . .

DR. MATHIS: What happened to her?

MAE: She died.

DR. MATHIS: When was this?

MAE: Almost a year ago. On the harvest moon. Our harvest moon's usually the end of October or early November.

DR. MATHIS: I'm so sorry to hear that. How old was she?

MAE: Five.

DR. MATHIS: Did she die from an illness?

MAE: No. [A pause.] From pain.

DR. MATHIS: Pain? What do you mean by—

MAE: Drowning . . .

DR. MATHIS: She drowned?

MAE: I don't want to talk about it.

DR. MATHIS: Okay, I understand. You don't have to talk about anything you don't want to.

So your brother told you about a boy named Victor, who they also—did the same thing to as they did to you. But you said no one else ever talks about it.

MAE: That's right.

DR. MATHIS: Then why did your brother tell you about it?

MAE: To warn me.

DR. MATHIS: Warn you about—?

MAE: Running away myself. He said that's what would happen to me, if I ran away. He tried to make me stay. [Pause.] But I still left.

DR. MATHIS: Why did you want to leave?

MAE: It was—hard there. They made us work a lot. On the farm, or watching the other kids. I didn't get to go to school that much. But I really liked to read. I found a few books and hid them under my mattress. I wrote too—poems. I had found a book of them, and tried to write my own. They weren't very good. But then Mother discovered them. She got so angry. She told Father, and he—

[A quiet moment.]

They were hard on us. If we did anything wrong.

DR. MATHIS: How so?

MAE: They—beat us. With belts. Or whips, same ones they used on animals.

DR. MATHIS: They punished you corporally—on your body— if you did something they didn't approve of?

MAE: Yes. Like if you said anything bad about a person, or questioned one of the leaders.

DR. MATHIS: Who were the leaders?

MAE: Older men, and a few younger ones. They were in charge. And they ran the ceremonies.

DR. MATHIS: What kind of ceremonies?

MAE: Rituals. They've done them since the town was started. They say they're from the dawn of time, but who knows . . . They do them in church. Ceremonies for different holidays, or full moons—those are important.

DR. MATHIS: And what do the church ceremonies consist of?

MAE: Singing, some prayers. And people confess anything they did bad. Then they get punished.

DR. MATHIS: They get punished in front of everyone?

MAE: Yes.

DR. MATHIS: Why?

MAE: To keep Him happy.

DR. MATHIS: Him?

Who's "Him," Mae?

[Pause.]

MAE: I'm not supposed to say his name. [Pause.] But you'd call him the Devil.

[Silence.]

DR. MATHIS: They would employ corporal punishment on people publically—including children—to keep "the Devil" happy.

MAE: "Pleased," they'd call it. And we'd say prayers, give sacrifices.

DR. MATHIS: What kind of sacrifices?

MAE: Usually animals. Rabbits, foxes, coyotes. Sometimes bigger ones too, like a deer. I saw that once. There was so much blood.

DR. MATHIS: And they kill them? The animals? [A moment.] Note that Mae is nodding yes.

MAE: Then they drink the blood.

[Notes being scribbled on paper.]

DR. MATHIS: Mae, I've noticed that you have scars on your palms. Could you tell me where you got those?

[Quiet.]

MAE: My mom. They do it to all the kids. Babies.

DR. MATHIS: Do what?

MAE: Make them hang upside-down. Overnight.

DR. MATHIS: Let me get this straight: When you're a baby in the town of Tisdale, they make you hang upside-down overnight?

MAE: Yes. More like toddlers, actually. A little older than a baby.

DR. MATHIS: Is this in front of the church congregation also?

MAE: No, it's in your own home. But then they bring you to the church and they do a ceremony. It's like a rite of passage.

DR. MATHIS: Where do they hang in your home?

MAE: On a cross. They use nails.

DR. MATHIS: Through your palms?

MAE: Yes. [A moment.] They don't give you any food or water. Everyone has to do it. It makes you stronger. If you can stand the pain, then you can withstand anything. The Lord only wants the strongest of the flock. That's what they say, anyway. It doesn't always work.

I mean, not everyone makes it. Overnight. Or if they do make it, they get infections after—in their hands or feet. That's why there aren't a lot of kids in the town. Or as many as there should be. But the ones who do survive are the strong ones. The ones strong enough to serve Him. That's what they try to make you think, anyway.

[Silence.]

DR. MATHIS: That must have been very painful for you.

[Sniffling is heard.]

DR. MATHIS: I'm so sorry this happened to you, Mae. When they did this to your younger siblings, did they—

[Sound of shuffling.]

MAE: I need to go outside.

DR. MATHIS: Oh. It's dark out—

[A door opens.]

DR. MATHIS: Can you just tell me one thing before you go?

[Footsteps stop.]

DR. MATHIS: The other boy who they marked on his back—
Victor. Was his last name Peterson?

CHAPTER 25

DANI WAS AT A SLEEPOVER, AND MAE WAS holed up in Mom's bedroom. I'd put my ear to the door, and it sounded like Mom was asking her questions or something; I wasn't sure why. In my/Dani's room, I worked on the finishing touches for my interview with the pianist Sebastian had suggested, Michael Wells.

Meanwhile, I tried *not* to scour social media for every post Sebastian liked and investigate if he had a girlfriend at his old school. He had a bunch of photos with a pretty cousin, but that was about it. He and I had started texting, mostly about *Regal* stuff, but sometimes we'd just go back and forth a bunch making jokes. We hadn't gone on an actual date yet, but it felt like that's where we were heading, and I would just have to be patient until he got up the courage to ask me out.

I did think about kissing him sometimes, though. . . .

Spell check! I had to run through my article one more time. Must stop distracting myself with All Thoughts Sebastian.

When I finished work I went to the bathroom to brush my teeth. As I passed Mom's closed door in the hall, I could hear Mae still speaking quietly with my mother. They did that sometimes, stayed up late talking to each other. One time I saw Mae come out of my mom's room in the morning—I guessed she had fallen asleep in there. I wondered what my dad thought about that.

Turning off the light and climbing into bed, I made a mental note to tell Sebastian about an article I had found on the impact of James Dean on 1950s cinema, which I thought he might like.

———

I awoke to a pressure near my feet.

Thinking I must have imagined it, I closed my eyes again to go back to sleep.

Then I heard a sound. A breath?

I opened my eyes to the dark room. Adjusting to the gray light, a poster for *Hamilton* came into focus on a nearby wall.

The sheets felt tight on my left side. I turned to see:

Mae, sitting at the foot of my bed.

I was startled, but immediately attempted to calm myself, trying not to act too alarmed.

She was sitting perfectly still, like a statue. Her long black hair was loose, hanging down past her shoulders. It glinted in the light from a streetlamp that filtered through the window. Mae was staring at me.

"You all right?" I ventured, seeing if she would give me a clue as to why she was sitting on my bed in the middle of the night.

She was wearing a white nightgown. It wasn't mine, so I guessed Mom had bought it for her.

Mae didn't say anything. She just kept staring at me through the darkness.

I tried again. "Are you okay, Mae?"

Mae looked down at the pink bedspread, took a handful of material into her hand, and squeezed it. She shook her head.

I pushed myself upright, hoping it was nothing serious.

"What's wrong?" I asked.

After a quiet moment, she finally spoke.

"I think . . . I think they're trying to get me back."

"They?"

Mae nodded. "My family."

Right. Her family from the satanic cult. Mae was becoming so integrated into my family and life, I often forgot she'd had a whole other life before us.

"I doubt they would be able to find you. They probably don't even know where you are," I offered.

"They'll find me," she guaranteed.

"How?"

"They followed me, to the cemetery," she insisted. But that just couldn't be true. How could they have known we were going there? *We* didn't even know we were going there.

"That was just some noise from the woods, Mae."

"They cut down the branch—"

"The one in front of the house last month?"

She nodded.

"It's an old tree. Branches fall all the time," I reasoned.

Mae shook her head adamantly. "They made it *look* like it fell down," she explained.

"Why would they do that?"

"As a warning."

"Warning for what?"

"That I should go back to them. That I'm not safe here, or anywhere except with them."

Then she looked me in the eye.

"And neither is anyone around me."

My heart froze. Why would anyone want to hurt us? We were the ones trying to help her.

I shook the idea off, sitting forward. "Mae, you're staying with us now. You go to Remingham High, you have friends. No one's going to hurt you here. You're safe."

Her face took on a thousand-yard stare. "I hope so."

I hoped so too.

"Have you told my mom?" I asked as the idea of possible danger started to sink in. "That you're scared about this?"

"She knows about them," Mae revealed. But then she admitted, "I don't want to do anything that would make her send me away."

Mom knew that Mae had come from a possibly dangerous community but hadn't said anything to us? Maybe that meant she wasn't really worried and Mae was probably just imagining things. She'd had a traumatic past, as my mom would say, and so she was just scared that it might happen again—even though she was safe in the suburbs now. It was like the soldiers we had learned about in school who, after returning from war zones, had nightmares even though they were back home safe.

"I'm sure it's all fine," I said, convincing myself and her that she was okay.

"Yeah," Mae agreed half-heartedly. She didn't make a move to go back to her bedroom.

"You okay?"

"I—" Mae started. "I don't want to be alone."

"Oh."

Since Dani was at a sleepover, there was an extra bed in here. . . .

"Do you want to sleep on the trundle?" I finally offered. I didn't mind sharing the space, but something made me pause at sharing a bed with her.

"Yes," Mae answered without hesitation, as if she'd been waiting for me to ask. She climbed into the bed on the floor next to me.

Her face was extra pale, looking like a ghost in the gloom.

I lowered myself back under the covers, staring at the ceiling. The streetlight cast a shadow from the ballerina figurine that hung in Dani's window.

"Could I hold your hand?" Mae asked quietly.

I wasn't sure I'd heard her right.

"Just until I fall asleep?" The question hung in the air for a moment. It was a strange request but seemed harmless.

"You don't have to," she backpedaled, but seemed sad about it.

"No, it's fine," I assured her.

I reached my hand down the side of the bed to the trundle and felt Mae's cool, soft skin envelop mine.

"I used to hold my little sister's hand so she could fall asleep," Mae explained in the quiet darkness.

"That's sweet." Dani would never want me to hold her hand falling asleep, and I might've wanted Helen to hold mine when I was little, but I doubt she would have.

"What's your sister's name?"

"Amelia," she answered. "Amelia" was what Mae had accidentally called Dani. Maybe Dani reminded Mae of her sister, who must be back in Tisdale. Dani annoyed the crap out of me, but I'm sure I'd miss her if I had to move away and couldn't see her anymore.

"Do you miss her? Amelia?"

"Oh yes," Mae answered. "A lot." Mae's palm closed around mine a little tighter.

"Does she get along with your parents?"

"No," she said sadly, "but she's in heaven now. They said she's not but I know she is."

My stomach sank. I'd had no idea her sister had died, and now suddenly I was desperate to find out more but didn't know what I could say to draw Mae out.

"I'm so sorry, Mae."

"It's okay. Now she can finally be at peace."

After a few quiet moments, I couldn't help myself. "How did she die?"

Mae took a slow, deep breath.

"She couldn't withstand the pain," she answered, as her hand gripped mine even tighter.

Then, Mae started to sing softly:

"*Rock-a-bye baby, on the tree top. When the wind blows, the cradle will rock . . .*"

I didn't sleep a wink.

CHAPTER 26

THE NEXT NIGHT, DANI COULDN'T STOP SINGING THE whole ride home from the restaurant. She wanted us to hear all the cool parts of the song she was going to sing in the musical, but she didn't want to spoil the whole song so was only singing phrases. It was majorly annoying.

I pulled out my phone and typed a text.

After a moment, Mae pulled out hers, hearing a *DING*. Mom had gotten her a cell phone a few weeks ago. While she was still getting used to having a cell, at least she wasn't jumping every time it rang like she had when she first got it.

She looked at the screen and smiled at the wide-eyed emoji I'd sent her in reaction to Dani's belting.

She tapped back a laughing-while-crying smiley face.

I couldn't complain to Mom directly about Dani. It was my little sister's twelfth birthday. She had been super irritating all day, extra bubbly and doubly loud, knowing full well that she could get away with just about anything. She even ate the last of the cornflakes at breakfast, leaving me the remains of a gross-looking muesli. Not to mention the fact that for her birthday meal, she had made us all suffer through dinner theater. It had been a murder mystery where, surprise surprise, the butler did it. These people needed to watch some Hitchcock and get tips on . . . suspense.

Mae had thought the whole experience was very strange but seemed to enjoy being out with the whole family. She talked to my mom and dad about school in the car on the way there, and even got Helen—who had kindly graced us with her presence—to chat with her during intermission. Mae ate all her chicken and then even had my potatoes. I wondered how she consumed so much food and still managed to stay so skinny. She also ate two pieces of birthday cake, which had been brought out by the "maid" in the play, which thrilled Dani.

Mom was trying to put on a good face, but the dark circles under her eyes told me she hadn't been getting much sleep lately. A few nights ago, I'd gotten up to go to the bathroom in the middle of the night and saw the light on in the living room downstairs. I leaned down the steps to see her reading over work files and typing on her laptop. She seemed to be working all the time these days, and always seemed distracted. I wondered if it had to do with Mae.

Thankfully Dani reached the finale of her car performance as Dad pulled his Toyota Land Cruiser into the driveway.

As we filed out of the car and down the stone path to the front door, Mom rummaged in her purse for her keys.

"I got it," Dad assured her. He stepped up to the door.

"Larissa wants to know if we want to go shopping next week for Halloween costumes," Mae said to me, looking at her phone. "Jessie and Christine are in."

"Totally," I replied, digging my hands into my pockets to check my phone, which had no messages. "They texted you?"

"Yeah," Mae said, texting back.

I wondered why I hadn't been included in the group thread.

"What the heck?" Dad stared at the lock on the front door.

I turned to see the metal door handle hanging at an angle. It was dented, as if someone had taken a hammer and smashed it sideways.

"Stand back," Dad warned, his voice lowering. He leaned down to inspect it more closely.

"Did someone break in?" Helen worried, pulling her attention from her phone.

I looked at Mae. Her face was pale.

Suddenly I remembered my late-night conversation with Mae. Was it possible that her family had tried to break in?

"I'm not sure what happened." Dad's response was measured as he checked out the frame of the door for signs of forced entry.

"Here." I went over and turned on the flashlight function of my phone so he could see better.

I looked back at Mae. Mom, who hadn't said anything, had stepped closer to her, almost like she was protecting her.

"Should we call the police?" I wondered. I glanced at Mae, thinking that the police would be a good idea if she thought it really was the cult coming after her.

Mae avoided eye contact, just stared at the ground.

"I'm texting Landon," Helen declared. "Their house got broken into a few years ago, so now they have the highest-end security system. I'm finding out what it is, 'cause clearly we need it."

"Look!" Dani said, pointing at a branch nearby. "It's from the tree!"

A new piece of branch had fallen from the oak in our front yard, which I was beginning to think was at least partially dead.

"That's probably what happened," Mom spoke up, trying to calm everyone. "A branch fell on the door handle. No one was trying to break in." She squeezed Mae's shoulder. "The door isn't even open."

"I think your mother's right," Dad agreed, jiggling the still-closed door.

Dad paced to the fallen branch, then tilted his head up, examining the tree. "Could definitely have dropped at that angle, especially with this wind," he determined. I knew it had cost a lot to repair the bay window from when a branch came down last month, so I'm sure he wasn't happy about having to do more repairs.

"I'm going to check out the house just to be safe," he continued, heading inside. "Stay here until I get back."

Mom put her arms around Mae. "There's nothing to worry about," Mom said to me and my sisters.

"We're all safe and sound," she went on. "Safe and sound . . ."

CHAPTER 27

AFTER DANI'S BIRTHDAY DINNER, PETER SAT AT HIS desk, searching on his computer in the lamplight.

He was researching security systems. He didn't want to worry Suzanne and the girls, but he hadn't liked finding that lock broken. Glancing at a photo of his family on his desk reminded him of who he needed to keep safe.

KNOCK, KNOCK.

"Hey, honey, I'll be done soon," he said without looking up, assuming it was Suzanne.

"Hey . . ." he heard a soft voice respond.

Peter looked to the door of his office to see: Mae.

"Hello there," he greeted her, surprised. He looked at her for a moment, not sure why she was there. "Anything you need?" he wondered, aligning the edges of some papers on his desk.

"No," Mae started, reclining against the doorframe. "Just the opposite."

Peter turned toward her, a perplexed look on his face.

"Not sure what you mean," he returned, his forehead creasing.

"Well," Mae purred. "You've been so kind to me. To let me stay with you, and paying for things for me. Food, clothes, dinner tonight . . ."

He waved her off. "Aw, don't worry about it. It's our pleasure. You're part of the family while you're here," he said, turning back to his screen.

But the girl didn't leave.

"I was wondering," she said, pausing to lower her voice, "if there was anything I could do for you."

Peter turned back to her.

"Do for me?"

"Yes," she confirmed, sliding her arm up the doorframe. "To—make it up to you?" The offer lingered in the air.

"I just told you, you don't owe us anything—"

"But maybe there's something that would—make you happy . . ."

Peter's face heated, not knowing how to respond.

She went on. "There were men in my town—elders—who liked to be made . . . happy."

Peter suddenly felt extremely uncomfortable being alone with this girl.

"I have some work to do," he blurted, standing abruptly. The move knocked a stack of papers into the framed photo of the Mathis family, tipping it over.

Peter reached for the frame and set it upright.

Mae looked at the desk quizzically. "Isn't that your work?"

"I have—other work," he backpedaled. "In the garage."

He stepped toward the door.

"Excuse me," he said as he squeezed past her in the doorframe, escaping the room as fast as he could.

Now alone, Mae remained standing in the doorway, her eyes glued to the picture of the Mathis family on Peter's desk.

CHAPTER 28

LATER THAT NIGHT, POST—BIRTHDAY DINNER, WE HAD all peeled off on our own. While I was catching up on homework and tasks in the living room, Mae had been in the kitchen, talking with Mom, Dad was working in his office, and Dani was I'm sure video chatting upstairs, telling her friends all about the branch drama and soaking up the last few moments of birthday attention.

I messaged Isaac about our Social Studies presentation, still trying to pay my penance for standing him up at the library. I knew he wasn't super happy with me these days, so I was trying to be extra thoughtful, and even brought him an orange soda the other day, which he loved. Then I worked on the portfolio I was continuing to compile for my photography application, which I was really starting to get excited about. *(It's) Still Life* was coming together. And now I had all the "People You Don't Know" portraits I could include too as additional material.

Sebastian had approved my column questions for next week's "People You Don't Know," so I went over them one more time before I sent them to Norman Bellinsky, a junior who played chess competitively. I'd already taken his picture outside at a picnic table where he played with a few other, well, nerds.

I shut my laptop, realizing it was after eleven. I guess we hadn't gotten back from dinner till kind of late. I yawned, heading for the stairs.

As I approached, I heard quiet voices.

"—make it up—?"

I looked down the hallway toward my dad's office. Mae was standing in the doorway, illuminated by the desk lamplight coming from within. I heard my dad say something back to her.

Why was Mae talking to my father? And what did the two of them have to talk about privately?

After more quiet talking that I couldn't make out, Dad hurried into the hallway, pushing past Mae. He looked upset.

He saw me standing by the stairs.

"Hey, Jules," he said, avoiding eye contact. "I'm gonna grab some air," he excused himself as he stepped outside, sweatered but jacketless.

Mae started toward me from my dad's office.

"Everything okay?" I asked her.

"Oh yeah," she answered casually as she passed. "Everything's great, Jules." Her voice was calm and placid, almost unnervingly so.

"Have a good night," she called over her shoulder, gliding up the stairs like a smug ghost.

What the hell was that about?

———

I couldn't sleep. The events of the night swirled around in my mind, like a song playing too fast.

Had Mae's former family really come after her and tried to break the lock on our house? And why had Mae been talking to my dad?

I flung the bedsheets off. My skin had started to perspire, even though it was a chilly night.

Dani was snoring away on the trundle as I climbed out of bed and dragged myself down the hallway.

Sometimes when I had trouble sleeping I made myself go to the bathroom. For some reason, if I did that, when I went back to bed it was easier to fall asleep.

As I passed Mae's room, I shivered. A cold gust of air slipped through the cracked door. Why was it so chilly in there? It was a windy night, but it shouldn't be breezy inside. Had Mae left a window open?

Knowing full well that it was super creepy to peek into Mae's room while she was sleeping, I did it anyway.

As my eyes adjusted to the darkness, I saw that everything looked normal—except the bed.

It was empty.

I nudged the door open all the way. There was no one in the

room. Maybe Mae had gone downstairs for a snack or something. Should I go check? That was a super-stalky thing to do.

A freezing gust ruffled the purple curtains on the open window. The leaves rustled on the tree outside, making a shimmering crinkling sound. I stepped across the carpet and looked out at the edge of the first-floor rooftop, which extended under the bedroom window.

I saw a sock.

I was pretty sure it was Mae's. It was a pink-and-purple argyle one that she'd borrowed from me and not given back. She said all the clothes she used to wear were brown or gray, so she loved wearing colors—even on her feet.

Had Mae climbed out the window and down the side of the roof? Why in the world would she do that? Or had the sock always been there, and no one—i.e., me—had noticed? I couldn't remember the last time I had looked out over that part of the rooftop.

I turned back inside and peered around. A few of Mae's schoolbooks rested on the desk, a bath towel hung on the back of the door, a few crumpled sheets of paper lined the wastebasket. I stepped over to pick one out, curious to see what she had written.

"Ow!" I yelped before I knew what had happened.

I glanced down at the floor and saw something under my foot. It looked like a thin stick or something. A pencil? But it had pierced my foot.

I reached down to retrieve:

A long-stemmed white rose, with thorns all down the stalk. It was lying on the floor near the bed. The white petals glowed in the faint light from outside.

I wiped a spot of blood off my foot and put my finger in my mouth. The metallic taste of blood covered my tongue. I should probably go get a Band-Aid so I wouldn't bleed all over the carpet.

As I headed for the bathroom I glanced down at the flower. I realized that I never really saw white roses. Usually they were red or pink—a romantic display of some kind. What was a white one doing on the floor of Mae's bedroom?

And then it dawned on me:

The front door lock. Maybe the house really had been broken into earlier. Had the cult come in and left Mae a white rose? Had she escaped out the open bedroom window?

I had to find her.

Quickly heading downstairs, I searched the kitchen and living room to make sure I wasn't missing her in the house. Then I hurried out the back door, grabbing a pair of boots along the way.

A light rain met me as I stepped outside. I sped across the grass toward the front of the house as the wind picked up, rolling dead leaves Dad hadn't raked up yet across the lawn.

Arriving at the road, I looked down the tree-lined asphalt. I had to shield my eyes from the rain, which was quickly coming down harder.

In the distance, I saw a small figure in white.

I raced down the road, as fast as my pricked foot would let me. I had stupidly forgotten my jacket, and now the rain was soaking through, weighing down my flannel pajamas, making it harder to move.

"Mae?" I called as I tried to get closer.

But she kept walking away from me down the road, her nightgown flapping in the wet wind. Where was she going? This road was desolate for another half mile till you reached the main road, and even then the nearest stores were a ten-minute drive away.

"Mae," I cried again, jogging now to close the gap between us. One-socked, she kept marching forward at a steady pace, almost robotic. Was she sleepwalking?

Finally catching up to her, I shouted, "Mae!" as I lunged forward, laying my hand on her shoulder.

"Ahhhhhhh!" Mae shrieked, whipping around, her eyes wide with fear.

"Sorry, I didn't mean to scare you. Are you okay?"

Mae stared back blankly, her face awash with rain and confusion.

"Were you sleepwalking?" I ventured, trying to figure out what in the world was going on.

Mae looked down at her now nearly see-through nightgown. She gazed around at the wet pavement and billowing trees, bewildered.

"Are we outside?" she asked.

Duh, I thought, but didn't say that.

"Yes," I answered. She must have been in a trance, like the one she'd had in the cemetery.

"I was worried about you," I continued, explaining why I'd followed her out. "I saw the rose in your room and—"

"Rose?" Mae glared at me, as if remembering it herself. "The rose," she repeated, her voice dropping.

Her body started to shake. *Oh no*, I thought. *This is not good.* I doubted I could carry her back in the rain if she had another seizure.

"Come on, let's go back inside. You're soaked." I pulled at her, trying to physically move her back toward the house.

But she grabbed my pajama top in her bony fingers.

"It's from them!" she yelled, shaking me. "The rose—they put it there!" Fury filled her thin frame; water streaked down her face.

"They did it to remind me!" Mae cried. "To make me go back!"

I stared at her. My lungs filled with air, but I wasn't able to respond. I had no idea what to say.

"They're coming for me!" She desperately clung to the fabric of my clothing even tighter, her hair wild in the rain. Then her voice lowered to a whisper, her green eyes staring straight into mine.

"They're coming for me. . . ."

Suddenly, I was the one shaking.

CHAPTER 29

SUZANNE KILLED THE ENGINE AND CLICKED UP THE parking brake, an unnecessary move in the flat land they lived in but something that she had always done out of habit.

She peered out the windshield through the crisp morning air. Across the parking lot stood a few gas pumps and a small convenience store. A lone Honda Civic refueled.

Over on the passenger seat sat Suzanne's files. She picked one up and opened it.

"What the Devil Happened?" read the title of the old newspaper article she had printed out. It chronicled a mysterious young boy from the small town called Tisdale, who had arrived at Remingham Regional Hospital, then disappeared. It didn't mention the carving on his back, since that was private information, but Suzanne had cross-referenced the dates with the confidential files she had covertly swiped from Connie's computer.

Victor Peterson didn't have a Facebook page, or any social media presence for that matter. Not the Victor Peterson she was looking for, anyway.

Suzanne leafed through the records she had pulled as she waited in her car, including Victor's confidential medical charts. Most of the information the papers contained was irrelevant at this point, since he had been a young boy when he had come to the hospital, and there were no current photos of him anywhere.

But Suzanne had found one very helpful clue in his file: the boy had red hair, which would make him much easier for her to spot. Mae had confirmed that Victor's hair remained red.

Using his last name, Suzanne had traced his family name to a local dairy. She'd checked business registries in the town of Tisdale and discovered the name of the dairy and a business address. She'd called the number associated with the company, but all she got was a full voicemail box. She'd even driven out to Tisdale a few days ago after work, telling Peter she had an emergency department meeting she had to attend, but the strange thing was—she couldn't actually find the town of Tisdale. Where the GPS told her the exit to the town should be was nonexistent. It was just a row of trees leading back into thick woods.

So Suzanne tried a different method. She'd driven to the gas station closest to the town "exit" on the map, in hopes of finding another lead.

The *CHUG-CHUG-CHUG* of a delivery truck pulled Suzanne's attention across the asphalt: Peterson Dairy.

Suzanne observed as the truck came to a stop in front of the convenience store. A tall young man stepped out of the gray vehicle, followed by a younger man, probably late teens, who hopped down from the passenger seat. They both wore brown jumpsuits.

And they both had red hair.

Suzanne dropped the files, unclicked her seat belt, and opened the car door. Zipping up her coat as the chilly air hit her neck, she hurried across the parking lot.

She approached the back of the truck, where the double doors were now open. The younger of the men reached into the truck and heaved out a crate of milk bottles. He carried them to the entrance of the store.

The older redhead grabbed another crate and slid it toward himself, tossing a clipboard on top. He lifted the crate onto his knee and swatted one of the doors shut.

"Victor?" Suzanne called in the friendliest manner she could muster.

"If He be pleased," Victor replied habitually, turning in her direction. His auburn brow furrowed when he realized he did not recognize Suzanne.

"Hello!" she said, speaking quickly. "I know you don't know me, but I wanted to talk to you about—"

"Not interested," he declared, slamming the other back door shut. He headed for the minimart entrance, where the other man—whom Suzanne assumed was his brother—was on his way out, holding the door.

"I just have a few questions if you wouldn't mind answering—"

Victor ignored her, continuing inside. She followed him into the store past the younger brother.

"It won't take long," she reasoned as Victor continued to the refrigerator case. He began to unload his crate contents onto the chilled shelves.

She pressed on. "I just want to—"

The door jingled behind Suzanne, startling her. She turned to see the younger redhead standing in back of her, arms folded.

"Help you with something?" the woman over behind the counter demanded more than offered.

Suzanne looked at the woman. Her gray hair was pulled into a tight bun. She was also wearing brown—a long, plain dress. Suzanne then noticed a young girl at a coffee station brewing another pot. Another customer was in the process of selecting a shaving razor.

Everyone in the store was dressed in dowdy, dark, old-fashioned clothing.

And they were all staring at Suzanne.

Used to people in Ohio being pretty friendly, she felt it was odd to get the cold shoulder these people were giving her. And what was with all the dark clothing? Were they all from Tisdale? Were they all in the cult?

"'Less you have some business I can help you with," the counter woman warned, "best make yourself scarce."

The woman's face revealed she was stone-cold serious.

Suzanne glanced at Victor, who gave absolutely no indication that he was willing to talk to her. She knew making anyone around here angry would not help her cause. She was not on friendly territory.

"Okay," Suzanne conceded. "Have a good day."

Stepping back toward the door, Suzanne moved past the younger redhead brother and pushed herself out of the store.

She strode back to her car, balling her fists in frustration. Victor had probably been too afraid to say something in front of anyone. If she wanted to get answers from him, she'd have to try to talk to him alone.

Back at the car, Suzanne checked the clock, then rummaged through her purse for her cell and dialed work. As the person on the other end of the line answered Suzanne sighed.

"Hey, Tammy, sorry to be so last minute like this, but I'm running a little late. Can you go ahead and reschedule my first appointment?"

CHAPTER 30

THE RED DEVIL HORNS GLINTED IN THE LIGHT. "We worship you, O Lord of Darkness!" chanted a girl's voice.

"Ohmygod. Love it!"

Larissa adjusted the devil horn headband on Jessie's dark brown curls.

"You're slutty Satan!" Larissa declared. "You should totally get that."

Jessie pulled at the strap of the turquoise halter top she was wearing even though it was October. "You think?"

The headband horns were the defining piece of a Satan costume, which also included a red leotard and tights. What devil wore red tights, I wasn't sure, but neither me, Mae, Larissa, Jessie, or Christine questioned the costume supply contained in the small shop.

"You're gonna get lice," Christine predicted re: Jessie wearing the headband, as she was leafing through outfits for herself on a rack.

"Ew." Jessie squirmed, tearing off the headpiece.

The purpose of our venture into town was to get costumes for the Halloween party in the woods next week. There was a handful of shops that ran through the center of town, and this place was pretty well stocked when it came to carrying seasonal items—Santa hats in winter, bunnies and baskets at Easter, and they were known for having a good Halloween selection. But nothing had caught my eye yet. I usually went DIY for Halloween since I just stayed in and gave out candy with Isaac—and stock personas weren't my thing. However, Larissa had insisted we come here together to look, so I went along with the group, since I was actually part of one. Smiley face.

My phone rang: Isaac.

I couldn't quite fill him in with everyone around me, so I sent it straight to voice mail.

Mae and I hadn't talked about what had gone on the other night with the rose thing. The next morning she'd seemed okay, like nothing had happened, and I didn't know what to say, so I just went along pretending everything was fine.

My phone rang again.

Larissa glanced up at me. "You're popular," she smirked.

"Tell me about it," I joked back flatly, switching the ringer to vibrate.

I fired off a quick text to Isaac.

busy now

The bubble of his texting back appeared immediately.

where are you?

shopping

—I responded quickly.

shopping?? You hate shopping!

I didn't answer him. He was right—normally shopping was not one of my top ten favorite things to spend time on.

waited for you at bus

Crap. I didn't want to deal with this right now. I slipped the phone into my pocket, leaving his text unanswered. I needed to focus on finding a good costume. I'd text him back later.

"What should I be?" Larissa mused. She picked an extremely short white dress off the rack, which had a little white nurse's hat. I'd been to Mom's hospital many times and had never seen a nurse dressed like that.

"You can give Travis a checkup," Christine joked, applying lip gloss to her already glossed lips. "Jules, who are you going with?"

"What?" I had been distractedly pushing costumes around the rack, trying to ignore the fact that I felt guilty about blowing off Isaac.

"The party. Who's your date?" Larissa pressed.

"Oh, I—no one yet."

"You better hurry, everyone good is almost taken," she warned.

My phone vibrated in my pocket. Isaac was not taking the hint. Maybe something was wrong. I quietly answered the call, ducking a few shopping racks away.

"What's up?" I asked.

"What do you mean, 'what's up.' What's up with *you*?"

"What's up with *me*?"

"Yeah, why are you totally avoiding me?"

"Oh, I'm not . . ." I trailed off, even though I kinda was.

"Where are you?"

"I'm shopping for a Halloween costume in town," I explained quickly.

"Why? We always stay in."

"Because." I paused, bracing myself. "I'm going to the Halloween party in the woods."

Dead silence emanated from the other end of the line.

I had never been invited to the Halloween woods party before. It was usually meant for, as with most parties, upperclassmen and cool underclassmen, of which I had been neither. And neither was Isaac.

"Let me guess," Isaac started. "You're going with Larissa and Jessie and Christine and—surprise, surprise—Mae."

He knew the answer, so I didn't deny it.

"I didn't think you'd want to go," I defended.

"Did you even ask me?" he spat back.

I fiddled with the hanger of a Wonder Woman costume.

"Precisely. What's happened to you, Jules?"

"What?"

"You used to be thoughtful, care about other people. Especially, um, your *best friend*," he emphasized.

"Isaac—" I started.

"No. I'm done. I don't need to be friends with a social climber who only cares about hanging out with the cool kids. Have fun with *Mae*."

The other end of the line went dead.

Damn. I hadn't meant to make Isaac feel bad. It really wasn't intentional. I was mad at myself for letting that happen—again.

"What is this?" Mae asked, holding up a long black dress to me.

"Oh," I said, shaking off the conversation with Isaac, "I think it's supposed to be a witch. You wear it with a black pointy hat."

"Why?" she asked.

"Because that's what witches wear, I guess."

Mae's brow rose, signaling that she didn't think that's what witches wore at all—and maybe she actually knew. "I don't really get it," she admitted.

"The outfit?"

"The whole thing. Dressing up." She surveyed the racks of potential ghosts and goblins.

"It's just a tradition," I attempted to explain. "Did you not dress up for Halloween where you grew up?"

Mae shook her head no.

"I don't know where the tradition came from—probably to scare away evil spirits or something."

Mae eyed me. "There are other ways of doing that."

"Like how?" I probed.

"You know, rituals and things. Sacrifices." Mae's attention ticked toward the other girls and she stopped herself from saying more.

"So you dress up every year?" she asked, moving on.

"Yeah. When we were kids we'd go door-to-door trick-or-treating. But this party will be more about people getting drunk and hooking up."

"Sounds . . . What did you say the other day? 'Riveting.'"

I laughed. "Exactly. Excellent use of sarcasm."

"Thanks," she smiled.

I scanned the shop. Not wanting the other girls to hear, I whispered to Mae, "These all seem pretty basic, though. I want a costume that's more original."

"Yeah, definitely," she agreed. "I want something original too."

"Mae!" Larissa called, striding over. "Try this on."

Larissa reached the red devil horns out to put them on Mae's head. Mae whacked Larissa's hand.

"Ow!" Larissa cried.

Larissa stared at Mae. No one pushed Larissa away. Christine and Jessie looked on.

"Sorry," Mae apologized after a moment. "It's just . . ." She didn't finish her explanation.

Silence. No one moved.

"No, I get it," Larissa finally replied. "You lived with devil worshippers, and these bring back bad memories. You probably have PTSD like my cousin Brad. He was in the Marines and he freaks every time he hears a car engine start." Larissa then added for good measure, "Jessie's the devil anyway, so she should wear it."

Larissa selected another outfit to signal that the whole awkward exchange was over. "You should be a nun!"

"What's a nun?" Mae wondered.

"What's a *nun*?" Jessie repeated, unable to believe that Mae didn't know.

"It's someone who's never had sex," Christine explained.

"That's not the only thing. They're, like, married to God. My aunt is one," Jessie added.

"I think I know people like that," Mae considered.

"Ohmygod, you're adorable." Larissa grabbed Mae's hand. "We're trying it on."

She led Mae toward the back of the store to a dressing room in which a curtain served as a door.

"Jessie, grab the hat!" Larissa ordered.

"It's called a habit!" Jessie corrected, obeying regardless. Christine followed.

I was relieved that the headband horn incident had blown over quickly and hadn't triggered Mae into another trance. I needed one day of normalcy this week.

A Princess Leia costume caught my eye, so I headed over toward the rack. I held it up, catching a glimpse out the window of the store behind it.

Sebastian was outside with Zeke, holding a fro-yo.

I shoved Princess Leia back onto the rack and practically raced out to the street.

"Sebastian!"

He turned toward me. "Jules!" he smiled. He was wearing his

glasses today, and a cozy-looking plaid shirt. I wanted to hug him, but I didn't.

I tried to play it cool. "What are you guys doing here?" I asked him and Zeke, in an effort to seem completely nonchalant.

Zeke held up his fro-yo. "New flavor—lychee mango. Not bad. What are you up to?"

"Just shopping for costumes for the woods party. Super-exciting stuff." I could feel my face flush.

"Find anything good?" Zeke asked.

"Not yet. I'll probably go the DIY route. I like making my own thing."

"Good call," Sebastian approved. "I'm doing the same."

"What are you going to be?" I asked Sebastian.

"You'll have to wait and see," he grinned. If air could be electric, I think it was right then.

Zeke must have felt it too because he suddenly said he had somewhere to be and took off, leaving me and Sebastian alone.

I knew I had to seize the opportunity, and forced myself to say something. Or at least tried to. *Deep breaths, Mathis.*

"Yeah, I went last year. It was entertaining," Sebastian went on. "Jason Kessler got so drunk he puked all over himself."

I was freezing up. Shit, I couldn't chicken out on this, it was the perfect opportunity. I had to ask I had to ask I had to ask.

"Would you—" I began.

Do it, Jules! Just say words!

I tried again. "Would you—want to go to the party? With me?" I clarified.

Boom. Confident Jules, that's who I was now. The Jules who asked boys out to parties.

Sebastian adjusted his glasses. The wait for a response felt like an eternity.

"Umm—" he finally replied.

Suddenly I felt nauseous. *This is why you keep your mouth shut, Jules!*

"We can all go together!" Sebastian finished.

What? Who was "all"? Was he going with a group of people from the paper or something? I had imagined the two of us going together, but if we still went as a group that wouldn't be all bad.

"I actually already asked someone to go with me," Sebastian explained.

I tried to stop my expression from falling into Biggest Disappointment of My Life face. I was devastated. How could I not have known that Sebastian already had a date? I was mortified.

"It's no big deal," I said, trying to brush it off. "It was just an idea."

"No, I'm glad you asked. I'm flattered."

Awkward. Silence.

"Who are you going with?" I tried to stop myself from asking, but I had to know.

Sebastian looked behind me, a grin widening across his cheeks. I turned to see what he was looking at. Or more important, who.

And there, standing on the sidewalk, was the answer to my question.

Mae.

She had come out of the costume shop with Larissa and company, a few of them holding shopping bags.

"Hey." Sebastian beamed at Mae.

"Hey." She waved, a blush warming her pale skin.

This. Was. Not. Happening.

"I'm already going to the Halloween party with Mae," Sebastian informed me, loud enough for the whole group to hear. *Please let me disappear right now* was all I could think.

"But we can all drive together! Although Mae gets shotgun," he offered his future date.

I closed my eyes, hoping that by not seeing it, it would make it not real. I had to extricate myself from this situation immediately.

"Gotta go!" I exclaimed, giving absolutely no reason at all. I didn't even know how I'd get home.

I started down the sidewalk before anyone could ask me questions. Hot tears hit my cheeks.

CHAPTER 31

I'D HITCHED A RIDE HOME WITH STACY AND her mother. It wasn't ideal, but I was out of options and couldn't ask Isaac. Stacy asked a lot of questions regarding my puffy cry-face, but I refused to answer and sat in stony silence.

As soon as I got home, I burrowed up in Dani's room. I couldn't believe Sebastian and Mae were going to the Halloween party together. I felt so stupid.

Like a movie montage, my mind raced through every interaction between the two of them I could remember. Sebastian had just seemed like he was being his usual nice self to her, but maybe there had always been something more going on. But how could it have all happened under my nose and I hadn't seen it?

What was even worse was that she knew I liked him. I had been nothing but nice to her, and this was how she acted in return? I had offered her friendship, and she rewarded me by going behind my back and stealing the one guy I actually liked.

"Dinner," Dani declared, lifting the headphone off my left ear.

Instinctively I threw a pillow at her.

"Jeez, chill out," she snorted. She exited the room, grabbing some sheet music on her way.

I wasn't feeling very hungry, but I knew family dinner was obligatory. Plus, something smelled good.

I paused the Carmen McRae album I was using to calm myself and pulled off my headphones.

Down in the kitchen, Mae was standing by the stove, wearing an apron.

Helen sauntered in, finishing off a text. "Smells good in here." Her perfectly straight hair was pulled into a sleek ponytail, which swayed as she walked.

Mom put a hot plate in the center of the table. "Mae made us all dinner! Isn't that sweet of her?"

Barf. Sweet, my ass. Mae was a two-faced, conniving traitor.

"I just wanted to do something nice for you," Mae smiled. "You've all been so kind to me."

The faux modesty was ridiculous. What was she trying to do, win points with my family after knowing she'd destroyed my life? They might have bought it, but I saw right through it. I'd watched Ingrid Bergman get duped in *Gaslight*; I knew exactly what Mae was doing.

"Have a seat, Jules," Mom insisted.

"Where's Dad?" I wanted to know, remaining standing. Maybe I could talk to him about Mae.

"Working late," Mom returned, putting out some plates. Dad had been working late a lot these days because of the merger and his new responsibilities from his promotion. But I'd detected increased tension between my parents. The other morning when I'd come into the kitchen I thought I heard them arguing, and they fell into a steely silence when I entered. I could count on one hand the number of times I had seen them fight, so this was weird.

"Mae, would you do the honors?" Mom asked, regarding the hot plate on the set table. She was clearly impressed with whatever Mae had made.

Mae covered her hands with potholders, picked up a casserole dish from the oven, and set it on the table. She really was committing to this whole Martha Stewart act.

"Doesn't that look delicious?" Mom beamed.

Mae shrugged modestly. "It's just something I used to make. We called it a Farmer's Pie."

"It smells delish," Dani complimented her, taking a whiff.

"Thanks, sis," Mae replied. Then corrected quickly, "Dani."

No one seemed to notice Mae's slip.

"I'll take a piece," Helen said, pulling out a chair. Why was everyone buying Mae's I'm So Perfect act?

"I'm not hungry." I had to get out of this whole charade.

"Nonsense," Mom returned. "Dani, would you get utensils for everyone?"

"I have a lot of work to do," I tried again.

"Jules, you have to eat with us," Mae said. "I think you'd really like what I made."

I stared her down. After betraying me by being Sebastian's date, how dare she pretend she was my friend?

"What do you care about what I like anyway?" I challenged her.

Mom stared at me; so did Helen and Dani. They were surprised at my outburst, but I didn't care. They didn't know what Mae had done to me.

"Is something wrong?" Mom asked.

I glared at Mae, daring her to tell them what had happened. Mae looked back at me quizzically.

"Yeah, Jules, is there something wrong?" Mae inquired.

I was dumbstruck. I couldn't believe she was doing this, especially in front of my family.

"Jules." Mae stepped toward me, her voice saccharine. "We have to all eat together."

"Why?" I demanded, crossing my arms.

"Because," Mae smiled, "that's what families do."

My mom and sisters stared at me. Not wanting to completely rock the boat, I suffered my way through dinner. After I'd stuffed down Mae's stupid Farmer's Pie, which I hated to admit was actually pretty good, I excused myself and hurried up to Dani's room where I stayed for the rest of the evening.

When it was time to get ready for bed, I listened closely to make sure no one was in the hall so I didn't have to run into anybody.

It didn't work.

As I exited the bathroom, I nearly smacked right into Mae.

"Hey, Jules."

"Are you serious?" I balked. " 'Hey, Jules'?"

She stared blankly. "I don't understand." She should win an Emmy for acting like she didn't have a clue.

"That's all you have to say to me?"

She didn't answer.

"About Sebastian?" I pressed.

Mae's eyes ticked to the floor. I folded my arms, awaiting her reply.

Finally, she returned, "What do you want me to say?"

I shook my head. "I seriously can't believe you."

Her forehead crinkled. "Really, Jules, I don't understand why you're upset."

I was so consumed with anger I couldn't speak. Didn't she understand that she'd betrayed me by agreeing to go to the party with Sebastian? A) She hadn't even told me herself, which was totally sketchy. And B) She knew I liked him!

Needing to get out of this interaction immediately, I stepped around her.

"Good night," she called after me as I sped down the hall.

As Dani and I got ready to go to sleep, I ventured to ask, "What do you think of Mae?"

"What do I think of her?" she returned, climbing under her pink bedspread.

"Yeah, like, do you trust her?"

Dani turned to me as I switched off the light. It was easier to talk in the dark.

"Totally. I mean, she's kind of odd sometimes—like stiff or something. Like she doesn't know how to act. But then again, you're like that too sometimes."

That wasn't the answer I was looking for. I heaved a sigh as I lay down on the trundle.

"I wouldn't worry about it, Jules," my sister offered. "She's just getting used to being in a new family."

"I guess." I didn't want to agree with her, but she was actually making sense.

"Plus," she added, "she's taking me horseback riding this weekend."

"What?!" I suddenly felt wide-awake.

"She knows how to ride, so she's going to teach me. Mom's driving us on Sunday. We talked about it after you practically ran out on dinner. Helen might even come too!"

I couldn't believe it: Mae was icing me out of my own family.

———

That weekend, I had a volleyball game on Saturday. I'd reminded Mom about it in the morning as she put her travel tea mug into the sink without rinsing it. I wondered why she'd already been out so early. She agreed she'd be at my game, but Mom didn't show up.

Stacy gave me a ride home again. If this kept up she was going to start thinking we were actually friends. I went into the kitchen to grab some juice and saw Mom there putting the kettle on for tea.

"Why weren't you at my game?"

"What game?" Mom asked.

"The one I told you about this morning. You didn't show."

"Oh, I'm so sorry, honey. I had some shopping to do with Mae. The boots we got her fit so well I thought we should get a second pair."

It was very unusual for my mom to forget about something like this.

"You should have texted me, at least."

"You're right. I should have," she admitted. Which made it hard for me to stay mad about it, she looked so upset about forgetting. "How can I make it up to you?"

Well this finally seemed like progress.

"We need to go over our trip," I reminded her.

Mom and I still hadn't settled on a game plan for our Chicago trip. There were so many museums, galleries, exhibits I wanted to see, we had to make a plan so we could book tickets and not miss any of it.

"And," I added, "we have to discuss something else." I wanted to get the idea in her head of giving me a new camera before Christmas, so that I could use it on the trip and for my "People You Don't Know" portraits.

"Sure," Mom answered, distractedly removing some files from her bag.

"Cool, I'll go get my notebook!"

"Oh, not right now, honey." Mom's words stopped me. "I have too much work to catch up on. Let's do it another time."

"When? You never have time for anything anymore!" I burst out.

Mom could see that I was distraught. "I'm sorry, Jules, there's a lot going on. I apologize for missing your game; that wasn't right."

I could tell she wasn't lying; she did seem like her brain was constantly spinning silently, like an old film projector.

She stepped over to me and smoothed down my frizzy hair.

"I'm so proud of you—how great you're doing in school, and the column, and all your new friends. And most of all I'm really happy you've taken Mae under your wing. It really means a lot to me."

This hadn't been where I'd expected me calling Mom out for not coming to my game would go.

"Okay" was about all I could answer.

The teakettle whistled. Mom removed it from the burner and plunked two green tea bags into mugs.

"You know I don't like green tea," I reminded her.

"Oh, this is for Mae. Did you want some?"

I stared at my mother. "No," I answered flatly, and walked out.

CHAPTER 32

PETER ENTERED THE BEDROOM AND LOOSENED HIS TIE. "Honey?" he called, pulling the silk fabric off over his head.

Suzanne stepped out of the bathroom, brushing her teeth. "Hi," she managed through cleaning her molars. "How was your day?"

"Long one, that's for sure," Peter returned, changing out of his suit into a pair of flannel pajamas. He'd been at work all day, even though it was a Saturday. "Merger's going well, there's just so many details."

"God is in the details," Suzanne replied.

"I thought the devil was in the details," he mused.

Suzanne returned to the bathroom to rinse. "You missed a really good dinner," she called to him over the water. "We had left-over Farmer's Pie that Mae made."

She headed back into the bedroom, wiping her face on the

sleeve of her bathrobe. "I would have saved some for you, but we ate it all. There's a frozen pizza, if you're hungry," she added.

She removed the bathrobe and climbed into bed in her light blue nightgown.

"Thanks, I ate at work," he returned. "How was your day?"

She paused a brief moment, wondering if she should tell him about what she had actually done early this morning—trailing Victor Peterson from the convenience store where she'd tried to talk to him before back to his family's dairy in the town of Tisdale, and almost getting out of her car to talk to him, until he had become surrounded by some fellow farmers so she couldn't get him alone.

But she didn't tell her husband any of that.

"The usual," she answered, pulling the downy covers up around her. "I took Mae to get some new shoes this afternoon."

"How was Jules's game?"

"I didn't go," she admitted. "Got caught up running errands."

"Why didn't you tell me? I would have gone to watch her play," Peter replied, disappointed. He headed into the bathroom.

"It slipped my mind. I'm sorry. Oh hey, get this," Suzanne called, trying to quickly change the subject. "Mae told me there are no newspapers in Tisdale. Literally. I mean, they don't have TV or movies or anything, and hardly any books, but no newspapers! Can you imagine? It's wild. They're so disconnected from the outside world. It's like nothing can get in."

Peter returned from the bathroom and sank onto the edge of the bed next to her.

"Honey," he started softly. "I think we should talk about Mae."

"What about her?" Suzanne's voice had an edge to it. Peter

recoiled almost imperceptibly, unaccustomed to this kind of reaction from his wife. But he went on.

"Well, I'm concerned," he confessed. "There's something kind of—off about her. I know she's been through a lot," he continued before Suzanne could interject. "But she tried to—"

He struggled to figure out how to say this the right way.

"She tried to what?" Suzanne almost challenged.

He paused, then finally said, "Talk to me."

Suzanne stared at her husband. "She tried to talk to you? What's wrong with that?"

"'Talk' isn't the right word." He picked a piece of lint off the bedspread, then forced himself to just say it.

"She came on to me," he admitted.

Suzanne was confused. "What do you mean, she came on to you?"

"The other night, after Dani's dinner. You were in the kitchen, I think, and she came to me in my office. Asked if there was anything she could—do. Anything she could do to—repay me."

Suzanne stared at him a moment, then laughed. "Peter, I'm sorry, but that doesn't sound like she was coming on to you."

This wasn't easy for him, but he couldn't keep it to himself anymore. "She was—propositioning me," he explained. "I know what she was doing."

Suzanne took this in, not sure how to respond.

Peter went on. "I assured her there was nothing she needed to do to stay here. We were happy to host her. But—that's what happened. And I thought you should know."

Suzanne attempted an explanation. "She was just trying to make a connection with you, Peter. As a father figure. That's all."

"Suzanne, I hate to say it, but I think this girl could have—different ideas about what the role of a father figure might be."

Suzanne fluffed her pillows. "You're overreacting," she concluded. "You can't blame her for being grateful to you for hosting her. It's just a polite thing to do to offer to repay someone."

Peter felt his frustration rising. "You're not seeing things clearly, Suzanne! Since Mae got here you've been so distracted by your work, and all you've been concerned about is Mae. You haven't been paying attention to your own family. To Helen, Dani—Jules."

"That's not true!" Suzanne argued. "How dare you say that I don't love my children—"

"That's not what I'm saying—"

"I admit I've been focused on work lately, but this is important, Peter. Mae is important. I have to help her. She's been through a lot of trauma with her family. I need to help her through that," she reasoned.

Peter looked his wife in the eye. He was still so in love with Suzanne. Had been ever since the moment he'd met her in high school when she'd moved to Remingham.

He softened his voice, then suggested kindly, "Are you sure this isn't more about you?"

CHAPTER 33

A FEW DAYS LATER, I WAS SLOGGING THROUGH Spanish in the living room, but my mind kept spinning.

What was Mae's deal? She was kind of nice but she was also kind of not. Was this the definition of a "frenemy"? At school, she was hanging out more and more with Larissa and her friends, and I kept "happening" to get left out of group texts and plans.

And with the whole Sebastian thing, she hadn't brought it up again, but I noticed them together a lot, and she was even getting rides with him now. Traitor.

Around the house, Dani was consumed in her musical world, practicing incessantly in her room. I'd decided that musical theater on loop was a method of cruel and unusual punishment, forcing me to spend time in the living room exposed to interaction.

Helen was obsessed with her college applications and wouldn't talk to anyone unless it was about entrance statistics or how Landon would go to whatever college she wanted to attend. Dad had been working a ton, and Mom only seemed to have time for Mae.

I was starting to feel more alone than ever.

"Hola," I typed to Isaac on iMessage. He didn't answer.

I messaged him again.

Hola . . .
Hola.
Hola.
Hola.
Hola.

I knew if I bugged him long enough he'd answer. Social media revealed that Isaac was indeed alive and liking things.

Hola.
Hola.
Holaaaaaaaaaa.

I was wrong—no one had time for me. At least I had my column, and thank goodness I had my trip to Chicago in December with Mom to look forward to. I couldn't wait to get away from everything. Everyone.

"Hey," a soft voice cooed.

Mae was standing in the entrance of the living room.

"Hi," I answered back flatly. I had no interest in speaking to her right now. Or possibly ever.

Not taking my hint, Mae made her way over and slumped down next to me on the couch.

She glanced at my screen.

"Spanish?"

I shut my computer.

"What's up?" I could hear the harsh tone in my voice.

"Oh, nothing," Mae returned casually, running her fingers along a strand of black hair. She was wearing it down mostly these days, probably due to Larissa's encouragement.

"Did you see what Jessie did in Bio? She, like, sliced through the whole frog. Mr. Gately almost gave her detention."

I stared ahead, unwilling to engage with her.

"What are you going to be for Halloween?" she asked, attempting more small talk.

"Carrie," I answered, folding my arms.

"Who's that?"

"She's from a movie. She kills everyone."

Mae thought about that. "Oh," she said quietly. Then continued, "I think I'm going to be a fairy."

Of course—the most innocent, beautiful creature of them all. She could prance all over the party and be gorgeous and mysterious and everyone would love her even more. Perfect.

Mae twisted the necklace with the half-heart pendant that I'd lent her for Chelsea's party, which was weeks ago. I had said she could borrow it for a while, but she still hadn't given it back.

"I want my necklace back, by the way."

Mae agreed with a nod.

"You're mad at me," she stated.

I didn't know what to say. I couldn't argue—I *was* mad at her. I'd barely spoken to her since last week on what I was now calling the worst day of my life. Unacceptable behavior for a friend, especially someone living in their friend's bedroom.

"Jules," she started. "I didn't realize Sebastian was asking me out on a date. I thought, you know, he wanted to go to the party as friends."

"But you knew people were going to the party with dates," I challenged her.

"Yes, but I didn't get it. I'm sorry. I'm new to all of this. Where I'm from, we weren't allowed to date. Or even talk to boys. So I don't understand it all. I'm sorry."

That made sense, but it still didn't make the whole thing feel much better.

"He clearly likes you," I assessed. "I saw him helping you with Geometry at lunch."

"He likes you too," she offered.

"Yeah, but not in the same way," I returned. She didn't argue with me.

The wind rustled the leaves outside. There weren't too many left on the branches.

No one said anything for a while.

"I know you like him, Jules, and I wouldn't have agreed to go if I knew that he was asking me out. I would never do anything to hurt you."

I snorted. "Yeah, right."

"Seriously, Jules. You mean so much to me."

I turned and looked at her. Her eyes were wide, and her pale face more earnest than I'd seen it. Should I believe her? Could I trust her beyond a reasonable doubt, as Isaac would ask?

Mae went on. "If it bothers you, Jules, I'll tell him I can't go. Then the two of you can go together. Really. You've been such a good friend to me, and I don't want to go with him if it's going to upset you."

I stared at her. Did she mean that? Or was she just saying it because she knew I wouldn't take her up on it—even Slightly More Confident Jules would never ask that.

"The last thing I want to do is cause problems for you, Jules. Especially—" Mae looked down at the couch pillow. "Especially after you've been so kind to me."

Tears welled in her green eyes.

I felt a weight in my chest. Maybe Mae did actually care about me. Maybe I had been acting like a jerk. How was she supposed to know any better? And, the truth was, if Sebastian really did like her, and not me, as much as it hurt my feelings, it wasn't her fault.

"You—" I began. *Ugh, Jules, just be the bigger person and get it over with.*

"You didn't know any better," I said, forgiving her. "I get it." I took a deep breath. This was hard, but I had to do it. "You should go with him."

"Really? Are you sure?" She seemed relieved. Maybe because she actually liked Sebastian, or was glad I wasn't holding it against her, or both.

"Yeah." I felt like crap about the two of them going together, but being mad wasn't suddenly going to make Sebastian interested in me.

DING-DONG, sang the doorbell.

"I'll get it!" Dani called, heading down the stairs toward the front door.

"I have no idea who I'm going to go with," I confessed to Mae. "At this point everyone probably already has dates."

"What about Zeke! He doesn't have a date yet. He's really nice."

I didn't think Zeke was that cute, but Mae was right, he was nice at least. Maybe it was better to go with someone rather than by myself. Was something better than nothing?

"We can all ride together!" she insisted. "Sebastian's driving."

"I don't know. Let me think about it—"

"AHHHHHHH!"

Before we could finish our conversation, Dani shrieked at the front door. I bolted from the couch to see her standing in the doorway—

Covered in blood.

———

I sat in the hospital waiting room, obsessively refreshing my Instagram feed, not knowing what else to do with myself. What had happened to my sister was so strange, I still didn't know what to think of it.

Danielle had answered our front door to find a puppy. She reached for it, reading the puppy's name off its tag.

"Bingo," she'd read out loud. But no sooner did she say the dog's name than it attacked her. It started biting and scratching her, in a way that seemed like it had been triggered to do, Dani had described. Dani also had a huge phobia of blood, so she freaked out even more when she saw herself bleeding from the injuries.

Even though Dad had installed a new security system after that branch broke the lock, it didn't protect against cute puppies on our doorstep.

I thought about what Mae had told me the other night in my room, that she was afraid the cult would do things to trigger her to go back to them. Now it was beginning to seem very possible they had left that white rose for her. Had they left the puppy too? Was it meant to scare Mae, or attack her, instead of my sister? I had noticed that Mae did like dogs.

A more disturbing thought seeped into my mind. What if it wasn't actually meant for Mae? What if this incident was intended to scare my family? Maybe the cult had figured out that we were harboring Mae, and they were angry about it. Maybe it was an "eye for an eye" thing. You took one of ours, we'll take one of yours.

My mind swirled with a million different thoughts. Dad stepped into the waiting room. He was still in his suit, having rushed to the hospital from work.

"Is she okay?" I asked, pulling my attention away from the hypnosis of my phone.

"She needed a couple of stitches on her forehead, and she's pretty scratched up, but she's going to be okay."

"Did she have to get a rabies shot?" I asked.

He nodded. I'd heard those hurt, and felt sorry for my little sister.

"She'll be fine," Dad assured me.

But his sigh on the way down to sitting in the uncomfortable chair next to me gave away that worry still plagued him. It was just the two of us in the waiting room. Helen was in the middle of playing a field hockey game, and Mom had suggested that Mae stay at home—she didn't want her coming to the hospital if she didn't have to.

"What do you think happened?" I probed, wanting to see if he would shed any light on the situation.

He bit the inside of his cheek, mulling it over. "I'm not sure yet," he admitted.

Although I hadn't heard him say anything directly, he seemed less than pleased that Mae was still staying with us. I'd noticed that he and Mom hadn't really been speaking to each other, and I was sure it was the issue of Mae that was causing the rift.

Mom stepped into the room. Her face was a mask of worry.

"She's going to be fine," Mom assured, trying to calm herself as much as us. "The stitches are small, and Dr. Pfizer said she'd be able to perform in the musical."

Mom headed over to the vending machine. "Anyone want a snack?" she offered.

I shook my head. Dad declined too. Mom got herself a granola bar and tore open the wrapper. She ate the snack like she was looking for a distraction, rather than actually being hungry.

"Dr. Mathis," came an authoritative voice. A woman in a bad pantsuit stood in the entryway. She saw me and Dad.

"Peter, Julia," she said, nodding.

I wasn't sure exactly who she was, and her lime-green blazer and slacks were way too bright, but I said a polite hello.

"Nice to see you, Joanne," Dad returned.

The woman looked to my mom. "May I have a word?"

Mom nodded, then started to follow her out. Dad touched her arm as she passed.

"Everything okay?" he asked, concerned.

Mom put her Everything's Fine face on. "Yup, all good," she answered, then continued out.

I looked at Dad. I could tell he knew my mom was being avoidant with him, and it bothered him. He stared down at the buffed waiting room floor.

And so did I.

CHAPTER 34

JOANNE LED SUZANNE TO A QUIET AREA OF the hallway. "I'm very sorry about what happened to your daughter," she started.

Suzanne took a bite of her granola bar. "I appreciate your concern."

"It's difficult for me to tell you this now, knowing the stress you're under at the moment. But I thought you should know."

Suzanne's face darkened. "Know what?"

"Why don't we go into my office," Joanne suggested.

"Why don't you just tell me what you have to tell me right here?" Suzanne challenged her. Whatever this was, she wanted to get it over with as soon as possible.

"Very well." Joanne glanced around to make sure no one was in direct earshot.

"The thing is, I know what you did." Joanne's eyes narrowed at Suzanne.

"What I did?" Suzanne scoffed. "My daughter just got mauled by a puppy. You think I had something to do with it?"

"Of course not. This isn't about that."

"Then what is it about? I'd like to get back to my daughter."

Joanne pursed her lips at Suzanne's attitude, then revealed, "I know you broke into confidential patient records. For Victor Peterson."

Suzanne tried to keep her face still so that it wouldn't confirm that her boss was absolutely right.

"And," Joanne added with emphasis, "you used Nurse Connie's login. It set off an IT security alert when you accessed such an old, confidential case. I wondered why in the world Connie was pulling up records of a boy who came in here over a decade ago, so I decided to have security pull up the video feed."

Suzanne folded her arms, as if trying to fend off guilt.

"And the other issue is that you've been missing appointments lately."

Suzanne didn't say anything. She couldn't deny it—she had missed an appointment here and there, but she'd been so busy taking care of Mae and trying to figure out how she could build a case against the cult.

"I'm not sure what's going on here," Joanne continued, "but if you want to keep your job, you'd better watch yourself. I can't have this kind of behavior from my staff."

Suzanne was about to protest, but Joanne wouldn't allow it.

"Whatever you say, it doesn't matter, Dr. Mathis. You're under review by the board."

Being a seventeen-year veteran of the hospital, Suzanne was too shocked to reply.

Joanne shook her head. "I'm sorry about this, I really am, but it's the way things are."

Joanne turned to head back to her office.

"Oh," she remembered before leaving. "Since you're on review, Dr. Brenner will be representing the hospital at the psych conference in Chicago in December. I hope your daughter feels better soon," she concluded.

Joanne clacked off down the hallway.

Suzanne stared, lost in her thoughts. After a moment, she pulled out her phone and hurried off in the opposite direction. She was now determined to get Detective Nelson on board with Mae's case no matter what.

CHAPTER 35

"EVERYONE HAVE ENOUGH POPCORN?"

It was a few nights later and Dad was making a huge attempt to play Completely Normal Family.

Mom, Dani, and Mae were sitting on the couch. I sat across the room in the armchair.

Mae was being super friendly to me at school and everything, and I had agreed to go to the Halloween party with Zeke. He was nice enough, and everyone else had dates. At least I'd have company, so I wouldn't look like a complete tag-along loser.

But I was starting to count the number of creepy events that were piling up around Mae—the running out in the middle of the night, the chanting seizure, and most recently the puppy attack on Dani. The amount was high for a girl who had just appeared in our lives a month and a half ago. I still wasn't sure if that had anything to do with Mae, and when I tried to bring it up with her she blew it off, saying it was just a stray puppy who got scared and attacked. However, she had been the one who said the cult would do things to get her back.

"Dani, you good? More butter or anything?" Dad double-checked. He was being extra caring to Dani in the wake of the dog mauling. Her stitches from where the puppy had bitten her were healing well, but she still had a bandage on her forehead.

Dani smiled. "Thanks, Daddy."

"Jules, have enough popcorn? Mae?" She and I both nodded, each holding gigantic bowls.

"Suzanne? All good?" Dad asked, a slight edge in his voice I could tell he was trying to hide.

Mom gave a tight smile. "Thank you, Peter."

He moved on. "All right!" He clapped his hands together. "Now it's time for our favorite Mathis family pre-Halloween tradition!"

He stepped over to the DVD player and discreetly slipped in the disc. Dad always kept the film a surprise to us. He turned back to his captive audience.

"And now for our feature presentation! Jules, drumroll, please," he requested, dimming the lights.

I felt silly, but I wanted to go along with it, so I drummed my palms on my armrest.

"This evening, I present to you—the classic American cult film: *Carrie!*"

I couldn't help a grin. It was my favorite thriller, and my father knew that. The new remake version was okay, but the classic version was where it was at. I appreciated the small effort Dad had made to try to do something nice for me.

As the movie started, Dad stepped toward the couch to sit down. I noticed Mae scoot over, making room for him. Dad looked at the spot next to her, then pulled a wooden chair over from the corner, claiming it was better for his back. I thought I saw a flash of emotion cross Mae's face, but it was too quick to read. I wondered what that was about . . .

But this was one of my favorite movies and a Mathis family tradition—I wasn't going to let anything ruin it. I ate a handful of popcorn and stared at the screen, ready to sink into the comfort of the story.

ZZZZZTT, buzzed Mom's phone. She quickly reached into her pocket and scoped the caller ID.

"'Scuse me," she whispered as she launched herself off the couch. "Thanks for calling me back . . ." Her voice trailed off as she pressed through the kitchen door to take the call.

Instead of wondering who was ringing Mom so late at night, I let myself be swallowed by the dark coziness of the living room and got ready to enjoy someone else's problems.

CHAPTER 36

"WHAT'S THE EMERGENCY?" CAME DETECTIVE NELSON'S VOICE FROM the other end of the line.

Suzanne perched herself against the kitchen counter, ignoring the murmur of the movie playing from the living room. "I need your help."

Detective Nelson sighed heavily from the other end. Faint music drifted in the background.

"We don't have any more time to lose. We have to go and question Victor Peterson. I found him in Tisdale."

"You went to Tisdale?!" Detective Nelson balked through the line.

"Yes, I followed him there."

"Dr. Mathis, you can't be going to that town by yourself," he cautioned. "You shouldn't be going there at all."

Suzanne pressed on. "The point is, we need to talk to him, question him—build our case. These people might have attacked my daughter." Suzanne told him about what had happened with Dani and the puppy. He said he'd check out the report—he hadn't been on duty when it happened.

"You think the cult might have done this?" she pressed.

"It's hard to know. Or more important, hard to prove."

"Then we have to go after Victor. We can go back there and question him. With him and Mae, we'll have two witnesses. Then we'll have a good case and can get these people locked up."

Detective Nelson didn't say anything. She thought she heard some laughing in the background. She guessed he was probably outside a bar.

"You're going to help me, right?" she stated more than asked.

There was a brief silence from the other end. Suzanne paced nervously across the kitchen tile.

"You want my advice, get that girl into a shelter, away from you, or at least with another family. You've done your part. You have to let this one go, Suzanne."

Suzanne wouldn't hear it. She was furious that no one would help her.

"If you won't do anything about it, I will," she snapped, clicking off the phone.

CHAPTER 37

MY HAIR PARTED RIGHT DOWN THE MIDDLE FELT different. I'd used the straightener to get it as flat as I could, like Sissy Spacek had her hair in *Carrie*, and I thought it actually came out pretty good. Looking in the bathroom mirror, I gave myself a small smile.

The narrow dress straps on my shoulders made me feel, I don't know, sexy, I guess. I never showed that much skin, and it felt adventurous to wear it, even though it was only a costume.

The dress was actually lingerie, which I'd gotten at Goodwill and washed thoroughly. I'd taken the bus the other day after a volleyball game, where I didn't play once. The slip I'd found was cheaper than a real dress and looked like it would do the trick, so I bought it.

I ran my hands over my hair one more time to smooth it down.

All I needed to do was drizzle "blood" onto my dress and I'd be set: Carrie.

Stepping into the hallway, I stumbled into—

"Jules! You look adorable!" Mom complimented me, her voice rising.

"I was going for creepy, but thanks." I was annoyed at her for being so spacey lately and spending so much time with Mae. But whatever. My gaze fell to her hands.

Mom was holding a long blond wig.

"What's that for?" I asked. Before she could answer, Mae exited her room into the hall.

I couldn't believe my eyes.

"What the hell?" I nearly yelled.

"What?" Mae returned calmly, looking down at her outfit. She was wearing a long white dress, almost exactly like mine.

"It's my costume. I'm like you!" Mae smiled.

My breathing had become shallow. How could this be happening?

Mom held up the wig. "Mae is going to be Carrie too!"

I felt my face scrunch with fury. This had to be a joke. First Mae stole my guy, now she was stealing my Halloween costume?!

"Not exactly," Mae explained.

"What do you mean?" I challenged her. "You're dressed exactly like me," I said accusingly.

"Well, you're the Carrie from the old movie, right? The one we watched the other night?"

"Yeah. Why?"

"I'm the Carrie from the other movie. The new one! I looked it up on the internet. There's another version of the film that's more recent," she proudly informed me—as if I didn't already know that. "I'm the New Carrie!" Mae smiled.

No. Effing. Way.

Carrie was my favorite horror movie. And now Mae was copying me? She was a total imposter! She was taking over my life! This was some *Single White Female* shit.

Mom held up the wig and shook out the flaxen, synthetic hair. She placed it on Mae's head, completing the outfit.

"Looks great, Mae!" Mom beamed. "You girls are twins! I always wanted twins."

I stared down Mae, my anger prompting a loss for words. She had stolen my costume and one-upped me by being "New Carrie."

I couldn't deal.

"Where's Dad?" I demanded, turning to Mom. She suddenly became focused on smoothing out a strand of hair from the wig, avoiding eye contact.

"In the garage," she mumbled, then returned her attention to Mae. "Let's run a brush through this hair!" she suggested, heading into the bathroom with Mae.

I stomped outside and headed over toward the garage. I wondered why Dad was out here.

I knocked on the metal door.

"Dad?"

No answer. I stepped inside. The musty room was lined with shelves of cardboard boxes and some old tools—mostly crap that no one ever used and probably never would. I noticed that the ladder that led to the upper part of the garage was pulled down.

"Dad?" I called again, heading over to the ladder. I climbed to the upper floor, careful not to get dust on my white dress.

Up in the small, attic-like space, Dad was sitting on a cot. He looked up at me.

"Hey, Sweet Pea," he said. He hardly ever called me that anymore. Under normal circumstances I didn't love being called my sappy childhood nickname, but at the moment I didn't mind.

My eyes caught a pile of clothing slipping out of a duffel bag near the bed.

"Are you—sleeping here?" I ventured.

Dad glanced down at the unfinished wood plank floor.

"Uh, just for a little while," he admitted.

I knew my parents didn't seem to be particularly getting along these days, but I had no idea that they were sleeping in separate places. This was not a good omen.

I'm sure Dad could see it on my face that my brain was spinning.

"It's nothing to worry about, Jule-Jule; sometimes people just need some space. Clear their heads and all."

I supposed that made sense. I certainly needed space from Mae.

"Your costume looks neat!" he congratulated me, forcing himself to sound upbeat.

"Thanks," I answered, remembering why I had come in here in the first place. "I need some help pouring blood over my hair. Mom was too busy helping Mae," I added.

I could see a flash of annoyance cross Dad's face, or maybe it was disappointment. Whatever it was, he quickly stood up and clapped his hands, a habit he had when trying to shift gears.

"Let's pour some blood on your hair!" he rallied with enthusiasm.

Outside in the driveway, Dad dripped the fake blood over my straightened locks so it spilled down onto my white dress, exactly like I wanted it to. I felt the sticky red liquid sink onto my skin through the thin fabric of the dress.

For a brief moment, I thought about what Mae might have felt when blood from the cuts on her back dripped down her skin . . .

I quickly brushed off the thought.

"Sure I look okay?" I asked Dad, seeking reassurance. I wasn't sure why I was feeling so insecure. There was no one to impress at this party. I didn't care what Zeke thought of me, Sebastian liked Mae, and my costume had already been outdone.

Dad looked at me, then carefully reached over and pushed a strand of blood-clotted hair off my cheek.

"You look great, Sweet Pea," he smiled.

CHAPTER 38

THE BACKSEAT OF SEBASTIAN'S PARENTS' VOLVO WAS ROOMY, but I tucked myself against the door, trying to place myself as far away from this whole situation as I possibly could.

Zeke had already been in the car when Sebastian had picked us up. He was dressed as a Dwarf Paladin, which he explained was a Dungeons and Dragons thing. He wore a long cape and held a stick of wood, which he insisted was a staff. It seemed like a costume he already had.

Mom had been overjoyed when the boys arrived. Seeing me and Mae together, both with dates for the party, made her extremely happy, as if she was vicariously living through us. I mustered as much enthusiasm as I could. My tactic was to lay low, go along with everything, and just get through the effing night.

Halloween was my favorite holiday—most years. Usually I

celebrated with Isaac, marathoning scary classics at home and handing out candy to trick-or-treaters, although we didn't get that many on my street since it was far from the main road. Isaac and I would try to prank-scare each other throughout the evening, seeing who could outcreep the other. One year when we were eleven he had slept over, and in what had been an extremely calculated and time-consuming move, he hid out in the bathroom all night to scare me when I went to use it. However, I had been so tired that I'd slept through the night, and found him asleep in the tub the next morning. I wondered what Isaac was up to tonight. I had to admit—especially with all this awkwardness with Mae—I missed him.

Realizing a smile had formed on my lips, I quickly erased it, brushing off the thought of my best friend, who wasn't really my best friend right now.

I Don't Care face, I Don't Care face.

Mae sat next to Sebastian up front in the passenger seat. I could hear snippets of their conversation, which was apparently hysterically funny since Mae kept giggling. Sebastian was dressed in a pirate costume—triangular black hat, eye patch, and hook hand. And he'd added his THE FUTURE IS FEMALE T-shirt underneath.

"What are you?" I'd asked when he'd come to get us.

"A feminist pirate!" he declared proudly. That he and I weren't going to this as dates made me sure there was something wrong with the world.

During the ride, Zeke and I made small talk for a little in the backseat, but after a while our conversation fizzled. I let my head rest on the window and kept it there for the rest of the forty-five-minute drive.

Finally we arrived at the edge of thickly settled woods, where there were signs for a campground. Sebastian pulled the car into a dirt parking lot, cramming it next to all the other cars. He reminded us that he was committed to being the designated driver, so everyone could drink as much as they wanted—within reason of course. (Sebastian believed in personal responsibility.) I didn't really like drinking, but maybe it would help me get through the night. Or God forbid enjoy myself.

Exiting the car, the cool night air hit my skin. I instantly regretted my decision not to wear a jacket because I had wanted to show off my sexy dress. At least I'd have something going for me tonight. Plus, Mae hadn't worn a jacket, so I didn't want to look like I couldn't handle the cold. But I was absolutely freezing.

"Through here," Sebastian called, waving us toward a pathway at the tree line. Mae followed, and Zeke let me walk in front of him.

As we wove through the foliage, brilliant flashes flickered in the distance between the pine needles. When we finally reached a clearing, a large bonfire raged.

The party was in full swing. I recognized a lot of the same people who'd been at Chelsea Whiff's party last month, plus a bunch of other people I didn't know. There were vampires and Pokémon, short-skirted superheroes and devilish angels, all sipping from red plastic cups pumped from a keg of what I was sure was less-than-mediocre beer, even though I couldn't really tell the difference.

"Beverages?" Zeke offered.

Mae shrugged and I nodded. As Sebastian and Zeke headed

off to get drinks, Mae and I stood alone for a moment. We hadn't talked in light of the costume-copying situation.

And it was hard seeing her actually on a date with Sebastian. While I'd forgiven her and accepted it theoretically, seeing it in person and being around them was like an ice pick through my heart. I wished I could disappear.

I reached for my phone—maybe taking pictures would make me feel better.

"This is fun." Mae broke the silence before I could get my cell out of my purse.

"Mmm-hmm" was all I could respond.

She glanced around the clearing. "Zeke is nice," she said encouragingly.

I didn't reply. I guess she was trying to make me feel better about my consolation-prize date, although it could have also been to make herself not feel as bad about stealing Sebastian.

Luckily the awkwardness was broken by a "nurse."

"Mae!" Larissa called. She, Jessie, and Christine had arrived in the clearing like a pack of Halloween Edition Barbies. Larissa was in a short white outfit complete with stethoscope, Jessie was adorned as the devil, and Christine had opted to be a baby, her diaper showing off her long, athletic legs. Larissa eyed our costumes.

"Love it," she cooed to Mae. "You guys are twins?"

"No, Mae copied me," I clarified a little too loudly. I was trying to be funny but my voice betrayed an edge. No one laughed.

"I didn't copy you," Mae countered. "I'm New Carrie. Jules is the old one," she explained.

Larissa reached her fingers for Mae's long blond wig.

"Ohmygod, gorge," she gushed. "You need to wear this, like, every day."

"Aw, but I love your shiny black hair!" Jessie piped in. "It's so straight! I'm jelly."

"Isn't it more fun being a blonde?" Christine added, pulling at her natural fair-haired waves.

"Haha totally," Mae replied, flipping her wig hair off her shoulder.

"Shit," Larissa interrupted. "Travis is in such a bad mood. He's already on, like, his fifth beer apparently."

All the girls followed Larissa's gaze across the clearing to see Travis, wearing white shorts, a white short-sleeve shirt, and a sweat headband, complete with tennis racket—Richie Tenenbaum from *The Royal Tenenbaums*. It made sense, since he was captain of the tennis team in the spring.

"He thought I was flirting with Scott Vargas after the game last night because he scored so many points. And I totally wasn't, although I kind of was, but whatever. He's been texting me all day but I didn't write back. I should go talk to him."

Larissa adjusted her cleavage in the tight white vest and moved off. Christine reapplied her lip gloss.

"Mae," Jessie purred, "did you bring any more of that Xanax? I can, like, give you cash again."

"Oh yeah, sure!" Mae agreed, reaching into her white clutch, which my mom must have bought her too.

I hadn't realized that Mae was on meds, but it made sense that she'd be taking something to help calm her post-traumatic stress.

Mae handed Jessie and Christine each a pill from her orange prescription bottle.

"You're a lifesaver," Jessie oozed, popping the pill and washing it down with her drink.

"Hello, ladies," Zeke greeted as he and Sebastian arrived back with drinks for Mae and me. He saw that Christine and Jessie were drinkless. "Would you like us to get you libations?" he offered.

"We're good," Jessie replied, eyeing his nerdy costume. "We're going to get shots," she informed him, pulling Christine away. "Mae, come find us."

It was blatantly clear that these girls were only interested in being friends with Mae and not me.

Sebastian raised his cup of ginger ale. "Cheers!" he said, tapping beverages. I took a quick sip, which reminded my tongue that I hated the taste of beer even more than the taste of coffee. Sebastian clearly had no memory that I wasn't a beer fan.

Mae turned to Sebastian. "I watched the YouTube video you sent, of the Chihuahua riding a Newfoundland. It was so adorable!"

"Cute, right? I know how much you love dogs."

Sebastian turned to me, in an obvious effort to be inclusive. "Have you seen it, Mathis?"

"I have not," I returned coldly. The crisp air frosted. I took a long sip of my beer—fuck it. I stared at the bonfire. A dead tree fueled the center of the fire, orange and blue flames dancing upward from it. I had the unadvisable desire to step into it.

"Do you want something else?" Sebastian had noticed that Mae hadn't touched her drink.

Mae shrugged. "I don't really like beer."

I took an even bigger sip of mine. It was either an effort to prove how much cooler I was than Mae, or to get myself drunk. Or both.

"Let's find you something else to drink," Sebastian declared, chivalrously holding out his arm. I wondered if they'd kissed.

"So," Zeke vamped now that he and I were alone. "What's your favorite scary movie?"

"I'll give you a hint," I said, taking another long sip of beer. I pointed to my dress and blood-soaked hair.

"Oh," he laughed. "Duh. Sorry. It's a good movie."

He sipped his drink. I could tell he was embarrassed. I didn't mean to be rude to him—he hadn't done anything wrong.

"What about you?" I offered, to make up for it.

"Hmm, I think it would have to be *Scream*."

"That's a fun one."

A high-pitched giggle hit my ears. I turned to see Mae laughing at something Sebastian had said over by the drinks. Gross.

I glugged down the rest of my beer. Desperate to fill the silence, Zeke offered, "You want me to get you another?"

I looked at my empty cup and considered. Why not? *Live a little, Julia.*

"Sure." I handed him the cup.

"Be right back." He took it obediently and headed off to the keg.

I stood for a moment, watching the crowd around me. Even though I was surrounded by all these people, even with a date, even with my new quote unquote best friend, I still felt so alone.

A blinding flash of light caught my eye, as the goose bumps on my arm disappeared. I turned to see:

The bonfire had doubled in size. Flames shot up yards into the air. How had that happened so quickly?

Branches snapped in the woods nearby. A tree had caught on fire. Ghost and movie character party guests were frantically looking around, trying to figure out what was happening. The whole clearing was catching fire, the dry branches perfect fuel.

The smell of burning leaves filled my nostrils. I tried to cover my nose and mouth with my dress, but the thin white fabric didn't do much good. I couldn't stop hacking. I had to get away from this smoke.

I turned from the fire and headed into the woods, bumping up against other kids as we ran from the fire as fast as possible. I didn't see Mae or Sebastian or Zeke.

Pulling a clump of hair across my face to block the smoke, I stumbled through the trees. I was hardly looking where I was going; I was just putting one foot in front of the other as fast as possible.

BRUUUUUUUUHT! BRUUUUUUUUHT!

A siren wailed in the distance. Fire trucks. Thank goodness they were coming to put out the fire—their response time was impressive. The heat behind me and the crackling trees made it sound like the fire was quickly raging out of control.

I could hear firefighters behind me working to put out the blaze. There were other kids near me running away from the fire too, all scattering in different directions. As the dark woods grew thicker, the crowd thinned. My eye caught something to my left. Was that Mae?

Suddenly my face felt the cool dirt. I must have stumbled over a branch on the forest floor. The fall knocked the wind out of me, my breath pausing for a heart-stopping beat.

And then the coughing returned with a vengeance. My throat gripped for air, like I had no control over my lungs. I would give anything for a glass of water. Even beer. I lay on the ground, trying to catch my breath. I'm not sure for how long.

Suddenly, a warmth embraced my shoulders. Before I realized what was happening, I was lifted up off the ground and into someone's strong arms.

Slung over a brawny shoulder, my body started bobbing up and down.

It dawned on me that I was being carried through the woods, away from the fire. Black branches began racing past my peripheral vision as my head thumped against a man's back.

I could no longer see other kids around me. I shifted my body upward, straining to see where we were going. As I moved, the carrier adjusted his grip so that he was now carrying me in front of him, like a baby.

Starchy material rubbed against my cheek. A uniform. I was being rescued by a fireman! I glanced at his chest and caught a glimpse of the division name of his fire department.

TISDALE.

What were they doing here? I didn't know exactly where we were, but I knew that Tisdale wasn't the name of the town these campgrounds were in.

I looked down at my dress: white. Blood in my light-colored hair.

I was dressed exactly like Mae.

Holy shit: this guy was from the cult. And he was trying to kidnap me, thinking I was Mae!

I couldn't breathe. I had to get away. But how? His grip was like iron, holding me immobile.

By now we were far from the fire, and I couldn't hear or see any other people from the party. The trees had begun to thin, and I could make out a road in the distance, where a fire truck was parked.

Oh no no no no. Everyone who has seen a horror movie knows that you cannot get into a vehicle with your kidnapper. It equals certain death.

Panic sent my brain spinning. Did they set this fire to steal Mae back in the commotion? What would they do when they figured out they'd gotten me instead of her?

I couldn't wait to find out. I struggled to free myself from the man's thick arms, but the more I struggled, the tighter his grip became.

"Let me go!" I screamed, pressing against him with all my might.

Arriving at the fire truck, he whipped me around to the front of the vehicle and shoved me into the passenger side of the cab.

"Ow!" I yelped as my head smashed against the steering wheel on the driver's side. He reached and pushed me farther in. The sleeve of his shirt lifted, and I saw on his bicep—

A pentagram tattoo.

He forced my legs in so he could shut the door and trap me, but I flailed my feet, kicking him off me.

"No! I'm not her!" I yelled.

I aimed my leg at the bridge of his nose. Isaac had once told me that was a vulnerable spot on the human body. But it didn't work. He heaved the door against my leg, sealing the compartment shut.

I was trapped inside. I had to get out.

As quickly as I could, I crawled across the seat to the driver's side, reaching toward the door. Through the windshield, I glimpsed him walking around the front of the truck. It was risky, but something crossed my mind.

Waiting until he had arrived at the driver's door—

WHAM!

I flung the door against him, whacking him in the chest. The impact surprised more than injured him, but this was my chance.

I scrambled out of the truck and raced away, not daring to look back. I knew I had a few seconds' head start on him and sprinted through the trees. My heart was beating so fast I felt faint.

But I made myself run faster.

Faster.

Fleeing for my life.

I raced through the foliage, aiming for whatever sound and light I could make out. Finally, I saw the clearing where the bonfire had been, and stumbled back, barely able to breathe.

As I heaved air, I looked around. Everyone was huddled around the now-extinguished bonfire, and there were firefighters on the scene—the real, local firemen. No one in a Tisdale uniform. They must have left, unable to get what they had come for.

Mae/me.

"Jules!" Mae spotted me and hurried over. "We lost track of you. Are you okay?"

"No!" I hurled back, furious. A few heads turned. "I am not okay!"

Mae tried to calm me. "It's cool. The fire's out now, and Sebastian's ready to take us home," she soothed.

I pulled Mae aside, out of earshot of the other shivering partygoers. "What the hell?" I whisper-screamed.

Mae stared at me, green eyes wide. "What?"

"Your creepy cult came to get you but thought I was you and tried to kidnap me!"

Mae's face paled. "No" was all she could manage.

"All because you copied my stupid costume!" I accused her. My whole body was pumping with rage, or pain, or both.

"You're ruining my life!" I shouted, unable to keep my voice down.

"Jules, I'm so sorry," she whispered, clutching her arms to herself. "I'm so sorry."

"I'm telling my parents, and they'll send you to a foster home, or back to Tisdale, or wherever—I don't care! I just want you out of my fucking life!"

Mae's hand grabbed my arm. "Please don't tell your parents! If I get sent back, they'll punish me!"

"Good! You deserve it!" I spat. I couldn't care less what they did to her at that point. I wanted her gone.

"Please, Jules," she pleaded. "I need to stay with you and your family to be safe. Don't you understand that now?"

I turned toward the black embers of the fire, trying to ignore what she was asking me to do.

"Don't you understand, Jules?" She put her hand on my cheek, forcing me to look at her.

"Please, Jules. You're my friend! I need your help. You can't tell your parents, I need to stay safe!"

Her green eyes begged forgiveness.

"You have to save me, Jules!"

PART THREE

[I]t was written I should be loyal to the nightmare of my choice.

—Joseph Conrad, *Heart of Darkness*

CHAPTER 39

RINGGGGG!

We weren't allowed cell phones at the table, but someone had neglected to turn hers off.

Mae looked down at the caller ID, then up to my mom, hopefully.

We weren't supposed to "engage with technology" during meals, and Mae knew that, but Mom just nodded as she ate her salmon, while Danielle talked her ear off about the "scene work" she was doing in rehearsals.

Mae smiled and answered her phone, stepping away from the table.

I kept quiet. I had been doing that a lot the last week since Halloween. The attempted kidnapping in the woods still freaked me out. At night when I was falling asleep, I kept feeling like I was bobbing up and down, a tight grip clutching my body. I'd even started locking the door to Dani's and my room at night. Dani had complained about the locked door this morning and I tried to tell her that the cult might be after Mae, but she looked at me like I was an insane person and rolled her eyes.

I didn't know what to do. I knew I couldn't condemn Mae back to the cult, but I couldn't not say anything about what happened. It was too dangerous.

The Sunday before—the day after the Halloween party—Mae had been out teaching Dani how to ride a horse again, so I went to the garage to find Dad.

He was sorting through an old toolbox.

"Dad? Can I talk to you about something?"

He turned to me. I could see that his eyes were a little puffy. Had he been crying?

"Of course, Sweet Pea," he agreed, wiping his eyes. "Why don't we go for a walk. Little dusty in here."

Dad and I had strolled along our tree-lined street toward the main road. The few houses scattered along the pavement still had Halloween decorations up—jack-o'-lanterns and ghosts. I was sure they'd switch over to Thanksgiving decorations soon enough.

I told Dad about what had happened in the woods the night before. About the fire breaking out, about getting taken by a fireman, about breaking free and running back to safety in the clearing.

"Kidnapped?"

"By a fireman."

"You sure he wasn't trying to rescue you?"

"He was from Tisdale. Where Mae is from."

"And you're sure about this?"

I considered his question. I thought I'd seen *Tisdale* written on the fireman's shirt. However, it was dark and we were moving quickly, so there was a chance that wasn't exactly what it said.

"That's what I thought I saw. It was dark out, I guess."

"But you think that a fireman was trying to *kidnap* you?"

Dad's inquiry was making me rethink what had happened. It had been a chaotic scene.

"If that's true, we should get the police involved," Dad evaluated.

Suddenly, the thought of talking to officers about the incident and having to give testimony seemed like more than I wanted to sign up for. Who knows what else they'd ask me about. And I had been drinking—not to mention underage. I didn't want to get into that—with Dad or the police.

"Never mind," I told him. "It was a hectic night. I was probably imagining things."

He nodded, unsure, but let it go at my request. "So how's it going with Mae?"

"Not great," I admitted. I told him about her and Sebastian, about Larissa and Co., about my falling-out with Isaac.

"Aw, that's a shame," he said. Dad liked Isaac, and I could tell it bummed him out that he and I weren't talking. I was too. I'd tried to make small talk with him a few times, but he'd apparently become "extremely consumed" with debate and wasn't speaking to me, not even to bring up the Social Studies project. I'd seen him hold grudges before, which he was quick to do; he'd just never done it to me.

"See what you can do, Sweet Pea. Isaac's a good friend. And Mae—" He thought about what to say next. "Just get along with her as best you can for now. I'll talk to Mom."

Later that night I heard my parents screaming at each other in the kitchen. Since then, over this past week, nothing had changed. And Dad hadn't come home for dinner all week.

I now looked down at the salmon my mom had overcooked and took a bite, while Mae continued to gab.

"No way," Mae giggled into her phone. I knew exactly who she was talking to.

Mae's confidence and social standing had mushroomed, like one of those capsule foam dinosaurs we put in the bath when we were kids that inflated exponentially. Everyone wanted to sit with her at lunch now, and the whole school thought she and Sebastian were the World's Cutest Couple. I had been sidelined for best friend conversations in favor of cheerleaders, which was fine with me because Mae had become so self-absorbed and fake I couldn't stand talking to her anyway.

Mae and Sebastian had been full-on dating all week since the Halloween party. They'd been eating lunch together and hanging out after school, and he'd even lent her poetry books, I'm assuming because she had expressed a shred of interest so he'd jumped at the opportunity. Sebastian prided himself on being "old-fashioned" and actually talking on the phone rather than just texting, and Mae loved it. Which was super annoying to everyone else. Everyone else probably just meaning me.

"No, I haven't seen that movie," she answered into the phone. "Saturday? Love it!" She sounded just like Larissa. Mom smiled at Mae and gave her an enthusiastic thumbs-up at the future film date.

I couldn't bear it.

"Mom," I called, trying to get her attention. She turned to me, like she'd forgotten what I looked like.

"We need to talk about Chicago after dinner. You keep putting it off."

Going to Chicago was about the only thing in my life that I was looking forward to. It wasn't for another month, but I couldn't wait. I needed to get out of town, get away from it all for a few days. The Chicago trip was my lifeline.

A shadow crossed Mom's face.

"Jules," Mom started. Uh-oh—it was sometimes bad if someone started a sentence using your name. It was like they were trying to soften whatever was about to come next.

"I'm not going to Chicago," my mother revealed, using her trying-to-calm-someone-down voice.

It didn't work.

"What? Why!" I shrieked.

Mae had finished her call and was staring at my outburst. So was Dani.

"It's complicated, honey," Mom tried to brush off.

"So are you letting me go by myself?" I challenged.

"You know I can't do that."

"You promised to take me!" I was practically shouting.

"I know, but now they're sending Dr. Brenner to the conference instead of me." Mom was clearly annoyed by that fact. "It wasn't my choice."

255

"But you go every year!"

Mom crumpled her napkin onto her half-eaten salmon.

"I'm sorry, Jules" was all she could manage. "I forgot to tell you."

"Wait. You've known about this? For how long?" I was enraged. I couldn't believe Mom had known about the trip cancelation and not told me.

"I'm very sorry. I know you were looking forward to going." She stood up and went to put her plate in the sink, attempting a half hug on the way. I ignored her and pushed myself away from the table.

Dani gazed at me. I could tell she actually felt bad. I was glad to at least have some sympathy, but sympathy wasn't the thing I really wanted. I wanted my mother to pay attention to me. I wanted to not have a lying fake friend from a cult living in my bedroom. I wanted to go to Chicago and get out of my crappy life.

How had this happened? Why would the hospital have changed their mind? Or, maybe Mom didn't want to be away from Mae. That was creepy. And what the hell was wrong with my mom? Why was she so freaking obsessed with Mae?

"We can go another time," Mom offered, rinsing the leftovers from her plate.

"When?" I challenged her, rising from my chair. "When have you ever taken me anywhere?"

She turned to me but had no reply.

I didn't wait for a response. I could feel my face getting hot. I didn't want to have a breakdown in front of Mae. I was embarrassed enough about how she'd messed up my life; I didn't need to feel even worse by humiliating myself further in front of everyone.

Leaving my half-eaten plate, I stormed out of the kitchen, devastated.

———

School continued to be miserable. Mae and Sebastian glided through the halls hand in hand like the king and queen of All We Care About Is Each Other. And I had to work with them both at the *Regal*, since Sebastian had given Mae a full-time position.

I had also been avoiding Zeke. I hadn't talked to him much after our Halloween party "date." I didn't know if he liked me or not—probably not, since I'd barely talked to him at the party—but I ignored the whole situation and just went about my days looking at the floor. It was like before Mae had arrived, except worse now, because I didn't have Isaac. I'd even stopped wanting to take photographs, leaving my portfolio for the summer program application unfinished.

The next day at lunch, Mae took a seat at Larissa's table before I could sit down. I had been sitting with Larissa and her pack most days too. Although I'd been practically mute, at least I was hiding under the cover of being with a group. But today there was nowhere to sit.

"Oh, sorry, Jules," Mae consoled me, making a half-hearted attempt to find another chair. She'd tried to be extra nice to me the last few days, but I couldn't stand to look at her lying face.

"Forget it," I quickly replied, and fled the cafeteria. My tolerance for trying to act okay with everything had worn out.

In the girls' bathroom, I stared at myself in the mirror. Black rivers streaked my cheeks as the tears snaked their way down. It was no use trying to stop them.

My life sucked. I was no longer a Nobody, so I couldn't float by on anonymity anymore, but I didn't fit in with the Somebodies either. I hung out with them, but what had happened between me and Mae created a crack between us that seemed too wide to repair.

But the worst part was I had tasted coolness, and the sweet, confident comfort it granted, only to be betrayed by the very person who had brought me with her into popularity.

It made my ears hot to think I was the only one who could see through Mae's falseness. Everyone else loved her. No one would even believe me if I said something bad about her. I'd look like the crazy one.

Mae had become social Teflon.

I reached for a paper towel and wiped my face. I just had to make it through a few more classes and I could go hide in the privacy of my own home.

Oh no, wait—Mae was there too.

Maybe I was the one who should run away.

Keep it together, Mathis. You can do this, I pep-talked myself. *Just get through the rest of the day.*

Composing myself, I trudged out of the bathroom, passing two Goth girls as they entered, probably to reapply their too-dark lipstick.

I turned into the hallway and nearly smacked into—

"Isaac!"

He stared back at me, taking in my bloodshot eyes. I immediately looked away, wiping my nose on my navy boiled-wool jacket.

I braced myself for a rant. He probably hated my guts. And I didn't blame him. I'd been a total asshole to him.

"Come on," he instructed, grabbing my arm, all business. "You need some fresh air."

Surprised, I let myself be led outside, keeping my face tilted low in an effort to not make eye contact with anyone in our path.

When we got outside, the cool air felt soothing on my skin. He pulled me over to a bench and instructed me to sit.

"Here," he said, handing me a chocolate bar. A peace offering.

I could feel my eyes well up again, like a faucet being turned back on.

"I'm so sorry, Isaac. I know I acted like a jerk. I thought those stupid girls were my friends, but obviously I was wrong, and I understand if you hate me forever. It's just been so much with Mae coming into my life so quickly and taking over everything. I didn't mean to, but I pushed my best friend away . . . and I don't know how to get him back."

There was a long silence as we watched a few chilly seniors smoking across the street.

"You are guilty of hurting my feelings," Isaac finally deemed. "But I know you've been under—extenuating circumstances."

"What can I do to make it up to you, Isaac?"

"Um, promise you'll never be a jerkface like that again?"

"Deal," I smiled. The wind blew a flurry of leaves down the sidewalk. "There's something about her, Isaac. I don't know what it is."

Isaac nodded. "Yeah. You haven't been the same since she showed up."

"She's nice, but like, not. And everyone is obsessed with her! Including my mother!"

"The horror!" he exclaimed. "That's from *Apocalypse Now*, right?" he added, just checking.

I nodded, smiling through sniffles. I proceeded to tell him absolutely everything that had happened, like I should have all along. His eyes widened as I told him about the white rose, the running out in the middle of the night, the puppy attacking my sister, the fireman carrying me away. He listened carefully to my testimony, and believed me—which was such a relief.

"She completely messed everything up," I concluded. "My family is barely talking to each other, and get this: my mom's not even taking me to Chicago anymore."

Isaac shook his head, agreeing that Mae's actions were criminal. "Verdict is in: she sucks."

"Before she came into my life, I know I wasn't cool. But at least I was happy." I took a breath of cold air.

"I wish I could expose her, à la *All About Eve*, and Mom would see how two-faced she is and kick her out."

"You should expose her," Isaac agreed. "Show everyone what a bad seed she really is."

Could I really do something like that? Expose Mae in the hope that Mom or Dad would send her off to live with other people?

I shivered, mulling over what Isaac had suggested.

He stood. "You need a hot chocolate. Come on, I'll buy you one."

"I don't deserve you." I smiled.

"I am aware," he returned smugly.

CHAPTER 40

"LADIEEZ. OBZEHRV!"

Dani and I broke out laughing at Dad's horrendous imitation of a French accent.

It was later that night, and Dad had decided to give us a tutorial on how to brew coffee in a French press. He'd reasoned that if I was going to drink it—and I had been a lot lately—I should at least know how to make it. Dani had enthusiastically volunteered to participate, even though she'd never even tasted coffee. But I think it was more about wanting to spend time with Dad, since he was hardly in the house anymore.

A waft of morning hit my nose as Dad opened the bag of coffee beans and scooped two spoonfuls into the grinder.

"And zen—" Dad went on.

"Dad, that is the worst accent I've ever heard," Dani interrupted.

"What?" He grinned. "I went to Montreal once."

"And they will never let you back," I cracked.

"All right, all right." Outvoted, he moved on with the tutorial. "Okay, this is going to get loud," he warned. He switched on the grinder, which cracked to life, decimating the beans.

Dani put her hands over her ears.

When the beans were done grinding, Dad lifted the plastic container of brown coffee dust and emptied it into the French press carafe.

"Zis is where it gets ex-ay-tang!" he said, relapsing.

"Dad!" Dani and I both shouted through smiles.

"What's so exciting?" Mom wondered, entering the kitchen as she arrived home from work.

Dad didn't say anything, avoiding eye contact with her. Silence fell over the room.

"Dad is showing us how to brew zie pehr-fect cup of coff-ee," Dani finally explained. She attempted a better version of the accent herself, but it was just as bad.

"Fun," Mom said flatly, putting her travel mug onto the counter without rinsing it.

"Where's Mae?"

Of course. Everything with Mom was about Mae.

"Outside," Dani answered. I wondered if Dani had noticed Mom's lack of attention toward us as well. She hadn't said anything to me about it, and I doubted she would, but the sharpness in Dani's voice made me suspect I might not be the only one Mom's behavior was affecting.

Mom's attention turned toward the kitchen window over the sink, which looked out onto the backyard. Dusk was falling.

Mae was sitting out there, swinging back and forth on our old swing set. She wasn't wearing a coat. At school Mae was always upbeat, but sometimes at home she sequestered herself in her room and was a little moody. I used to care and try to make her feel better, but at this point I thought she could keep her two-faced mood swings to herself.

Mom walked over to the door to the backyard and pulled two fleeces off the hooks. One of them was mine, although I hadn't worn it in a while.

Mom opened the door and stepped outside. A gust of cold air swept in through the kitchen.

Dani, my dad, and I watched as Mom crossed the dying back lawn to the swing set. Danielle and I used to play out there when we were kids, but we never did anymore.

Mae looked up at my mother, who held out my old jacket. Mae smiled as Mom wrapped the jacket around her, then took a seat on the swing next to her.

They swayed in the fading light.

"What's next?" I asked Dad, trying to get away from the distraction of Mae, never mind the attention Mom was giving to her and not us.

Dad clapped his hands together. "Next, we do the hot water," he said, forcing enthusiasm.

Dani and I turned back to Dad. At least he was paying attention to us.

"Jules, you mind heating up the kettle?" Dad asked.

I picked up the container from the stove and walked over to the sink. As I filled the kettle with tap water, I stared out the window at Mom and Mae.

Rather than mother and foster girl, they looked more like sisters.

CHAPTER 41

LANGUAGE ARTS. 8:02 A.M. *THE GREAT GATSBY.*

We had a quiz today, so tension in the room was high. Ms. Ramsey was stapling together pages of questions at her desk in the front of the room, while I was picking my cuticles and listening to Isaac brag about how hard he was going to beat Victoria in their mock debate after school.

"Love it!" I heard Mae compliment someone from her desk in the aisle next to me. She was admiring Jessie's lavender halter, which Jessie wore under a puffy coat.

"Hey, do you have any more of those Xanax?" I heard Jessie say. "I'm, like, so freaked about this quiz. If I don't do well my grade's gonna suck."

I glanced over to see Jessie trying to score drugs off Mae again. It seemed like this had become a regular thing. Mae probably didn't even know that the prescription was just for her and she wasn't supposed to share it with people.

"Sure," Mae responded, reaching into her backpack.

I felt a jab in my arm. Isaac's elbow.

"What?" I said, turning back to him.

Isaac's eyes widened at me—he'd witnessed the exchange too. He tilted his head toward Ms. Ramsey.

"Tell her," he said out of the corner of his mouth. I had told Isaac what a fake Mae was and how I wanted to expose her—maybe this was my chance.

Isaac urged me on with his eyes.

Ticking back to Mae, I saw she was still rummaging through her bag for the bottle.

"Ms. Ramsey!" I called. She looked up from her stapling.

"We'll start in a few minutes. I'm almost done, but this thing keeps jamming," she said, tapping the stapler.

"Actually, I have a question," I vamped.

She looked at me expectantly.

"It's—about a passage in the book," I said, picking up the paperback off my desk.

Unable to resist helping someone, Ms. Ramsey sighed and stepped over in her furry snow boots, which were finally approximate to being weather-appropriate.

As the teacher walked over, Mae pulled her orange pill bottle out of her backpack.

Ms. Ramsey approached my desk. I could hear Mae open the bottle and shake the pills out. I had to get Ms. Ramsey to look at Mae.

"Um." I leafed to a page, then angled the book out so that she'd have to turn toward Mae's direction to see it.

"So is Nick Carraway—"

"Excuse me!" Ms. Ramsey demanded. I followed her eyeline to:

Mae, handing pills from her prescription bottle to Jessie and Christine. Jessie was holding a twenty dollar bill.

Mae was caught red-handed.

Ms. Ramsey stared down Mae, who had no idea she'd done anything wrong.

"Principal's office. Now."

———

I couldn't believe that *I* had been called into the school counselor's office too. What did Mr. Towers need to talk to me for? Mae was the one who had been selling drugs.

Although it was my fault that she'd gotten caught, Mae needed to be exposed for the lying, deceitful hypocrite she was. Maybe then Mom would come to her senses and send Mae away.

Sitting there in the yellow-and-puke-colored waiting room, the thought of Mae leaving made me feel like Dorothy in the *Wizard of Oz*, stepping into Technicolor.

Mae paced out of Mr. Towers's office. Her black brow furrowed as she glared at me, her green eyes cold.

I couldn't care less.

I waited for her to say something, but she didn't. She continued past me and out of the waiting room.

"Julia?" Mr. Lance Towers, the school counselor, stood in the doorway to his office. He was tall and thin and dressed like he'd lost a bunch of weight but never bothered to buy new clothes.

"Thanks for coming in," Mr. Towers started, as we settled into his office. His fake leather couch was slippery on my vintage silk pencil skirt.

He glanced down at some notes. "So, you've had some—changes in your life recently. Is that correct?"

"Um, yeah. Well, one change," I amended.

"Mae," he said.

"Yeah." *Duh.*

He looked at me for a moment, then scribbled down some notes in pencil.

"Tell me more about that."

And I did. I told him how Mae had come into my home, taken the boy I liked, stolen all my mother's attention. It felt so good to talk to someone about it all. Someone else had to know how much Mae was messing up my life.

He listened to it all intently, carefully taking notes.

I wondered why this was all about me, though.

"But *she* was selling drugs," I reminded him. "I've seen her do it before."

Mr. Towers took a deep breath, scratched his pink cheek with the eraser end of his pencil.

"Julia, your teachers have noticed that you've been—despondent lately. That you haven't been giving school your full attention, and your grades are slipping. Now, I know there are things that have changed in your home life—"

"Well, yeah," I defended myself. "I just told you how Mae messed everything up."

"I understand," he said thoughtfully. "That's why I'd like you to come in for counseling once a week."

"What?! Why should I get punished for something Mae did?" I could feel my face getting hot.

"It's not a punishment," he clarified. "It's for your own well-being."

"Is she even getting punished?" I asked.

"That's being discussed at the administrative level. But she was unaware of the policy."

Anger rose from the pit of my stomach. I couldn't stop it from boiling over.

"That's not fair! She gets away with everything! She barged into my life, she ruined my family, she even stole the boy I like!"

"I understand, Julia," Mr. Towers responded evenly. I hated when people acted all calm and measured after something emotional happened. It was like they were denying what had just gone on.

"I believe that your actions—"

"*My* actions?!"

"—are a call for attention. We'll now have the opportunity to discuss the things that are going on in your life so they don't build up emotionally. How about Thursdays at three fifteen. Will that interfere with your volleyball practice?"

My plan had completely backfired.

———

I got a ride home later with Stacy after our volleyball game. I didn't even want to play, but if I had skipped the game I would've had to ride home with Mom and Mae, and that was something I clearly wanted to avoid. It was just my luck that the coach actually put me in the game. However, I was so angry that I tomahawked the ball right over the net and scored a point.

When I came back to the house, my heart sank as I entered. Mae and my mom were sitting on the couch in the living room, drinking tea.

I started for my room.

"Jules!" Mom called, hurrying over to the stairs. Mae made herself scarce and slunk into the kitchen.

I had made it up the first few steps when Mom put her hand over mine on the banister.

"Why don't we sit down and talk?"

"What do you care anyway?" I shot back. "You don't care about anything I do."

"That's not true," she started.

"You don't care about me anymore! You even missed another volleyball game today!"

"I'm sorry, honey. Mae had to get a checkup at the hospital."

"Of course she did," I scowled. I noted that she was wearing the necklace with her half of the heart pendant she'd given me, my half of which Mae still had.

Mom took a deep breath. "Can we please sit down and talk?"

"No," I hurled back defiantly, even though sitting down with my mother was exactly what I wanted. I just couldn't admit it in the moment. "Say whatever you have to say to me here."

She nodded, then put her other hand on top of mine. I steeled myself.

"Jules, I know you're upset about our trip to Chicago getting canceled. I completely understand that, and I empathize. I will try to make it up to you. I promise. Maybe we can go in the new year."

I was glad she was making the effort, but she was missing the point.

"It's not the trip, Mom. It's her! She's ruining everything!" I didn't even care if Mae was hearing me in the next room. "And now I have to see the school counselor because of her!"

"Well, I don't think that's a bad thing—"

"You don't get it!" I screamed.

She was oblivious! She was so enamored with Mae she had no idea how she'd been acting. I couldn't stand talking to her.

I tore my hand from under hers and bolted up the stairs.

Up in Danielle's room, I slammed the door behind me. Danielle had been practicing a ballad.

"Get out!" I shouted.

Too surprised to object, Dani obeyed.

CHAPTER 42

"SUZANNE?"

Hearing her name, Suzanne opened her eyes. It was still dark, and her mind searched for a reason for being woken up in the middle of the night.

A floorboard creaked under the carpet near the door. Suzanne looked over and saw a shadow.

Mae stood in the doorway, wearing the white nightgown Suzanne had bought for her. Her long, dark locks fell past her shoulders, and her face was pale. She looked like a ghost.

"Are you okay?" Suzanne asked, worried that the intrusion might mean something bad.

Mae shook her head. "Sorry," she apologized quietly, "I didn't mean to wake you."

"It's okay," Suzanne reassured her, pushing herself up to sitting.

"I just couldn't sleep."

Suzanne scooted over so there was room on the bed. Mae padded over and sat down next to Suzanne.

"I had a nightmare," Mae admitted.

"Again?"

Mae nodded. She picked at a fiber on the bedspread. "I just—feel bad," she confessed.

"About what?" Suzanne tucked her legs up, wrapping her arms around her knees, making her look almost girlish.

"Jules," Mae answered, distraught. "I know she's mad at me."

"Oh, sweetheart," Suzanne soothed. "She's adjusting to a new situation. It's normal to have a few bumps along the way."

"I didn't mean to cause trouble for her. Or you, or your family. I'm so grateful for all you've done for me."

Suzanne shook her head. "No, Mae, I'm sorry Jules has been acting out toward you. You've been getting a lot of attention, and she's jealous. It's a natural dynamic between siblings. Even though that's not exactly what you are," Suzanne amended. "But—you are becoming part of our family."

Mae looked at Suzanne and smiled. It made her happy to be welcomed into a family who was kind to her—who didn't want to hurt her.

"I'm really proud of how well you're doing," Suzanne complimented her. Mae was surprised.

"Really?"

"You've been integrating socially, making friends at school. You even have a boyfriend. I'm very impressed. It's not easy, what you're doing."

"I bet all those things were easy for you."

"Actually," Suzanne began, "they weren't."

Mae looked at her expectantly.

"When I started at Remingham High," she went on slowly, "I transferred in freshman year."

"That's when you met Peter."

"Yes. But I used to live a few states over. My family—my mom, my brother, and I—moved. So I started at the high school new, in the middle of the year. I didn't know anybody. Peter became my first friend."

Suzanne glanced at the unused end table on Peter's side of the bed.

"Why did you move?" Mae asked.

Suzanne turned and looked at Mae through the darkness. "Because just like you . . . I was abused."

CHAPTER 43

I WAS IN THE MIDDLE OF BOMBING MY Social Studies presentation. I could not remember one thing that had to do with Cold War USSR, which was the topic of our presentation. My brain was in Siberia.

Thank goodness Isaac was doing it with me so he could carry the weight, but I knew my individual grade would be crap. I'd been so distracted lately I'd hardly prepared anything.

Then Mr. Towers, the counselor, knocked on the classroom door.

"Sorry to interrupt. If I could just borrow Jules Mathis." His voice was solemn.

I turned to Mr. Towers, surprised. "Me?"

The Social Studies teacher, who for some reason always smelled like pickles, nodded his approval for me to step out of the class. We went into the hallway and headed toward another classroom.

"Let's go get your sister," he told me.

What was going on?

When we reached her classroom Mr. Towers bailed Helen out of her French class.

"There's been an accident," he informed us.

"What happened?" Helen asked before I could.

"It's your mother."

———

Dad left work and picked me and Helen up at school, along with Danielle, and brought us to the hospital.

Mae came too. Mr. Towers had gone back to our Social Studies class and told her, after he'd told me and my sister.

Mom was in the emergency room.

"She was in a car accident," Dad explained. "Her brakes went out, and she hit a tree."

Danielle cried the whole way to the hospital, even though Dad told her Mom was going to be okay.

My stomach tumbled as I sat in the back next to Danielle, making her sit between me and Mae. I had been so angry at Mom lately, but the last thing I wanted was for her to get hurt. I hoped she hadn't been injured too badly.

When we got to the hospital, we all rushed to her room.

Mom was lying back in the bed, her face pale. She had a bandage on her forehead, and her foot was in a cast. An IV dripped into her arm.

Helen, Dani, and I filed in, Dad and Mae following behind. Seeing us, a smile spread across Mom's face.

"Mommy, are you okay?" Dani reverted to her little-girl self in the wake of seeing our mom like this.

Mom reached for my crying sister and hugged her with her non-IV arm.

"Yes, sweetheart, I'm going to be fine," she assured Dani. Her words were a little slow, most likely from painkillers.

Mom looked up at Dad, who gave a tight smile. He was still living in the garage, so I knew that they must be keeping up appearances for our benefit, but I could tell he was genuinely upset about Mom's accident.

"What happened?" I needed to know.

"Yeah, Mom, how did this happen?" Helen chimed in.

Mom's glassy eyes blinked. "I was driving home from work, and when I got onto the highway, the car felt like it kept accelerating too fast. I couldn't get it to slow down. I realized that the brakes weren't working right. So I tried to pull over to the side, but I swerved, trying to avoid the other cars. I went off the road and crashed into a tree. Totaled the car."

"You could have been killed!" I realized, putting the pieces together of how dangerous this had been.

Mom brushed it off.

"It's just my ankle," she explained. "It's fractured, but other than that I am completely fine," she slurred.

"What about your head?" Dani looked at the bandage.

"It's just from getting bumped around."

Dani looked at our mother with skepticism.

"Seriously, I am going to be just fine. I'll be on crutches for a few weeks, and then with a little physical therapy, I'll be good as new!"

She gave us all a wide grin.

"I can cook so you don't have to," Mae offered. I'd forgotten that she was there.

"Thank you, Mae," Mom cooed. "That's so sweet of you."

"Yeah, we'll all help out, Mom, don't worry about anything," Helen assured her.

The doctor needed to run some tests, so we filed into the waiting room.

Helen was texting, and Dani and Mae were also on their phones. I'm sure Mae was group texting with Larissa, et cetera. I went over to Dad and sank down next to him. My mind raced as I sat there stewing.

"How exactly did her brakes go out?" I asked him.

Dad took a moment. "I don't know," he answered slowly. I could tell he was disturbed by that. He then added, "I'm sure the insurance investigators will look into it."

I let that sink in: Mom's brakes mysteriously went out, causing her to get in a dangerous car accident. It was only a few weeks since we'd been here for Dani's puppy attack incident. And now my mother was injured. Not to mention the fact that I had nearly been kidnapped. Mae had said the cult would come after her to try and get her back. Were they causing all the bad things that were happening to my family?

It was there in the hospital waiting room—staring at Mae—that I came up with my ultimate plan.

CHAPTER 44

IT TOOK A FEW DAYS TO GET THE timing right. I needed a day when everyone would be out of the house for a while, so I had to wait until Mom was back at work the next week. She still was on crutches and couldn't drive because of the cast, so a colleague who lived nearby was driving her. I knew Mae was out with Sebastian covering a model UN meeting for the paper, Dani was at rehearsal, and Helen had a game tonight and so was at practice. Dad was at work.

It was also the full moon, which I knew had some significance for Mae.

Tonight was the night.

As I walked into our house, I called out to see if anyone was home, just in case.

Silence.

I slipped into Mae's room.

Right before this, Isaac had jacked his aunt's minivan, and I'd skipped volleyball practice and he'd driven me into town. We'd stopped at a shop on the main street. What I'd bought had cost a lot more than I'd expected, but I didn't care.

Getting my life back was worth it.

Now, moving around my bedroom setting up, I surveyed my things. I'd lived without my stuff for two months already, and I could hardly wait to have my space again. Get back to my normal life. With what I was about to do, that was going to happen once and for all.

After I'd finished my task, I stepped back and looked at what I'd done. Surveying the room, I smiled at the sight of:

Dozens of white roses.

I'd laid them all around the room. On the bed, the desk, the floor, bedside tables. There were so many flowers filling the room, it smelled like a garden.

A garden that would trigger Mae to go back to the cult, and give me back my life.

———

"Ahhhhhhh!!"

My mother shrieked from upstairs. I was sitting down in the living room later that night, calmly working through my homework. I'd finished editing my list of questions for this week's "People You Don't Know" and sent it off to Sebastian for approval. I assumed he'd dropped Mae home a little while ago after they'd worked together covering the model UN.

I took precautions to go back out of the house after I left the flowers, so that no one would suspect that I had been here, or that I had anything to do with what was happening.

After I'd secretly adorned Mae's room in flowers earlier, Isaac and I went out for fro-yo. Hanging out with my old friend and knowing that things were going to resume normalcy soon, I finally started to feel like myself again.

I'd gotten home around eight and did a quick sweep through the house. Everything was according to plan. Mae's backpack was in the kitchen but she wasn't anywhere in the house.

Before I'd closed the door to my/her room, however, I had caught a glimpse of something on my bed: the necklace. The half-heart pendant I had lent Mae now sat on my bedspread—a parting gift from Mae, I assumed. I almost felt bad for what I had done, but I stopped myself. This needed to happen.

Mom's scream right now coming from the second floor was exactly what I'd wanted.

"You okay?" I yelled up.

"Mae? Is that you?" Mom called as she hopped down the stairs on her good leg. She'd been bad about using her crutches, mostly just holding them and jumping around on her noninjured foot. Dad was out and had taken Dani to Helen's field hockey game a few towns over.

"What's up?" I asked, looking up at my mom—with impressively effortless nonchalance, I thought.

"Oh," she said, disappointed at seeing it was just me. "Have you seen Mae?" Desperation cracked her voice.

I shook my head innocently. "No. She was hanging out with Sebastian after school and then he dropped her here after that. Why, she's not here?"

"Her backpack is, so she must have come home. But there's . . ." Mom's voice trailed off as she looked up toward Mae's room. Her face was stormy.

"Maybe she went out with Dani, or Dad. I wouldn't worry about it," I added. I wanted to give Mae plenty of time to get away. Far away. I had even thought to leave her the number for a taxi and a handful of twenties for the ride, hoping she'd assume they were also from the cult.

"Dad took Dani to Helen's field hockey game in Perkville," Mom informed me.

"I'm sure she'll be back soon," I assured her. Mom might have been injured, but that didn't stop her from attempting to pace.

"This is not good. And they knew it was a bad time of year for her."

"What do you mean by that?" I asked, starting to feel like something was going wrong.

"It's the full moon—their harvest moon." Mom hobbled over to the window and peered above the trees. "This is going to destroy her," Mom worried.

"The harvest moon is bad for Mae?"

"This is when her sister died! Last year on the full moon," Mom nearly yelled.

I froze. My mom hadn't yelled at me in ages. It made me feel even worse than I'd felt with her ignoring me for the last couple months.

Mom must have seen the scared look on my face because she softened. "She was very close to Amelia, and to have something like this happen on the same day . . . Anniversaries are always a fragile time."

I'd had no idea it was the anniversary of her sister's death. I felt bad about the timing, but I had to stay on task. Mae needed to not be with us anymore, and this was the best way I could think to have that happen.

My family was falling apart; I was going to make it right.

"Mom, I'm sure it's all going to be fine. Maybe she misses her family and just wanted to go home," I assured my worried mother.

This was exactly what I'd wanted. The white roses had triggered Mae to go back to the cult. I couldn't believe it was happening. Only, now that it was, it didn't feel so great.

Mom stopped her crutch-pacing. "I'm going to get her back."

"Are you serious?" My eyes bugged at Mom. Not only was she on crutches, if the cult really was dangerous, why would she go near these people?

"I'm going to get Mae." Determination set into Mom like a plague.

"Mom, you can't go to Tisdale," I attempted to reason. "It's a cult!"

Mom pulled out her cell and dialed.

"Plus, you're on crutches!" I added, trying to use logic, which clearly was nonexistent to my mother at the moment.

"Peter, it's me," she stated into the phone. "Mae is gone. I'm going to find her. Call me when you get this."

Dad being at Helen's game sitting in loud bleachers meant that he would probably not have heard his phone—if he even had the ringer on. And he was the worst at listening to messages. Also, Perkville was at least an hour away, so even if he did get it, it would be a while before he got back to Remingham or made it to wherever Tisdale was.

"She cannot return to her abusers!" Mom declared. "I won't let it happen, Jules." She grabbed her coat.

"Mom, you can't even drive. How are you going to get to Tisdale?"

She looked at me. It dawned on my brain what she was thinking.

"You want *me* to drive?" I balked. This was crazy. "There isn't even a car to take," I added. "You don't have a new one yet and Dad's out."

"We can take a taxi," she spitballed.

"Isn't it like an hour away?"

Mom looked back at me.

My mom going to Tisdale to go after Mae was the last thing I wanted to happen. But having to drive her there on crutches was even worse.

"Stacy!" Mom blurted. "Go ask if you can borrow her car."

"Mom! You know she can't keep a secret. Do you want everyone to know you're driving off on crutches to rescue Mae from a cult?"

"What about Isaac? Can you call him?"

"You want his aunt to drive her car over here and let us borrow it?"

"Do you have a better idea?" she asked.

"Yeah, how about *not* go chase after a girl from a satanic cult. She's going to get us killed!"

Mom looked at me and shook her head. "I'll do it myself."

"Mom, you can't even walk!"

But there was no talking her out of it. Mom had become a woman on a mission. She hopped to the coatrack and grabbed a parka, ignoring my logic.

"Why don't you just stay here? Dad will be home later and then you guys can call the police. They'll take care of it."

"Detective Nelson!" Mom pulled out her phone and dialed again, zipping up her jacket.

"Mom, you're acting crazy. Why don't you just sit down for a minute—"

She ignored me, speaking into her phone. "It's Dr. Mathis, please call me. Mae went to Tisdale and I'm going to get her back."

She pocketed the phone, making sure the ringer was on high, then turned to me. Resolve was fastened to her face.

"Mom, why are you so obsessed with Mae? You have to tell me what this is—"

"I was abused, Jules!"

The revelation knocked the wind out of my lungs.

I stared at my mother.

"I'm sorry to—tell you like that." Mom sank down onto the arm of the couch.

"My father . . . was not a nice man. He . . . hit me. And he hit my mother, and my brother."

"Uncle Albert?"

"Yes," Mom said of her off-the-grid sibling, who lived in Portland, Oregon, I think.

"My father drank a lot of alcohol. He'd get drunk and beat us. It was very painful, in so many ways..." She paused a moment, then took a breath. "He'd done it since I was little, so part of me just thought it was normal. But as I got older, it got worse. The beatings became harder, and more frequent. My body was always covered in bruises.

"One day," she went on, "things got really bad. My father had beat me so hard I couldn't walk, and I had to stay home from school. I begged my mother, please take us away! We can't do this anymore. My mother was terrified to leave him—he'd kill us if he found out, but I knew what he was putting us through was already killing us.

"So my mother finally caved. One night, after my dad had passed out, she stole his keys and took my brother and me, and we left in the middle of the night. We drove far away from him and never looked back. We stayed in cheap motels for a while, then finally settled in Remingham."

"Did he ever come after you?" I asked, dumbfounded by hearing all this.

"Yes. Once. After Helen was born, I started working at the hospital. He found me there. I was a resident, and was working with a patient. He started to attack me, right there on the hospital floor, telling me it was all my fault. I had ruined his family. Security came and threatened to arrest him on sight if he ever came around again." She paused. "I never saw him after that."

Silence fell. My tsunami of emotions had swallowed my thoughts.

"I'm sorry to tell you all this, Jules. I just—it's hard for me to see someone get hurt like that, you know?"

I looked at my mother, feelings welling in my eyes. I nodded in understanding.

After a moment, I finally managed, "I'll call Isaac."

CHAPTER 45

I CONCENTRATED ON THE ROAD. I DIDN'T DRIVE often—it made me nervous, thinking about moving thousands of pounds of metal down asphalt at high speeds. Plus, everything my mom had told me was reeling in my head. I felt so sad for her that she'd been hurt like that. I felt protective too, like I never wanted anything bad to happen to her again. I wished she hadn't had to go through all that. And I also admired her for going through such hardship and coming out the other side.

I could now see—my mother wanted to save Mae the way she wished someone had saved her.

"It's not on the GPS," Mom informed me. "The exit. I'll tell you where to get off."

"Cool." I nodded.

Isaac's aunt's minivan was much older than our cars. She

didn't mind coming over and letting us borrow it. She was taking an online course to get her accounting degree, so she said she could study from our house, no problem.

We drove the rest of the way listening to the tires speed across the asphalt. After we had driven past about an hour of cornfields, Mom advised, "It's coming up."

She kept her eyes peeled as we passed a few exits for other towns.

"There it is." She finally spotted it on the right. "Turn here."

I glanced at the side of the road where she was pointing. At first I couldn't see where she meant. All I could see was a narrow area between the thick trees.

"It's just dirt."

"That's the exit," she directed.

I quickly swerved to the right to try to make the passing "exit." The tires thumped as they hit the textured bumps that warned we were at the edge of the road. The car skidded, hitting earth.

I stared at Mom, catching my breath from the Formula One driving I'd just pulled off.

"How did you know that was there?" I wondered. Had she been here before? Or had Mae told her?

Not answering, she kept her eyes focused ahead.

"Follow the path. And watch out for deer," she warned.

As I navigated the car down the bumpy, remote road, adrenaline pumped to my palms, which tightly gripped the wheel. We trailed the road as it veered out to the forest's edge into a clearing.

Beyond lay a small, isolated farm town. Rows of rustic houses, with a few barns and a silo clumped on the outskirts. Farmland sprawled beyond the town. I caught a whiff of manure.

Mom and I were in Tisdale.

"Turn off the lights," Mom advised.

"How will I be able to see?"

"Turn them off, Julia."

Mom never called me Julia. I could tell she was scared. She and I had come to a cult town of known violent offenders with absolutely no backup. All to save the girl who had ruined my life.

"Pull over here." Mom pointed behind the largest barn.

I eased the car to a patch of dirt next to the wooden structure, red paint peeling off the side.

I looked around as I left the engine running. The place was desolate, and here we were alone in the dark night.

"Mom, maybe we should go home."

"I can't let her go back, Jules."

In the moonlight, I could see that Mom's eyes were wide with fear. Saving Mae was something my mother had to do.

And I had to help her.

"Okay." I nodded, killing the ignition. "What's the plan?"

Mom looked out the windshield. The gigantic moon shined above us.

"They'll all be in church, since the moon is full. I'll go in and find her," she determined.

"Mom," I protested. "There's no way I'm letting you hop around this town on crutches."

I took a deep breath. I had caused Mae to come back here. This was my mess—I should be the one to clean it up.

"I'll get her," I declared.

"No! Jules. I can't let you do that—"

"I'll be able to move more quickly on my own. Just let me go find her, and I'll bring her back. Then we can get away from this creepy-ass town."

Mom wasn't happy about it, but she didn't have much choice. She looked at me. "I'm so sorry for bringing you into this, Jules. I shouldn't have done that. I just—"

"It doesn't matter now," I interrupted. We needed to get Mae and get out. "Where's the church?"

"I'm not sure exactly, but the town is only a few streets. It's probably the biggest building."

"I'll find her," I confirmed, hoping that I actually could. "Is she going to be, like, in a trance or something?"

Mom's face was grave as she admitted, "Possibly. But here's what you have to tell her: Amelia was not her fault."

"Her fault? She thinks she had something to do with her sister's death?"

Mom didn't want to get into it. "We don't have time, Jules; you have to hurry."

She was right. "I'll call you if I can't find her."

"They block reception," Mom informed me.

I remembered that Mae had told me the town wasn't into technology. I didn't realize that meant there was no cell coverage or wireless signal. That was barbaric.

Leaving the keys in the car, I opened the door and climbed out.

"Be careful, Jules!" Mom warned with a whisper.

I nodded and eased the car door shut, venturing into the town on my own. The moonlight was bright, lighting my way past the barn and a silo.

Up ahead were rows of small houses—it looked like about four or five streets' worth. The darkened houses were made of wood and looked like they had been built a long time ago. Even though this place was mostly dirt roads and old buildings, the town was clean, organized, quaint—eerily perfect. Like Stepford meets *Little House on the Prairie*. It looked like it actually might be a nice place—minus the small fact that it was a cult.

Walking among the deserted streets, I noticed that there were no street signs. I guess if you belonged there, you knew where you were going. This was clearly not a place for people who didn't belong there. People like me.

Above the rooftops a few blocks away, I saw the steeple to the church. It looked normal, except on top I noticed that the cross was—

Upside-down.

A shiver swept down my spine. I had to get this over with quickly.

I made my way down the dirt roads, realizing another creepy thing: not only was no one out, besides a few tractors and delivery trucks over by the barn there weren't any cars. No one was able to get into this place.

Or out.

I followed the empty roads toward the church, figuring everyone in town—probably a couple hundred people or so—must be there.

As I got closer to the building, I could hear singing. It sounded like a hymn or something. I turned the corner and saw a large white structure. The church was the largest building in town, a few stories high. A handful of white passenger vans were parked in front.

Stepping onto the creaky porch of the church, I headed for the double doors. The hymn continued—a simple melody sung by men at the lower octave, and women above.

The thick wooden doors were heavy. I pulled the handle of one and quietly cracked it open. Warm light spilled out from inside. I looked in and saw rows of pews filled with people. I didn't want anyone to see me, so I leaned back and replaced the door.

I moved around the corner of the building to see if there was another way in. There was a side door, which led inside to a curtained-off side area of the chapel. I didn't see anyone looking, so I slipped in.

The curtains were actually drapes, which hung up to the rafters. I hid behind them. The red velvet smelled musty and strangely comforting, reminding me of my grandmother's vintage clothes in the attic.

As the hymn continued, I carefully peeked around the corner of the curtain into the church.

The large space was lit by candles and contained rows of wooden pews. Men sat on the right side of the aisle, and women on the left.

The men were dressed in dark clothes, mostly black. Heavy coats, with hats on the seats next to them. The women wore thick dresses in mostly brown, with a few gray and black mixed in. Some of them wore bonnets. They looked like they were out of the eighteen hundreds or something, like the Amish. I could see on some of the people nearer to me that they wore crosses around their necks.

Squinting, I could just about make out that the crosses were upside-down.

The observer in me wanted to pull out my phone and take pictures, but I didn't dare.

Up at the front of the room on a platform, a few older men stood in front of the congregation. They wore long black robes and black hoods.

These must be the elders Mae had told me about.

Behind them was a large upside-down cross.

The hymn started to crescendo, as the people singing put all their might into it. I couldn't make out the lyrics. It didn't sound like any hymns I'd heard before. It kind of sounded like they were saying *Ave Maria*. Then I realized it wasn't *Maria* they were saying.

It was *Satana*.

The melody started to slow down as the song came to an end. As the last strains echoed up to the rafters, the congregation took their seats.

While they settled, I scanned the backs of the women's heads, searching for Mae's black hair.

The priest-type people at the front stepped across the platform, getting ready for the next part of the ceremony. Besides the creaking ancient floorboards, the room became pin-drop quiet. Everyone in this congregation was extremely well behaved.

One of the priests stepped over to the side of the platform and took a small silver box from an altar boy, a fresh-faced kid of about ten. Another priest took a seemingly full silver chalice from another altar boy. It looked like it was time for communion.

Then, a man entered the stage. He was dressed like the other priests—long black robes—but on his head, instead of wearing a hood, he wore a mask:

A ram's head with horns spiraling upward.

He must have been some kind of high priest. All in black, and with the ram's head covering his face—

He was fucking scary.

They handed the high priest the silver chalice. He chanted some sort of prayer over the cup of what I guessed was wine. Although I didn't recognize the words, I heard "Satana" again.

Didn't take a genius to translate what that meant.

The men's side of the congregation shuffled to standing, and they filed toward the center aisle, forming a line.

I kept scanning the women's side for Mae but couldn't spot her. I had to find her quickly. I needed to get out of here.

As the male congregants moved forward down the aisle, they stepped up to the platform. There they each received a wafer from a priest, then sipped from the chalice of wine from the high priest ram guy.

As the men's line eventually started to shorten, the women stood and filed into line behind them. Through the crowd of women I saw a swath of black hair. My heart raced, but then the black-haired woman turned, and her field-tanned face revealed that she wasn't Mae.

Up on the platform, my eye caught sight of a teenage girl

stepping out onto the stage. There weren't any other women involved in the ceremony, so I wondered what she was doing up there.

A few other young women like the first walked over and stood next to her.

Then, each one of the young women unbuttoned the cuff of her dress and rolled her heavy sleeve up her arm, exposing flesh.

An altar boy carried another silver chalice over to one of the priests standing at the end of the row of women. He nodded to an older woman with a gray bun, who put something around the upper arm of the first woman. Was she tying something?

My eyes focused to see: a tourniquet.

The gray bun woman then put something into the arm of the young woman.

A syringe.

The needle of the syringe was attached to a tube, which snaked into the silver chalice held by the altar boy.

These people weren't drinking wine—they were drinking blood.

Holy shit.

The young woman's face drained pale. The older woman then removed the needle and placed something where the needle had been, a cotton ball or something.

The altar boy transported the chalice to the main priest, who was distributing the liquid to the congregation. He took the full chalice of blood and handed the boy the empty one. The boy then carried the cup over to the row of women, where the older woman had moved on to drawing blood from the second girl.

My stomach tumbled. This was insane. These people were

drinking human blood! I was glad I hadn't eaten dinner or I might have thrown up.

I had to stay focused. I had to find Mae.

I scanned the line of women waiting for "communion," but none of them looked like Mae. Mom had been convinced that Mae would be here. And where else would I go to find her? All the houses looked empty, and they were all the same.

The women's line in the aisle was starting to wind down, the last young woman on stage who was giving her lifeblood now anemically pulling her sleeve back down.

When they were finished, the altar boys began clearing up the chalices and wafers, and everyone took their seats. The high priest stalked behind a table and took out a wooden box.

He opened it and withdrew a long, thick horsewhip.

"Ave Satana, may the power of our great Lord of Darkness be upon you."

"And also with you," the congregation returned in unison.

The ram-headed priest addressed his flock.

"In the eyes of our Lord, we are all sinners. And it is our *duty*"—he paused for emphasis—"to confess to him our sins, so that He may forgive us—be pleased with us—and we may walk with him, into the darkness and beyond. Praise be to our great Lord."

"Amen," the group returned.

The congregation listened attentively.

"We invoke His name, so that he may be the great manifestor of justice, as we repent for our sins, and so please our Lord."

He then began to recite:

"O ye sons and daughters of mildewed minds, that sit in judgment of the inequities wrought upon me—Behold! The voice of Satan; the promise of Him who is called amongst ye the accuser and the supreme tribune! Move therefore, and appear! Open the mysteries of your creation! Be friendly unto me, for I am the same! The true worshipper of the highest and ineffable King of Hell."

The incantation sounded like what Mae had recited in the graveyard. I wondered if it was another one of those Enochian things Zeke had mentioned.

The priest then turned his attention to his captive audience. "Who before me lies in wait to confess their sins?" he probed.

A few members of the congregation stood up and shuffled into the center aisle.

The first man arrived at the front of the room. He was a brawny guy, in his thirties or so, his sandy-haired head hung low in shame.

"Brother Eli," the priest acknowledged.

"If He be pleased," the man returned quietly.

"Behold!" the high priest declared. "This sheep has confessed . . . to theft!"

The congregation grumbled its disapproval.

The priest went on. "He hath stolen grain from his brethren. He hath sinned in the eyes of our Lord. Only He will grant you forgiveness. You must atone for your offense."

The priest signaled for the man to lift his shirt. The man followed orders, lifting it up over his back, and knelt to the ground at the priest's black-booted feet.

The priest then raised the horsewhip and beat the man vigorously.

THWACK!

THWACK!

The whole congregation watched without a shred of sympathy as this man was beaten for his sin. After a few hits the man crumpled to the ground in agony.

"Face your master!" the high priest demanded. "Do not be a coward in the eyes of our Lord!"

Using all his remaining strength, the man lifted himself back up off the floor with a whimper, onto his hands and knees.

The priest *THWACKED* again. Blood spilled down the man's back.

I had to look away.

After the priest was done, the man crawled to the side of the stage, where the gray-bunned woman placed a blanket over his bleeding back. The able-bodied man had been diminished to a pile of trembling limbs and silent tears.

As the next man stepped forward to the priest to confess his sin, something in the back of the room caught my eye.

Behind the last row on the women's side, I saw someone enter. Black hair glinted in the candlelight.

It was Mae.

She was wearing a long strappy white dress, which might have been the one she had worn for her Carrie costume. They would surely punish her just for wearing something so exposing and clingy.

She adjusted the dress, readying to head toward the center aisle and presumably confess her sins. Which meant she would receive punishment.

I had to stop her.

It was too far to call to her without anyone hearing. My mind raced to strategize if I had enough time to sneak back out through the side door and around to the main entrance in the back of the hall.

Mae smoothed down her hair.

I had to get to her before she went up to that altar. I could crouch down, slip out from behind the curtain, and crawl my way over to her from behind the pews, but it was risky. What if one of these people caught me? I saw what they were willing to do to people they did know—what would they do to a complete stranger like me?

Everything went black.

CHAPTER 46

SUZANNE COULD BARELY KEEP STILL—SHE HAD TO FIND Jules and Mae.

Before she thought better of it, she opened the car door, pointed her crutches out, and heaved herself from the passenger seat.

As the cold night air hit her cheeks, Suzanne looked beyond the barn to where the church steeple protruded over the rooftops.

She crutched toward it, making her way down the eerily quiet streets.

She passed darkened home after home, until something caught her eye. Through a crack in the window curtains, Suzanne saw something and leaned her face to the windowpane.

Her jaw dropped:

Through the drapes, Suzanne saw a small child, suspended upside-down on an inverted cross.

The child was hanging in some kind of closet, but the door was left open. The child's feet were tied to the upper part of the cross, and the arms were fastened at the hands out to the sides. It appeared as though the child was gagged, but it was hard to tell because it was so dark inside, lit only by the flickering embers of a hearth fire.

Suzanne had been told about this ritual by Mae. It was a technique the cult used to weed out the "weak" children, so only the "strong" would survive. They had done it to Mae, which left her with scars on her palms—a sickening reminder of where she came from.

Suzanne had to get photographic evidence. She needed this to build her case against the cult, to get justice for what they had done to Mae, and to other children. People needed to be punished for this abuse.

Suzanne slipped her phone out from her jacket pocket and snapped a picture through the glass. It was hard to see what the image was from so far away. She tried zooming in, but the light was too low. She had to get a better shot.

The house looked empty. She glanced up and down the small street, checking that there was no one in sight, then—her heart pounding—she reached for the door handle. The cold brass fastener stiffly—

Unlocked.

She slowly inched open the door and, hearing only silence, crutched inside.

Suzanne looked around. There were a few pieces of uncomfortable-looking wooden furniture. There were no pillows or cushions, no artwork, no photos. Nothing that gave comfort.

A woodstove glowed in the center of the living room, burning logs fueling the low light. Suzanne made her way past the stove, over to the closet where the toddler was suspended.

The poor boy hung fastened upside-down. He was awake, but not crying. He had probably grown numb to the pain.

Suzanne's eyes welled.

It pained her, but she had to take his photo as evidence.

After snapping a few pictures, she stared at the boy. She couldn't let herself leave this poor thing there. She needed to take him down. But how? She had to get the nails out of his hands; was there a way to do that without hurting him further? Maybe there was something she could find to ease out the nails? If she could get him out of there she could call an ambulance once they got back into cell phone range.

"Well well well," a gruff voice came from behind her. "Still tryin' ta save the world, are we."

Suzanne turned to see: the sheriff.

CHAPTER 47

A QUIET CRUNCH FILLED MY EARS AS I slowly turned my head.

My forehead pounded. I tried to search my brain for why it ached so much, but I couldn't think.

I cracked open my eyes, but it was as dark as having my eyes closed.

Where was I?

I moved my hand to scratch my face, only to discover that it wouldn't move. I tried the other, but that wouldn't budge either. I slowly realized that my hands were tied together behind my back.

What. The. Eff.

I pulled myself up to sitting and heard that soft crunching again. I was sitting on something with texture, like a beanbag chair. Tilting my head up, all my eyes could see was darkness stretching high above.

I was not sitting on a beanbag. I was at the bottom of a grain storage silo.

I could now feel that my feet were also tied. Beyond my legs, I spied a dark shadow.

A man was standing over me.

My eyes were starting to adjust to the darkness. He appeared a few years older than me and was tall and muscular. I caught a glimpse of a marking on his bicep beneath his rolled-up shirt-sleeve: a pentagram.

"You two don't look that alike after all," he concluded, staring down at me. This was the fireman who had tried to kidnap me in the woods!

"I figured out you weren't her," he went on, "but by then it seemed a little late to let you go. You were a fast one, though."

I couldn't see his face, but the way he said it sounded like he was smiling, relishing this moment of power.

"But you are a traitor," he said, stepping toward me, his tenor voice almost kind. "Like her."

I could see his face now. Handsome, square jaw, jet-black hair. And green eyes—

Just like Mae's.

"Haskell, don't."

I heard a rustling a few yards away. There was another figure lying on the grain.

Mae. Tied up like me.

He turned to her. "And we always knew you'd come back. Couldn't stay away. You know where you belong," he continued, stepping over to Mae.

He knelt down and took her face in his hand. "Maybe that's because you always knew it was your fault."

What was Mae's fault?

Mae didn't answer. She sniffled in the darkness.

"You were supposed to be watching her, weren't you. You let her drown, right before your eyes. You let your own sister die."

He must have been talking about Amelia.

"And what's even worse"—his voice lowered to nearly a whisper—"you let me take the fall."

Mae didn't respond. I could hear her sharp intakes of breath. She was sobbing.

"I took sixty-six lashes. Sixty-six . . . Do you know how much that hurt? I still can't sleep on my back."

"It wasn't my fault!" Mae blurted back, her voice shaking through tears. "She wanted to do it. She wanted to die!"

"But *you let her*!" His voice rose, echoing off the circular metal walls. "You let your flesh and blood die, and blamed your own brother!"

He stood, seething. "If I had known better, I wouldn't have taken the fall for you. Especially if I knew you were going to betray us all." His heavy boots crunched the grain as he paced.

"I was going to turn myself in, Haskell. That's why I came back," Mae reasoned.

"Good," he concluded. "I've been trying to get you to come back for months. Glad you finally got the message."

So someone *had* been trying to get Mae back. Her very own brother.

"I knew you'd be back sooner or later. Of course you came back on the harvest moon," he smirked.

Mae sniffed again. I had no idea she'd had a hand in her sister's death. That's why she was so haunted by it. If I'd known it had happened this time last year, I never would've triggered her to come back now. Or, come to think of it, triggered her at all. The guilt I felt for causing this whole thing made my body feel like turning inside out. I ached to leave. Click my heels and get out of here. Disappear so this nightmare would end.

"Why didn't you let me turn myself in, then?" Mae challenged her brother. "That's what I was going to do in church."

"I wanted to bring you myself. Then you would have to tell them the truth: that it wasn't my fault. Then Father would finally forgive me."

Haskell's voice lowered. "Then I'd watch Father give you every lash he gave to me."

I wondered if their father was the high priest in the church wearing the ram mask. The one who had beat that man . . .

"I'd watch you suffer the way I suffered," Haskell condemned his sister. "Take every whip, tearing the flesh of your back apart—"

"No!" I shouted before I could stop myself. "Please don't hurt her."

I knew it was my fault that Mae had come back. I couldn't be responsible for her being dealt even more pain.

Haskell turned to me and stepped over.

"Too bad you had to drag your friend into it," he scolded his sister. "We'll have to punish her too."

He knelt down and looked right at me. My heart was pounding so loud but I couldn't breathe.

This was it. Mae's cult brother was going to kill me.

Mae kicked herself up to her knees. "Stop it, Haskell! Jules had nothing to do with this! I'm the one you want," she declared. "Take me. I'll do whatever you want. Just please, let her go."

Mae was offering herself up for me, risking her life. And I was the one who had put us in this situation. I could feel bile rising in my stomach, nauseous over what I had done.

"Always the brave one," Haskell tsked, shaking his head at his sister. "Mother used to say that was one of the great things about you. But how wrong she was. Now all she talks about is the shame you've brought upon our family. What a disgrace you are.

"But I'm going to bring honor back," he concluded. "You are going to be the sacrificial lamb to right the wrong. They'll whip you for your sins and then hang you on the cross to pay for what you've done. In death you'll be forever in service to our Lord.

"And in return, they'll make me a priest—just like Father." I could hear a smile in his voice. "Mother will be so proud."

I shivered. This couldn't be happening. They were going to kill us both.

Haskell headed for the door to the silo. "If I were you I'd take this time to make peace with Him. Your time has come . . ." The warning hanging like the last strains of a sermon, Haskell let the door slam behind him.

Now alone, I could hear Mae crying.

"Mae!" I whispered. "We have to get out of here!"

"I'm so sorry, Jules. I'm so sorry I got you into this—"

"It's not your fault. We have to leave—"

"Yes, it is. I deserve death. I don't deserve life with you and your family. I don't deserve people being nice to me. I killed my sister, and this is my punishment." She sobbed.

"No!" I scooted over to her across the slippery grain. "You were only trying to help," I assured her. "You tried to help your sister escape from torture and cruelty."

I remembered what my mom had told me. "And her death wasn't your fault. It's the monsters' who did this to you."

Mae's face turned to me.

"Really?"

"Yes. You have to forgive yourself."

Mae shook her head. "No, I'm ready to die. At least that way I can see Amelia again. And maybe I can save you—it's my fault I brought you into this."

The fact that this whole trip was my fault was hanging around my neck like an anchor. I had to confess. She had to know the truth.

"Those white roses on your bed—I put them there. It's my fault you came back here tonight."

Mae's wet eyes widened. "*You* put them there?"

"I shouldn't have done it. I was upset. I'm so sorry; it is all my fault and not yours."

Mae took that in, then shook her head.

"No, it's not. I ruined everything for you—your family, Sebastian. I know I did. I'm sorry. I copied you—I admit it," she went on. "I wanted to be like you. I wanted to be in your family. I wanted to be close to you. Close to all of you. You think your life is so nor-mal and boring, but it's *special*, Jules. You don't even know what you have. I wanted it. I wanted it all."

Finally, an admission that I wasn't crazy—that Mae had been trying to take over my life. I guess I understood why she'd done it, but it was such a huge relief to hear that it hadn't all been in my head.

"Thank you. For saying that."

I appreciated the sentiment, but we had to focus. We didn't know when Haskell would be back, or what he would do to us. We needed to leave.

"We have to get out of here, Mae. Both of us. Mom's waiting in the car. Come with me."

Mae didn't answer. I could hear her whimpering. If we were going to get away, now was our chance.

"I need you to turn around. Scoot your back so it faces mine."

She didn't move. Action Mode Jules sprang into gear.

"Mae!" I nearly yelled. "Move! We need to do this!"

Finally, she started to turn around. I propelled myself over to her, and we pushed our backs toward each other.

"I saw this in a movie once. Untie my hands," I demanded.

"What?"

"Do it!" I whisper-shouted. Confidence trumped my fear. "Haskell will be back any minute."

Mae hesitated, the thought of her brother weakening her will.

I made my final plea: "Mae, do it for me. You owe it to me to at least try."

Mae heaved a breath, then obeyed. Following my directions, she worked the rope around my wrists until I felt it start to loosen.

I slipped my fingers out of the ropes, then untied Mae's hands.

Then we sped to unbind our feet. Neither of us spoke, our hearts pounding so hard I could hear them both.

When our legs were free, we stood and stumbled across the slippery grain. Moving again made my head ache even more, but I pushed through it. We had to get out of the silo.

As we reached the door, it opened.

Mae and I both crouched down on opposite sides of the door.

Haskell stepped in past us. He held something in front of his face.

"I made it myself," he beamed, holding up a "wreath" he'd made—a barbed wire crown of thorns.

As my breath caught in my throat, I pressed on. I nodded at Mae across the doorway, behind Haskell's back. Since it was so dark, it would take him a few seconds to notice that we weren't there. This was our chance.

She nodded back, and we—

Bolted out the door.

CHAPTER 48

WHITE-HOT TERROR FILLED SUZANNE AS THE SHERIFF STOOD before her.

"Trespassing," he scolded. "Tut, tut."

Suzanne tried to discreetly slide the phone into her back pocket without him noticing.

"Take him down," she returned. Using her crutches, she tried to move around him, but he blocked her path.

"Shame you got yourself injured. Lord only knows how that happened," he said with a wry upturn of his lips.

"I don't want any trouble," Suzanne assured.

"Trouble," he said as he took a slow step toward her. "That's about all you've caused." His dark eyes stared her down. "You have something that belongs to me."

"I don't know what you mean by that," Suzanne replied, avoiding eye contact.

"Oh, ya don't? What were you doing in here? This is private property."

"That child is in danger." Suzanne felt her anger rising.

"I was just coming to take him down. Bring him in for his first confession."

Suzanne literally bit her tongue to withhold herself from commenting.

"Give me the photographs," he demanded.

She didn't answer. Her eyes darted around her, assessing whether there was any other way to get out than the exit behind him.

"I saw you taking them on your telephone."

"I'll just make my way out and let you get back to your business." She could call an ambulance to come and get the child.

"Give me the phone." He wasn't asking.

She needed the photos. It was her evidence—proof that these people were abusing children. These photos would make a strong case, and combined with Mae's testimony, she could make sure the townspeople were punished for the child abuse they'd caused. Since there was no signal anywhere in town, the data hadn't had a chance to back itself up to the Cloud—she needed the phone.

"I asked nicely," he warned, treading toward her. She could feel his hot breath on her neck.

He reached his hand toward Suzanne's back pocket.

She smacked his hand away with her crutch.

He snickered. "You're a feisty one."

Suzanne held her crutch out and tried to push him away, but he grabbed the end of it and yanked, pulling Suzanne off balance.

She tumbled to the floor at his feet.

Groaning as she hit the hard wood, she could feel her ankle pounding in its cast—the fall made her injury hurt even more.

She forced herself up onto her hands and knees, keeping the weight off her injured ankle, and began to crawl away from him.

THUD! She slammed to the ground again—he'd pulled her leg out from under her.

He laughed again.

Now lying flat on her stomach, Suzanne frantically flailed at him with her good foot. She heard metal clanging.

Her shoe had knocked over a set of fire pokers that stood next to the hearth.

Now she felt his weight on top of her. She tried to squirm herself free, but he flipped her over right side up. He kneeled over her, and pinned her wrists to the floor above her head with one hand.

She stared up at his dark eyes, terrified of what he might do next.

With his free hand, he reached around to her lower back and slid his hand into the back pocket of her jeans.

She gasped at the contact of his hand on her body.

He slipped the phone out from beneath her.

Still kneeling on top of her, he released her hands and opened the door to the woodstove to throw the phone in. Suzanne hurled her fists at him, but it was no use.

He tossed her phone into the fire.

"No!" Suzanne screamed as she saw her precious photos melt into the vermillion flames.

"Now," he said, looking back down at her. "What do I do with you?"

Suzanne was paralyzed with fear. Then her past came flooding back to her: flashes of her father beating her, her mother trying in vain to wrench him off, her brother sobbing in the corner.

"Time to teach you not to go meddling in other people's business." He reached for the thick leather belt at his waist.

Suzanne's body pumped with terror, anger, rage.

He unbuckled his belt and snaked it out of his pant loops and—

THWUNK!

The sheriff's eyes bulged wide, his jaw slackened. He looked down at his chest, bewildered.

Dark red trickled from the center of his shirt, the bloodstain blooming toward the edges of his open jacket. His face contorted in horror as he saw:

A thin shaft of metal protruding from his chest.

Suzanne had speared him with a fire poker.

CHAPTER 49

"OVER HERE!" MAE WHISPERED AS WE SPRINTED OUT of the silo.

I followed her through a warehouse, which was attached to the silo, as fast as my legs would carry me.

The big barn wasn't far, I believed, but we had to get there fast because Haskell was already coming after us.

As we passed heavy machinery used for processing grain, we reached the end of the warehouse. It connected to another building—a long barn with rows of sleeping cows in stalls. I could see that the animals were branded, with five-pointed stars on their haunches.

I signaled to the far end of the barn, where I was pretty sure the car was.

We sped through the odorous barn as heavy footfalls thumped behind us, getting closer.

Closer.

I had seen the sequence in *North by Northwest* where a man was being chased by a crop duster enough times to know that it was impossible to outrun things that were bigger and faster than you. I had to think of something.

Running past the stalls, I glanced to my right and saw an opening that led to another, parallel row of stalls. I quickly grabbed Mae's arm and ducked down around the corner of the opening to the other side, behind a stack of crates.

My heart was pumping so hard I thought it would explode.

Mae and I were kneeling close. She turned to me, and our eyes locked. My anger toward her, my frustration, melted away. She had been willing to give her life for me. And a few months ago, the last thing in the world I thought I'd be doing was rescuing a runaway from an angry cult. Albeit scary as hell, it was exhilarating. Spending time with Mae, and everything I'd gone through at school, had challenged me to be bolder, take more action, and here I was being that new person. I might not make it till tomorrow, but I was proud of New Jules.

Haskell's heavy treads whipped around the corner toward us. And then.

Past us.

I had a millisecond of relief. If we doubled back to the aisle we had been in and kept our bodies low, we could hopefully make it out of the barn without him seeing us.

I prayed to God my mom would be ready with the car running.

Mae peeked around the edge of the crates to see that Haskell was far enough past us to make a run for it. Now that he was in the second aisle, we crept back to the first. Hunched low, we sped down the row, careful not to slip on any wet piles of cow shit or wake any of the bovines.

When we reached the far end of the barn, there was a heavy door. Glancing to the right, I saw Haskell glaring around in the other aisle. We'd need to open the old wooden door to get out, which he was sure to hear. We had to do it fast and race to the car before he caught on.

Mae and I made eye contact, then looked at the door. Quickly, she turned the handle and heaved the door open.

It creaked loudly, causing Haskell to turn toward us. We fled out of the barn to—

An empty dirt lot; no car.

I was sure this was where we'd parked it. Mom should be here!

"It was right here!" I panted.

Had my mother left us? Where had she gone? How were we supposed to get out of here? Haskell would make his way out to us sooner than—

THUD THUD THUD, came his heavy boots.

Mae and I turned to him. Seeing us, he smiled, stopping to catch his breath. He was holding the razor-wire crown.

Shit, shit, shit. Where the hell was Mom? How were we supposed to get out of here? We'd have to make a run for it into the woods and head for the highway. Maybe there we could hitch a ride to safety before Haskell caught up to us.

I nodded toward the trees and she nodded back, silently agreeing to head for the highway. We took off sprinting.

MEEP MEEEEEP, Isaac's aunt's minivan blared.

The car reeled around the corner of the barn, my mother at the wheel.

Mom pulled the car up in front of us. Haskell was closing in. I hurled open the door before the vehicle stopped moving. Mae and I threw ourselves in.

"GO! GO! GO!" I yelled.

As I yanked the door shut we sped off in the minivan. A sliver of Haskell's image—a mere few yards away—disappeared as the van door swung closed.

We bumped down the dirt road as fast as the minivan would carry us, and barreled onto the highway.

As we sped away, whining cop cars passed us, headed for Tisdale.

EPILOGUE

"LIGHT OR DARK?"

The knife glinted in the candlelight, perched waiting for me to make my choice.

"Dark meat, please," I requested of my mother, who dove into carving a drumstick off the turkey for me.

It was our traditional Thanksgiving meal, which was one of my favorite holidays because it revolved around eating. And I was relieved to have a few days off from school to relax and binge as many classic films as I could stream.

"Marianne, what can I get for you?" my mom, now hobbling around in an air cast, offered to our guest.

"Oh, I'll have light, please," the woman said, her voice velvety soft. She wore a white silk blouse and long maroon wool skirt, which I admired.

"Oliver, what about you?"

Marianne's husband opted for light as well. His brown tweed jacket and khaki pants were a respectable combo, minus the pleats.

The young couple had joined us for dinner. Mom had invited them, seeing as they were going to be Mae's new foster parents, and I was curious to meet them.

"Mae loves turkey," my mom informed them.

Marianne stretched her lips into a smile. "That's very good to know. I want to learn everything you like," she said, gazing at Mae.

While the sentiment was nice, she seemed really into Mae kind of overly so.

But Mae seemed excited to have a new family to live with, and happy that they were looking to foster and hopefully eventually adopt her. Although of course, she was sad to leave us, and Remingham.

"You're only moving a few hours away," I'd offered to soften the blow of the move. "And we can video chat." I'd grinned, knowing that I'd been the one to show Mae how to use it.

I was bummed she was moving away, but I knew it would be good for her to get farther away from Tisdale, although still staying in state because of foster care laws.

And it would also be good for my family. The events of the last few months had caused a lot of strain on us, and I was glad to get some time back all together so we could become a close-knit family again.

Although I'd miss her, Mae leaving was kind of a relief.

"Pass the casserole, Jules?" asked Dani. I handed her the plate of green beans. The crispy onions on top wafted to my nostrils, making me so ready to eat this meal.

"Save some for the rest of us," Helen snapped at Dani as she piled green beans onto her plate.

"Jules, can you spoon some gravy on this?" Dad asked, reaching out his plate, heaped with stuffing. I was glad that he was living in the house with us again. It felt so much better to have things back to normal between my parents.

"Mae, would you like light meat or dark?" my mother offered.

Mae looked at the gigantic turkey on the table.

"I'll have light, please. Thank you, Suzanne," she smiled.

"Mae, we painted your room lavender," Marianne grinned. "That's your favorite color, right?"

"Yes." Mae nodded. "Thank you."

"And you're all signed up at the local school. A church friend of mine's daughter's going to show you around," Oliver added, pleased with himself.

"That sounds great," Mae replied, sipping her ginger ale.

"So do you have other children?" Dad asked the couple, adding mashed potatoes to his plate.

Marianne and Oliver looked at each other. "We don't," she said, sadly. "I'm not able to."

Oliver put his hand on his wife's leg. I noticed his hand fell pretty high up her thigh for being in front of other people.

I felt bad that they couldn't have their own kids. But then, being a young couple, why were they choosing to foster Mae? Wouldn't they want a baby so they could raise it like their own?

"That's why we're so happy to have Mae," Oliver replied, turning to Mae with a smile.

Mae had been happy when she'd met with the couple—she and Mom had gone to spend time with them on a few occasions, to make sure it was the right fit. Now, all the paperwork was finally signed, and after our meal, they were going to whisk Mae off to her new home.

But I couldn't shake the feeling that something about them was kind of weird.

"Marianne, could I have that gravy right near you?" Mom asked, extra kindly to our guest.

"Sure thing," Marianne replied, reaching for the porcelain.

As Marianne's thin arm stretched to pick up the gravy boat, her shirtsleeve lifted, revealing a small tattoo on her wrist of the delicate letters:

o.t.o.

It was a strange combo of letters. I wondered if it was someone's initials, or maybe it stood for something. But I brushed it off and enjoyed the rest of the meal with my family.

After we'd finished, Oliver and Dad loaded Mae's things into the young couple's car. I still thought something was strange about them, but maybe I was just sad that Mae was leaving. Saying good-bye to her was hard, especially after all we'd been through. However, I knew she'd be better off starting over somewhere else.

When all her things were packed up and the car was running, I hugged Mae.

"Keep in touch, like, every second, okay?" I made her promise.

"Pinkie swear," she grinned back. Then she bounced down our stone walkway to her new foster parents' car.

Hopping in, she blew me a kiss. I blew one back and waved.

And with that, Mae drove off to her new life.

And I went back to mine.

ACKNOWLEDGMENTS

First and foremost, thank you to the woman who shared her life experiences with me, on whom this book is based. Thank you for letting me tell your story.

I am indebted to my editors Anna Roberto and Liz Szabla and everyone at Feiwel & Friends. I could not have wished for a better home for *Devil in Ohio*. Thank you for your wisdom and guidance developing the book. It has been a joy to work with you bringing this adventure to the page.

I was extraordinarily lucky to have advisors on this project in the worlds of psychiatry, social work, and hospitals. Thank you to Dr. Amy Funkenstein, Katherine Bailey PhD, Moshe Ben-Yosef MA, LMFT, and Dr. William Reid, who all patiently answered my questions in order to help me tell this story as accurately as I could.

Thank you to my early readers, Neve and Anthia, for your keen eyes and teen expertise.

Special thanks to Les Bohem for your encouragement and support of my writing in all areas, and also to writing goddess Annie Jacobsen for your advice and camaraderie. Thank you to Carlton Cuse, Graham Roland, and the *Jack Ryan* team for your inspirational storytelling and lunch jokes.

Thank you to my mother, Betsy and sister, Ruby, for your unflinching support since day one. I'm grateful to the whole Polatin family for your encouragement over the years. Also a big thanks to the Danowski/Hoogewerf family for plying me with delicious holiday meals while I raced against the clock, unable to step away from my screen.

I'm grateful to my dear friends Jordana, Susanna, Taryn, Julie, Dahvi, Jamie, Lindsay, Courtney, Kat, Bekah, Julia, and Aditi for your years of friendship and support. A big thanks to my coffee-shop friends Sarah, Alex, and Shawn, whose caffeine-infused smiles encouraged me to keep typing day after day. Thank you to Myles for your loyal support, and for cheering me on when I needed to not hit the snooze button.

I'm extremely grateful to my book agent, Mollie Glick, for helping me hone this story and shape it into the book that it has become.

Thank you to my tireless managers, Jordana Mollick and Brendan Bragg, and the whole Haven Entertainment team, and my agents Tim Phillips, Lauren Fox, and Rachel Viola at United Talent Agency for your belief in me and advocacy on my behalf.

Last but by far the least, I offer my deepest gratitude to my manager and producer Rachel Miller, without whom this book would not exist. Thank you for the encouragement, the deadlines, and for bringing this story to life with me. Your relentlessness is inspiring, and I couldn't have asked for a better partner on this book. Here's to the next.